SEE
HOW
THEY
LIE

SUE WALLMAN

Scholastic Children's Books
An imprint of Scholastic Ltd
Euston House, 24 Eversholt Street, London, NW1 1DB, UK
Registered office: Westfield Road, Southam, Warwickshire, CV47 0RA
SCHOLASTIC and associated logos are trademarks and/or
registered trademarks of Scholastic Inc.

First published in the UK by Scholastic Ltd, 2017

ISBN 978 1407 16538 7

A CIP catalogue record for this book
is available from the British Library.

Printed by CPI Group (UK) Ltd, Croydon, CR0 4YY
Papers used by Scholastic Children's Books are made
from wood grown in sustainable forests.

1 3 5 7 9 10 8 6 4 2

www.scholastic.co.uk

To Mum and Dad, with thanks

ONE

This is a good place. Behind the kitchen building, far enough away from the vegetable garden not to be seen by any gardeners. The ground is summer-dry and the air vibrates with the buzz of insects. When we lie down we're hidden from view in the long, wild meadow grass. Too near the perimeter fence we'd be picked up on the CCTV cameras, but here is perfect.

It started a few months ago, Drew and me meeting alone in secluded areas to smoke. At first Drew smoked and I watched, but these days I have a cigarette so he doesn't think I'm a total lost cause. Drew negotiated the deal. The signed basketball jersey he was given on his last birthday in return for tobacco, papers and a lighter smuggled in by a recovering addict. We keep our smoking kit buried in a plastic ziplock bag in the Woodland Gardens, and pick it up on our way to wherever we're meeting. Our shared bad secret.

We're each propped up on an elbow, the ground already moulded to our bodies. I watch Drew's large tanned fingers roll the cigarette. He's become better at it. He lights it and hands it to me, and I suck the evil smoke into my lungs. Am I becoming addicted?

"The new teacher is super-demanding," he says as he rolls the next one for himself. "And she's *how* old? Barely college-age."

"She's all right," I say. He'll laugh if I say I like her.

"At least she doesn't spit when she talks like Miss What's-her-name," he mumbles, his cigarette still in his mouth. "That was grim."

"The guy before her was worse," I say. "At least Miss *Constable* didn't make us listen to audiobooks while she took naps."

"How does admin find these losers?" asks Drew. "They must have loads of applications and they choose idiots every time."

We're both aware that people love working here, even though it's in the middle of nowhere. We hear whispered conversations between assistants in admin when we're there for our individual computer sessions. They love their high salaries, access to all the facilities here and bonus payments for going above and beyond to promote Creek values.

"All I know is it's a complicated process," I say. It's what Dad told me one time when we were between teachers.

Drew shrugs, bored with the conversation, as he always is about lessons and teachers.

Limb by limb, I feel myself relax. I know where I am with Drew. I've known him pretty much all my life. With my finger I trace the healed graze on his leg, just below the line of his running shorts. An old basketball injury. Everyone here is fit, or soon becomes fit, but some people's muscles suit them better than others. Drew's body is near perfect.

He bats my hand away. "Hey, that tickles."

He doesn't touch my body as much as I touch his. There are nights when I lie in bed and stroke the side of my face and pretend that it's Drew's hand touching me, except my body isn't fooled at all.

Pulling my hand away, I change position so that I'm at more of a right angle to him, and rest my head on his T-shirted chest.

"Geez, Mae. Your head is heavy. Must be all those brains."

I feel the steady rhythm of his chest rising and falling, and the heartbeat that I swear pumps in sync with mine.

"Don't go dropping your ash on me," he says but he doesn't push me off his chest.

I pull my arm away immediately – we don't want anyone to smell the smoke on us later. I check the pocket of my shorts for the little toothpaste tablets I swiped earlier from the freshen-up area of the spa.

We watch the only cloud in the sky change shape as

we smoke in silence. Tobacco, alcohol, drugs of any kind, junk food – they're banned from Hummingbird Creek, all nine square miles of it. The penalties of being in possession are harsh. But Drew and I are careful, and we only smoke now and again.

"I asked your dad again for permission to go running outside the gates on my own," he says.

"And?"

Drew sighs. "What d'you think, Mae? It was a straight-out no." He wriggles so I lift my head to allow him to change position. "Then I said I'd go running with you. The two of us. That we'd train for a marathon. Still no."

I move so that I can see his face properly. Study the grey-blue eyes. "That would be cool," I say. "Just you and me, outside the gates." I dig a burial place for my cigarette end as I shake the image from my mind because it's never going to happen. "I'm sorry," I say. "About my dad being . . . being like he is."

"He treats us like the patients." Drew looks away towards the perimeter fence. "Don't you want freedom, Mae? Tell me, what's so wrong with wanting to go running outside the grounds?"

"Nothing," I say. "But—" I bite my lip.

"You're going to tell me we're lucky, aren't you?" Drew jabs his cigarette into the ground. "That we've got everything here."

"I just think. . ." I try to find the right, placatory words, ones that won't make him cross. "You'd be happier if you stopped wanting these things so badly."

Drew makes a snorting noise. He's finding it harder and harder to accept the rules.

"Two more years," I say. "That's all." When we're eighteen we'll be off to college. I lie on my back, one hand behind my head. The sky is vast. Swimming-pool-blue and beautiful.

Count your blessings. It's one of the Creek phrases. Sometimes in group sessions we actually do count them.

I have a lot more blessings than the patients. Not just because I don't have problems the way they do, but also because I've lived here longer. Dr Hunter Ballard met my mom when he was working in England, and we moved to America when I was six. He bought this land and had Hummingbird Creek built: a psychiatric treatment and rehabilitation facility for teenagers. His philosophy of masses of exercise, perfectly balanced organic food prepared by top chefs, brain training and positive thinking, with regular health checks in a highly structured, stunning environment, is so popular that parents will pay enormous sums of money to keep their children here for extended periods.

"Two long years," says Drew. He pushes the tobacco towards me. "Want to make the next ones?"

I roll two cigarettes, but the lighter's almost empty. We're never given outside money and there's no lighter on the Creek's limited shopping site, so we'll have to arrange

5

for one to be smuggled in through the post, hidden inside another item, and exchange it for something else. I think Drew gets a kick out of living these prison-movie moments.

Drew manages to light one, and we smoke and peer at the bugs in the grass until his watch bleeps and the screen lights up with a reminder message. "Ten mile run, here I come," he says. "My exercise schedule is crazy today." He takes one last drag of his cigarette before stubbing it out and leaving it for me to bury, peeks above the grass to check it's clear, then leaps to his feet.

"Have fun." I blow a kiss at him and he smiles, so perfectly that my stomach tightens. I watch him bound over the long grass to the vegetable garden to pick a few herbs. He'll chew those to rid his breath of tobacco. I check my watch, which is the same as Drew's but with my name engraved on the metal back. I still have free time left until my computer session, and enough tokens for a spa treatment.

I have the spa to myself because the patients have scheduled time. I squiggle my signature on the payment screen and within minutes I'm lying on a treatment table with a cooling detox cream on my face.

"Would you like music, miss?" asks the beauty therapist.

I shake my head, gently so that the cream doesn't gloop down my neck, and she slips from the room while the cream does its work. Outside I can hear the birds and the low rumble of distant machinery in the fields beyond the perimeter fence. After this I'll go to the juice bar and order a carrot-and-ginger juice and do more of this week's mega-jigsaw of an ocean scene. I let my arm dangle off the edge of the table. It feels so good to be done with my exercise for the day. To be relaxed. Content.

An hour later, in the juice bar, someone's completed the jigsaw. All 4,700 pieces are in place. There's already a photo of it on the noticeboard alongside the other jigsaws we've completed this year. On our annual open days Dad tells people they're a metaphor. Pieces of different shapes and sizes that don't make sense are put together at the Creek to make something whole and amazing. I run my finger over the bumpy surface of the ocean bed, and change my mind about the juice. I'll see if Jenna, my favourite receptionist, is on duty.

I walk back out into the sunshine and take the long way round to reception. The outdoor pool, twice the size of the indoor one in the spa area, gleams. The lawns are immaculate, the flowers like a bold new fashion collection in their early summer glory. We rarely have visitors, but the Creek is always in perfect order regardless. It's because we have high standards and personal pride.

I turn the corner to enter reception by the formal entrance. Across the drive and the next expanse of lawn is the staff accommodation block, Hibiscus Hall, where I live. There are five floors visible from the outside, and two further basement floors. The first basement floor, which my dad has fitted out to the same high standard as the patient accommodation, is for support staff. *A harmonious society is one where every single person is valued.* That's one of his favourite sayings, and it's printed in big letters in the lobby. The second basement floor is for the underground complex of fully-equipped gym, sprung-floor exercise studios, break-out spaces, movie theatre, games room and breakfast cafeteria. Underground corridors lead to the main building and to the patient accommodation block, Larkspur Hall. Drew says there could be a nuclear disaster outside and we'd all be fine for months.

I'm in luck – Jenna is on reception. She's tapping at the keyboard on the large dark-wood desk, the short sleeves of her top digging into her plump arms. When she looks up, she says, "Why Mae, honey, how nice to see you. How are you?"

"Good," I say and settle into the black leather swivel chair next to her. "I've got twenty minutes until my computer session."

Jenna beams. "You want to do some helping?" She treats me like I'm still a little kid, but it doesn't stop me liking her. She plunks a pile of envelopes in front of me, then a few sheets of white labels printed with addresses, and nods towards an open cardboard box of glossy brochures under the table. "Make sure you keep the address labels straight. When you're done, I'll fix us both some tea." Jenna's one of the few members of staff who live outside the Creek, which means she has more interesting things to talk about when she has a tea break. We're kind of friends, despite our massive age difference. I'm one of six staff kids and we're not encouraged to mix with the patients, so my friendship pool is limited.

I stuff envelopes while Jenna carries on typing. As she's waiting for her document to emerge from the printer, the phone rings. She leaves it the regulation two rings before picking up.

"Good afternoon. Hummingbird Creek. How may I help you?" There's a pause, and she says, "Certainly, sir. I'll put you through right away." When she's replaced the receiver, she checks her puffy hair is still in place and says, "Peppermint tea coming right up. I won't be long."

When Jenna's gone through the side door towards the kitchenette, I glance across at the printer and read the top of a patient referral form that she's just printed. *Noah Tinderman. Paranoia. Anxiety. In need of a calm, nurturing environment. Requested length of stay: two months.* That's short by Creek standards. My eye leaps to the address. *England.* I remember very little about my first few years in England, but one day I'd like to go back.

The phone rings. I leave it. The voicemail fails to kick in after two rings. Jenna must have forgotten to switch it over. It keeps ringing. On and on, echoing in the empty, marble-floored lobby.

I'm not supposed to answer the phone, but I know

what to say. I'm nearly sixteen, so of course I'm more than capable of taking a message. A million times I've watched how Jenna transfers calls. I lift the phone. "Good afternoon. Hummingbird Creek. How may I help you?" My voice sounds fancy.

I hear a man give a cough, then, "Right. I've been fobbed off enough times." The accent is weird. British, but odd. Perhaps he's connected to the new patient, Noah. "I want to speak to Louelle Ballard, and this is about the sixth time I've called. Would you put me through, please?"

"Er. . ." I bite my lip. Should I forward the call to the grounds staff office? Could he be one of the reporters Dad tells us about, trying to sell stories about a celebrity's son or daughter being here? But if he was, I don't know why he'd want to speak to Mom.

"I only need to speak to her for a few minutes." He sounds less sure of himself now.

"Who are you?" I ask as I look round for Jenna. I shouldn't have picked up. "I could take a message?"

The man sighs. "How do I know you'll give it to her?"

While I'm trying to think how to answer, he says, "All right. Tell her that her brother called. Frank."

Is he saying that he's my *uncle*? "Pardon?"

"Tell her Frank called. Tell her our mother died a couple of days ago."

What's going on?

Mom has no family other than me and Dad. Her parents died before I was born, both of them addicts. Her mom abused drugs, her dad alcohol. Dad says Mom and I have a predisposition to addictive behaviours but it's not something we should worry about while we live here. His job is to protect us.

The man's voice is softer now. "If Louelle wants to speak to me, tell her I'd love that. I'll give you my number."

I reach for a pen and pull a Hummingbird Creek memo pad towards me. "OK," I say, my brain spinning. Out of the corner of my eye, I see Jenna, carrying two white bone-china mugs of tea. She speeds up when she sees I'm on the phone, her eyes wide with *What are you doing?* I've missed the first few numbers Frank's told me. Jenna's closer. Her cheeks are redder than I've ever seen them.

"Thank you for your call, sir," I say and hang up, not having had a chance to write anything down.

"Who was that?" Jenna asks. She barely glances at where she's placing the mugs on the desk.

"An inquiry," I say.

She frowns. "What about?"

"The next open day. I told him that he could find the details on the website." I'm shocked by my lie but I know I've done something wrong, and I don't want to upset her.

"We could have sent him a brochure, but OK." She places a hand on her chest and breathes out dramatically. "Don't do that again. You nearly gave me a heart attack." She takes a gulp of tea. "I have a very expensive mortgage and a husband out of work. My job has rules, honey, and I have to follow them or your dad will be extremely unhappy."

I cradle my hands round my mug and try not to let my confusion show. Is it true? My grandmother has been alive up until two days ago? Why would Mom and Dad lie to me?

Frank must be a reporter, or maybe some kind of con artist wanting to score money.

But, just to be sure, I'm going to pass the message to Mom when Dad's not here.

TWO

In the main building, admin takes up the whole of the first floor, and my computer session is in the main area, accessible through a glass door with swipe-card entry or by buzzing for admittance. Any staff-kid or patient using a computer has to be supervised. It's about learning appropriate boundaries. I switch on the gleaming computer on the desk next to the supervising assistant, and wait for the login prompt. The view up here is dramatic – the imposing drive to the gates, and beyond them the road to Pattonville, the nearest town an hour away. I'm always drawn to that long, straight road.

Earl, the head of admin and security, sweeps past me on his way to the corner desk, his long, sinewy arms full of files. Earl's been at the Creek as long as I have, but he hardly ever speaks to me. He prefers to stare with eyes that don't blink much. I still feel his eyes on me as I turn back to the keyboard to log in. We have one of the best computer and security systems in the world to ensure patients' maximum comfort and safety, and according to Dad that's mostly thanks to Earl. There was a rumour about how he strangled a man with his bare hands when he was in the army. I asked Dad about it once, and he laughed and said I shouldn't believe everything I hear.

I click to remove the box that appears on the screen. I know its message by heart: *You are logged in for one hour. Please note that you will only be allowed access to the sites listed below. These have been assessed by your clinician as the most suitable for your recovery and/or well-being. All forms of social media are blocked as Hummingbird Creek strives to provide as non-toxic an environment as possible. Emails are subject to filters and may be read for diagnostic or intervention purposes. Ensure you have enough tokens before making any purchases on the shopping sites ($1 = 2 tokens).*

I've heard it's possible to search for anything on computers outside the Creek, that a lot of people don't even consider the dangers of what they might come across. In the search box I type *Louelle Ballard family*.

No results.

I have two emails. One tells me that the vintage fountain pen I ordered for my collection last week, through a website I've been given individual access to, has been dispatched from India. The other is from Greta. She used to be home-schooled with us until she got a place at college in Pattonville. She lives there in term time, in an apartment by herself. She's nineteen, old enough to do whatever she likes, but what she wants is to keep telling the rest of us what to do.

The subject of her message is: *Make sure you buy...*

The message says: *... a birthday present for Drew.*

Does she truly think I'd forget to buy him a present if she didn't remind me? I reply, telling her that I've bought a tennis racquet from the bespoke range in an exclusive online sports shop, and that it's already wrapped and waiting in my closet for him. I browse through a couple of the clothing sites to see if my favourite sneakers have been made in any other colours yet, and play a couple of games of Scrabble with the computer.

When my hour is up I leave the main building by the side entrance, past the grounds staff office and the schoolhouse for us staff kids, towards home, which is the fifth floor of Hibiscus. We — Dad, Mom and I — have the penthouse suite with a roof terrace and a view of the main lawn and the buildings: all that Dad built up over these last ten years after we moved here from England. Mom would probably have preferred the view from Greta's family's apartment on the floor below, with a large balcony looking out the other way, over gardens and fields, and no buildings in sight.

I take an elevator to the fifth floor. If Dad was with me, he'd make me run up the flights of stairs while he raced me in the elevator.

"Hey!" I call as I walk in through the front door. Doors in Hummingbird Creek are never locked, apart from admin and the solitary rooms in the medical suite, and occasionally rooms in Larkspur. It's a fact that's always mentioned on open days. *We work in a climate of trust.*

Mom is where she usually is at this time, on the sofa in front of the television with a guava juice and a pre-weighed bowl of roasted nuts on the polished wooden table next to her. "You OK, honey?" she says. Her eyes are bright. She must be having one of her better days.

"Yeah," I say automatically. "You?"

"Not bad," she says and tells me a story about somebody ripping their jacket. I don't catch the beginning of it, so I can't tell if she's talking about one of the grounds staff she works with, or someone in the TV soap she's watching. It doesn't matter. I smile anyway and study the silver-framed photos on the shelves by the TV. There's Dad with his parents on his graduation from medical school. They look pretty ancient in the photo – now they're too old to travel.

There's a photo of Mom with me in her arms as a chunky baby, a smile on her face so wide it makes my chest hurt. Mom and Dad in the reception lobby of Hummingbird Creek, when it was first opened. Me in a series of posed black-and-white shots when I was about five with my dark brown hair in two high pigtails, tied with ribbon: English me.

Mom's photo albums were damaged in a flooded basement before I was born. "It's a shame we don't have any photos of your family at all," I say. I don't just mean around the apartment. I mean in the slim leather photo albums in the bookcase in Dad's study. They begin with Mom and Dad on their wedding day, Mom just nineteen, Dad aged thirty-five. Dad conventionally handsome, and Mom like a model with shining brown eyes and a big red flower tucked into her long dark hair.

Mom shrugs. "My parents have been dead so long, I hardly remember them." She leans forward to take a sip of her drink. Her hands are shaking ever so slightly. "Let's talk about something more cheerful." She smiles – it's one hundredth of the intensity of the smile in that photo. "Has Drew chosen his meal for Thursday yet?"

"Think so." He usually has the same birthday meal: burger and fries with vanilla milkshake, followed by Key lime pie. His dad, who runs Creek catering, says people outside eat a junk food version which is crammed with fat and sugar and empty calories. Staff kids get to eat their birthday meals wherever we want in the Creek – in the movie theatre or by the pool or up a tree – and there are fireworks and goodie bags.

"Sixteen," says Mom. "It's a nice age."

"What were you like at sixteen, Mom?" She rarely talks about the past because we try to live in the moment, in order to appreciate the here and now.

Her forehead creases. "Hopeful. Full of energy..." I wait for more, but she picks up the bowl of nuts and offers it to me.

I'm not supposed to eat from her calorie allowance but I take one and nibble it slowly.

Our watches beep at the same time with the ten-minutes-to-dinner reminder.

"Where's your father?" asks Mom. "It's unlike him not to be home by now."

The folding glass doors to the roof terrace are open, so I walk past the dining-room table and step out on to the warm terracotta tiles to see if I can see Dad over the railings. I spot him straight away, striding across the lawn, talking into his two-way radio. He's never off-duty. Even when he's away from the Creek, he's at a meeting or conference, or doing something to promote the work he believes in.

I sit on one of the pale-grey outdoor chairs. From here I can see across the living room, down the hall to the front door of the apartment. I count the seconds from when I hear the main door of Hibiscus bang shut, to Dad walking in through the door. Ten. He's definitely taken the elevator. As he places his radio on the narrow table in the hall, our food trolley arrives, and he helps the catering assistant negotiate the heat-insulated trolley into the dining room end of the living room.

"Thank you, Dr Ballard," she says with a blush. She's one of Dad's many admirers, eager for his charm to be turned towards them. A patient once told me she saw Dad on a TV show about how to heal troubled teens. She says he's a household name, a doctor who's not afraid to tell parents where they're going wrong with their kids.

"Hello, you two," Dad calls to us. He hands Mom a couple of the pre-portioned plates and turns back for the third. The catering assistant hands me a platter of peeled and sliced exotic fruits, asks if we've got everything we need, and then disappears.

I pour water into the heavy crystal glasses while Dad fetches the multivitamins from the sideboard. Two clear glass bottles from the on-site pharmacy in the medical suite. He shakes out a couple of pills from the first bottle and hands one each to Mom and me.

"How was your day, Hunter?" Mom asks, before popping her vitamin pill in her mouth and gulping it down with water.

I swallow mine with a mouthful of grilled fish. Even though I'm used to the chalky, bitter taste of the pill, it still makes me shudder.

"Irritating," says Dad. He tips out one of his multivitamins into the palm of his hand. "A patient's anger-management issues are worse than I was told." He bites his pill. His are white, different to our beige ones because he needs more vitamin B than us.

I'd like to talk about the phone call, but Dad says never to speak about Mom's family because it upsets her too much. It's a rule.

Rules are for our own good. I need to remember that. But the curiosity is killing me.

"How was the new teacher, Mae?" asks Dad.

"All right," I say.

He raises his eyebrows for more, but out in the hall his radio bleeps. He drops his linen napkin on to the table, and goes to answer it. "Hi, Abigail," he says. "Austin? You want me to calm him down?"

Mom stops eating and gazes at her plant pots on the terrace. I wonder when she last thought about her family.

"I have to go," calls Dad from the hall. "Don't keep my food. I'll get the kitchen to make me something else."

After the front door slams, I abandon my fish and move on to the fruit. Mom talks about a new online boutique that Drew's mom somehow knows about, which is going to be added to the approved list.

I cut in and ask, "What was my grandma's first name?"

She looks at me, startled. "Pam, of course."

"*Your* mom, not dad's mom." She takes a long pause, and I laugh gently, trying to make a joke out of it. "It's not that hard a question, is it?"

She taps her fist repeatedly against her mouth. What's so problematic about recalling her own mother's name? She drops her fist a couple of inches. "Vonnie," she says, slowly as if she's a child trying out a word for the first time.

"Vonnie," I repeat. "Nice." I'm not sure it really is. I just want to encourage her to tell me more. "What was her last name?"

She pulls in her lips and says nothing.

I try something else. "What was the name of the place you lived in?" I move my chair closer to her, in case that helps. "Was it a city?"

Mom shakes her head and says slowly, "No. There were horses." She stands up and stacks the plates noisily.

"Tell me more," I urge. "Please. Did you have brothers or sisters?"

"I can't..."

I can see that breaking the rule about mentioning her family is upsetting her, but it's never felt important before. "I answered the phone in reception to a guy who said he was your brother, Frank."

Her eyes connect with mine and there's a flash of shock. "He said to tell you that your mom died a couple of days ago."

"What are you talking about?"

But I've seen her steady herself by gripping the edge of the table. I'm sorry for her, but my sudden anger makes me keep going. "He wanted to speak to you."

Her face is set in a stubborn line.

"Why did you tell me your parents had already died? Why didn't you say you had a brother?"

"Stop!" she yells. She slumps backwards into her chair, hands over her ears. "Just stop. I don't want to hear any more." Then she's sobbing and rocking back and forth, her head in her hands.

I crouch down beside her, and touch her arm very gently. "Mom, please. It's OK. I've stopped. I'm sorry."

She gulps for air.

"What's going on?" Dad's standing in the doorway to the living room, back way too early from his call-out. I didn't hear him come in above the noise Mom was making. She falls silent but remains bunched over in her chair.

I can't speak.

He walks towards Mom. "Why's she so upset, Mae?"

I spring up, away from Mom, my mouth dry and my stomach lurching. I'm going to have to say it. "We were talking about her family."

He frowns and places a firm hand on Mom's shoulder. Ever so slightly, she shrinks away from his grip. "That was a poor choice of subject. Why did you bring it up, Mae?"

I'd like to ask him why he's so sure that Mom didn't start the conversation, but the fury in his pale blue eyes unnerves me. "We were talking about family histories in lessons today. For a project. I want to write about both sides of my family, so I was asking Mom. . ."

Mom lifts her head. Her make-up is streaked across one cheek. "My mom died, Hunter," she says in a flat voice.

"How do you know that, Louelle?" I'm scared of the way he asks. Slowly. Ominously. He repeats, "I asked you how you know."

Don't tell him, Mom. Act like you're too spaced out. Say you dreamed it.

"Frank spoke to Mae. He phoned reception and she was the one who took the call." Mom reaches for her napkin and wipes her face.

"Is this true, Mae? That you picked up the phone in reception?" The room is silent apart from a creak as Mom shifts in her chair.

"I was helping Jenna. She had to step away from the phone for a moment."

"I see," says Dad. He sits at the table, apart from Mom, and presses the top of his nose.

I wait for my punishment. When he's angry there's always a punishment. It's how self-discipline's learned.

"I guess I have to do this." He places his hands on the polished table, in between two placemats. They are freckly with pale hair growing out of them. "This is something I'm going to say once, then I never want to talk about it again. We told you your grandparents were dead because they were dead to us. As you know, they had terrible addictions. They were toxic people who caused your mom great unhappiness." He looks at me. "Do you understand?"

I nod. "But Frank?"

"Frank was not a good role model either." He pauses. "Mae, you answered the phone without permission. You upset your mother, and almost let a damaging individual back into her life." He pauses again, then clears his throat. "I didn't want to bring this up, but you also did a search in your computer session today that demonstrates poor judgement, and you lied about a school project. These behaviours go against everything the Creek stands for. I'm extremely disappointed in you."

I should have kept quiet. I shouldn't have answered the phone. Rules are there for a reason. No more risks. I'm going to stop smoking. I'll tell Drew tomorrow.

Mom is on her feet now, pale and breathing strangely.

"Go to bed, Louelle," says Dad. "I'll bring you a pill

to help you sleep." Before she's out of the room, he turns his gaze on me. To say anything now would be classed as back-chat. "Your punishment is. . ." he says, and pauses. I know he has to do this – that when there are rules, there also have to be punishments. "You're banned from taking part in Drew's birthday celebrations."

My head is hot and I'm dizzy. I've been a part of Drew's birthday ever since he came here nine-and-a-half years ago, a few months after us and the Jesmond family. He's chosen to eat his dinner on the building site where the cycling track's going to be. Of course he's only doing it to be awkward. I can't imagine what it will be like to hear the fireworks in my room and know I'm not standing next to him, laughing at the crazy noises and the blistering bursts of colour in the sky. Being outside at night is a rare treat.

"*I* decide what you study and what projects you do, not your teachers," says Dad. His face is very close to mine but his voice is a whisper, and I have to strain to hear. "Don't ever try to pull a trick like that on me again."

THREE

The alarm on my watch startles me awake, as it does every morning apart from Sunday. A minute later the light starts to fade up. Today I feel even more sluggish than usual, so I stay in bed an extra five minutes to think about yesterday's phone call. I wonder how Mom's doing, but I won't see her until this evening. I force myself to move. If I'm late for my first fitness or brain-training session of the day I'll be fined twenty tokens, and dragged out of bed by an orderly anyway. It's only happened to me once, but it was humiliating.

I can't tell what the weather's like yet because of the automated metal shutters at the windows, which are controlled centrally, like the lighting and air conditioning. They roll up silently at exactly eight-thirty a.m., and shut again at eight-thirty p.m., locking into place. Established routines that follow our bodies' natural rhythms are essential for well-being. Once, a patient's finger was almost severed because she didn't hear the shutter coming down. Now every shutter has a cushioned strip at the bottom, but it's still sealed tight.

I'm not going outside, though, so the weather doesn't matter. I pull exercise clothes at random out of my sports closet, and when I'm dressed, I shove my hair into a hair elastic without brushing it. But then an image of Drew comes into my head, and I undo the ponytail and reach for my hairbrush, checking in the mirror at the same time that there's no gunk in the corner of my eyes.

After a quick brush of my teeth, I take a lift to the lower basement level. Patients are divided into groups and there are three start times, six-thirty, seven and seven-thirty. Staff kids are in a separate group, and we always start at seven-thirty. Having an easier start to the day is one of our extra privileges, like the birthday dinners and very rare trips outside the Creek to shop or participate in sports competitions.

I scan the list on the noticeboard quickly and see that I need to be in Studio 4. I'm in a distracted mood this morning, so I'm glad I'm not in a schoolroom for neurocognitive-reinforcement therapy, or brain-training as we call it, even if there's the chance of earning tokens.

Apart from Drew, everyone else is there: Zach, Greta's brother, who's fourteen, and then the youngest three, all from the same family: Ben, Luke and Joanie, ages ten, eight and five. Their dad devises the exercise programmes.

Other lower-ranking members of staff have children, of course, but they're not allowed to live at the Creek.

Joanie pats the empty mat next to her that she's reserved for me. I don't want to go there. I want to be on a mat next to Drew, so I can whisper that I've got something important to tell him later.

I have an uncle. And a grandmother who just died. Perhaps I have a grandfather too. Maybe cousins.

Joanie pats the mat again and I walk across to her and sit down. "Morning, Mae," she says and leans over to give my bare shoulder a quick kiss because it once made me laugh. She's a mini version of Ben, sturdy with a mop of blonde-hair. Luke, their middle brother, is thinner with brown hair that grows close to his scalp, as if his hair is as timid as he is.

I mumble morning back, but I'm looking at Drew who's just managed to walk through the door before our instructor. He hasn't pulled his sports top down properly. It's hitched up slightly on one side, and when he bends to grab a mat, I can see the line where his tan fades to white at the waistband of his shorts.

Our instructor today is a solidly built physical education grad student, one of several on internships, here for a few months to make a chunk of money and enjoy the lifestyle.

The student logs the heart-monitor readings from our Creek watches into one of the silver Creek laptops, and checks we've reset our calorie counter to zero. It takes him a while as he's still new to it.

27

During the squatting, Joanie gives up and rolls on to her mat.

"Get up," I hiss.

"I hurt," she says.

She's got a couple more minutes and then the student will have to note it down and she'll be fined. He's already looking at his watch. She's five, old enough to learn that you have to keep aiming high to reach your potential. Also that when self-discipline fails, life without tokens to spend isn't fun.

"Come on. Imagine you're somewhere else," I whisper.

Joanie rubs her thigh. "Like where?"

I shrug. "Outside? Painting under a tree. Or about to jump in the pool?" I hold out my hand and when she takes it, I haul her up to standing.

She starts again and I look away because I don't want to see her wincing.

"Mae?"

I turn and frown. "What?"

"I'm on the veranda with you. On the swing chair."

I smile. "That's nice. Are we reading?" I ask.

She nods. When I was her age, I was in England. I wish I had better memories of that time.

After the class the student logs our data and we make our way to the cafeteria, which smells of freshly baked bread and sweat. We queue up with the patients to choose our breakfast. Patients at Hummingbird Creek don't look like regular patients according to an article Dad let me

28

read, written by a journalist he hired. The journalist said they look as if they're on vacation in an exclusive resort. Moneyed, clear-eyed and energetic, they wear the latest hot labels and are comfortable around uniformed staff. Nobody here is out-and-out crazy. They just need support and structure. A holistic, non-drug-taking approach. A six-month stay is entirely usual. Dad says it takes time to fully appreciate the benefits of the Creek lifestyle, and to see the best results. Patients are occasionally allowed home for a couple of days and there are a few parent and guardian days throughout the year when parents are allowed to come for a special lunch and an afternoon of sampling the spa and other leisure facilities.

The made-to-order line is extra long today, so Drew and I scoot round to the breads, cereals and yoghurt section. Someone's complaining to the staff that the fruit platter needs topping up. We each fill a bowl with bran flakes, slosh over some milk, add a few blueberries, grab a glass of unsweetened juice and dodge the wrong way round the extra-supervised area where the eating-disorder crew sit.

I search the room for pink. For my friend Thet. She's inspecting the rim of her glass of juice before she takes a sip, her glossy black hair covering half her face. It's pink juice, naturally, to match her pink sportswear. She looks up and, when she catches sight of me, her serious expression changes and she waves. We've known each other for nearly three years. She was discharged once but came back four months later. She never makes me feel odd for having grown up here like some of the other patients do, and she's watched an astonishing amount of TV series which she can recall in great detail. She used to write something called "fan fiction" – stories about the characters from her favourite TV show – but recently she started a fantasy novel, loosely inspired by her grandmother, who fled a barbaric war that had killed Thet's parents.

Thet's the only patient friend I've ever had. Actually, she's my only female friend; I don't count Greta or Joanie.

"Move along, Mae," calls an orderly.

Although there's no rule against us staff kids mixing with patients, it's not encouraged. They might be a bad influence on us with their outside habits but, more importantly, they leave and we don't. No contact with patients after they've left is one of the most sacred rules. They need to be free of their past as they live their new lives.

The staff kids' table is next to the far wall, which is papered in a photographic scene: woodland with the early morning sun shining through. We all have our preferred places; mine is between Drew and Joanie. I sit, eat the blueberries with my fingers, and feel sick at the thought of telling Drew I can't be at his birthday meal. I'll tell him when we're on our own, not here with Zach, who's already making comments behind his hand about a patient who's being made to eat breakfast sitting on his own. I think it may be Austin, the patient with anger problems.

Drew pushes back his chair and grips one of his calves. "Ow."

I'm the only one who makes a sympathetic noise. We all have muscle pains from time to time because of the amount of exercise we do, but Drew's have been bad lately.

"You're such a baby," says Zach. He's a year-and-half younger but much bigger than me. I reckon he hates the fact that he'll never be as cool as Drew.

I reach across and tug the hem of Drew's shorts. "Perhaps you're growing too quickly. Look how short these have got."

"Mae," says Drew. "Leave my shorts alone."

Zach sniggers loudly and I turn back to my bran flakes with a flushed face.

When I return to the apartment to shower and get dressed for morning lessons, the shutters are up and a cleaner is vacuuming the living room. We say hello to each other politely. As I leave to meet Drew downstairs, she's dusting the collection of glass horse ornaments that Mom keeps in a cabinet in the hall.

Horses. A link to Mom's past. I have a small plastic horse in my bedroom that I've had for ever which I keep on my chest of drawers, in a pottery dish I made in art therapy. Mom often picks it up when she's in there. I think I only like it because she loves it so much.

I press the button for the elevator and wish I'd had time

to take Frank's phone number before Jenna came back. He must have been calling from England. I wouldn't be able to phone or write to him if I had his details now, but I'd have them for when I leave the Creek in a couple of years. Very few people have access to an outside phone line, and anyone coming into the Creek has to hand in their cell phones at the security building until they leave. We're a cell-phone-free environment. Not that there's any signal out here that makes them worth having. And all letters that leave the Creek are read to ensure the privacy of other patients, especially the celebrity ones who are here trying to stay under the radar.

Drew's waiting for me in the lobby, sprawled across the corner sofa and flipping through one of the new Hummingbird Creek brochures that someone's left lying around. He throws it in my direction, and it lands at the end of the sofa.

"*Allow us to give your teenager world-class care in the most exquisite of surroundings,*" he quotes from the brochure's strapline at the top, then grimaces as he stands up and puts weight on his aching leg.

We walk towards the schoolhouse and I take a deep breath. I tell him about picking up the phone to Frank and making Mom hysterical. Before he can comment, I tell him about my punishment.

He curses. "Your dad. . ." He shakes his head.

"I'm sorry."

Drew stops, which means I have to turn and face him.

32

"It's not your fault," he says.

"It is. I shouldn't have picked up the phone." Since we're not walking for a moment, I slip my feet out of my flip-flops and feel the soft grass. It's still slightly damp from the overnight sprinklers. "I think we should stop smoking," I add.

Drew walks past me. "God, Mae. Your tiny rebellious streak didn't last long, did it?"

I pick up my flip-flops. "I'm just refocusing on core values," I snap at his back.

Drew snorts. I push him and he pushes me back. I want to talk to him more about Mom's family, but by the time the pushing's over the moment's passed and we're at the schoolhouse.

Staff kids are separated from the patients for lessons, as well as sport and most activities, because it's considered less disruptive for us. We get the cute building. They get schoolrooms in Larkspur. Our teacher, Ms Ray, is sitting at her desk when we arrive, stapling pieces of paper together with Joanie. Ben and Luke are on the floor, playing a board game I've never seen before.

Ms Ray just started working at the Creek two days ago, and Drew's right – she does look young. I think it's because she doesn't wear make-up and her wavy hair is loose around her shoulders. Her pale blue shirt is plain but has different coloured buttons up the front. Perhaps she's more of a pre-school teacher.

"You're ten minutes late. I've already told you I want

you all here on time. And where's Zach?" she asks. "I thought everything worked to a strict timetable here."

"Lessons are different," says Drew. "No one minds."

Ms Ray frowns. "I mind. And I'm waiting to start a science test."

Ben looks up from the board game. "I don't want to do a test."

Drew says, "We never do tests. I mean we have health tests, and fitness tests. Verbal reasoning and non-reasoning tests. But not tests in lessons."

Ms Ray doesn't believe him. "Never?"

"We've never had one," I confirm. "Haven't you had an induction with Earl? The tall guy in charge of admin and security? He usually gives out a list of dos and don'ts."

We all look at her. She frowns and taps her stapled papers on the desk. "My induction's been delayed until tomorrow afternoon. I'm just seeing what you know. That's all. Joanie, your test is to see if you can colour quietly for forty-five minutes."

We start soon after Zach arrives. Ms Ray takes no notice of him when he says he's too tired to use his brain. I'm surprised he isn't curious to know what a schoolhouse test is like.

I don't mind the jumpiness in my stomach when Ms Ray says, "Turn your papers over now, please." But the test turns out to be impossibly hard, with graphs and diagrams. After twenty minutes I've done the only questions I can, and I spend the remaining twenty-five drawing an intricate zigzag round the edge of my paper.

While Ms Ray marks the papers, I listen to Joanie read out loud on the veranda, on the swing chair, while the boys read inside. After she's read me her boring chapter book about a dog who is always getting himself in trouble, she snuggles into me and I read her some of the adventure book that Ms Ray gave us yesterday, about two kids who go back in time to ancient Greece.

Mid-morning, when we take a break, Ms Ray asks me to help carry some books to her car. As soon as she hands over two not-very-heavy books, I know it's just a way to get me on my own without keeping me behind at lunchtime.

"How d'you think you did in that test?" she asks me once we're out of the schoolhouse.

"I couldn't do it," I say.

"It was mixed," she says. "You did brilliantly on the few questions that you had enough knowledge to tackle, but I'm worried about significant gaps in your learning. What are your ambitions, Mae?"

No one has ever asked me that before. Beyond leaving Hummingbird Creek for college, I have no idea.

"College."

Ms Ray nods. "Which one?"

"I don't know."

"If you work incredibly hard over the next two-and-a-bit years, you'll stand a real chance of getting into a very good one." She looks around. "I'm guessing tuition fees aren't a problem for your family."

I guess not. It hadn't occurred to me that tuition fees could even be a problem.

"Thing is," says Ms Ray. "I'd have to teach you topics that don't feature in the home-school booklets." We're walking to the small staff parking lot by the kitchen building. She points at the only ancient car. One of the side panels is a different shade of red to the rest of the car. "That's mine."

"Don't you live on-site?" I ask.

Ms Ray nods. "Yes, but my room's too small for all my books so I keep some of them in the car. I had to hand my keys to admin because I'm only allowed to drive Creek cars while I'm here but I keep it unlocked so I can use it for storage."

Her car could do with an inside-out valet service, or a sort-out at the very least. The floor at the back is covered with stacks of books, and on the seats there are candy wrappers, carrier bags full of science journals, some scrumpled clothing and a jumble of sandals. Ms Ray places the books we're carrying on top of the clothing.

"Don't look too hard in there," she says. "I'm not very tidy."

As she slams the car door shut, a car a couple of spaces away reverses out at speed. I see stiff blonde hair. A crying face. The wheels make a slight screeching noise as they turn. It's Jenna. She speeds down the path, past the restaurant building, towards the security building, then stops for the heavy gates to open slowly. I run towards the car.

Something's wrong. "Jenna!" I shout. "Wait."

I'm almost in touching distance of the trunk when she accelerates out of the gates, before they're fully open, on to the road towards Pattonville.

"I have to go," I tell Ms Ray as I pass her on the way back, and run to reception.

One of the newer receptionists is there. She narrows her eyes at me. "What do you want, Mae?"

"Why was Jenna leaving in such a hurry? What's happened?"

"You'll have to ask your father that."

"Tell me," I persist. "Please tell me."

"Jenna no longer works at Hummingbird Creek. That's all I'm prepared to say." She shifts her attention to the computer screen in front of her. "Now, if you don't mind, I'd appreciate it if you'd go. You aren't welcome in reception any more."

FOUR

Dad doesn't want to hear Jenna's name mentioned when I try to speak to him at dinner. He says she was no longer in tune with the Hummingbird Creek ethos, and I'd do well to remember that rules create structure, and structure is essential for good health. That's all he's going to say on the subject. Mom looks upset but carries on eating, slowly, looking at her food and not us.

After dinner I watch TV with Mom while Dad works in his study off the living room. Creek TV changes its selection of programmes and movies every month, and I want to see *ET* again before it's off-list. I sit on the sofa next to Mom. I'd like to ask her what it was like growing up with a brother who wasn't a good role model. Does she feel different, knowing her mom is dead? She stares at the screen, expressionless. I can't concentrate on the movie and, before ET goes home, I take myself to bed and doodle in a notebook with my favourite vintage fountain pen – a Dunhill-Namiki made in Japan in the 1930s. It has a black lacquered cap and barrel, and is decorated with an intricate golden dragon. The nib is super-fine and italic, and perfectly shaped to the way I hold the pen to write.

When the lights automatically turn off, I usually fall asleep straight away, but tonight guilt keeps me wriggling, unable to find a comfortable position. I wonder how easy it will be for Jenna to find another job. There's no way she'll find one that pays as well as the Creek. I remember the day she started here, soon after Joanie was born, and she couldn't stop smiling. She was in thrall of all the luxury facilities. "I feel like I've gone to heaven," she told me. And in all the years since, she was only ever kind to me.

At breakfast the next morning, there's a buzz in the queue about the imminent arrival in Larkspur of some clothing samples from a couple of fashion houses. A small group is arguing about a soccer match from the previous day. I want to speak to Thet but I can't see her – she must have had an early exercise session.

As I eat my second mouthful of berry compote, Zach says he's heard a rumour that I demanded Jenna was sacked because she said something rude to me. I tell him he's wrong and stand up suddenly so that my chair makes a scraping noise and everyone in the cafeteria looks round. Drew frowns but says nothing until we walk across to the schoolhouse together.

"Your dad got rid of Jenna because you took that phone call?" he says.

I nod. I can't look him in the eye. Jenna was his favourite too.

"What a control freak."

"She broke the rules. So did I. We went against what this place stands for. Dad was only protecting me from Mom's family."

"What's wrong with them?"

"Addictions. Damaging behaviours."

Drew raises an eyebrow. "You'd think he'd be more sympathetic."

Perhaps there's more to it. Things that would be too upsetting to know. I have to trust Dad.

Ms Ray reads out the day's announcements. One of the students is organizing a water slide beyond the basketball court between three and five p.m. All have permission to attend. There's a special offer at the spa for haircuts over the next three days: only five tokens for a trim.

Drew rolls his eyes and I smile back at him. Dr Jesmond told Drew his hair was too long the other day. It feels unfair sometimes that the patients are allowed to get away with much more than us concerning their appearance, but I guess we understand better how taking care of ourselves is part of good discipline and inner confidence. There are very few people who don't have five tokens in their accounts, when a basic weekly payment of fifty

tokens is paid into everyone's account (u_____
on zero privileges), with a chance to earn m_____
achievements, like getting high scores in brai_____
sessions.

I think how proud I used to be to tell Jenna my brain-training scores because she'd make more of a fuss about them than Mom would. I'm still thinking of her as Ms Ray begins a lesson about atoms. I only pay proper attention after she's asked me a question, and I'm unable to answer it. She's drawing on the whiteboard when the door to the schoolroom opens.

Greta. She's not supposed to be back until tomorrow evening for Drew's birthday.

"Hey, everyone," she says. "Who are you?" she asks Ms Ray. "How long have you been here?"

Ms Ray steps forward. "Hi, I'm Steffi Ray, the new teacher. This is my fourth day and you are...?"

"Greta, Zach's sister." She waves in his general direction. "You probably know that our dad is Dr Karl Jesmond." She walks across to Ms Ray's desk and leans against it. "I don't mind leading a circle time if you want a break. We usually pick topics at random from old work booklets."

"Welcome back, Greta," says Ms Ray. "Thanks for the offer, but this morning I'm teaching the class about atoms and molecules. Feel free to take a seat." She points towards the spare chair next to Zach, but Greta walks back down the schoolroom. "It's OK. If you don't need ne, I've got better things to do. I'll see you guys at lunch."

Ms Ray waits until she's gone, and then she asks Joanie if she can remember what the central part of an atom is called.

"No," says Joanie.

We wait for Ms Ray to tell her, but she doesn't. She says, "Go on, Joanie. Have a go."

Joanie opens her mouth. "Nu..." Her round face scrumples with effort. "Nu-cle-us!"

I clap enthusiastically. Drew and the boys look at me. Schoolwork isn't anything to be bigged up. It's only one section of our lives, and we need to keep the right balance or we're headed for emotional difficulties.

At lunchtime, I dread going to the restaurant, where I know I'll have to witness Greta's usual Queen Bee routine. She's already there at our staff kids' table next to the window when we arrive from lessons, talking in her loud voice to a waitress about how the table hasn't been set correctly.

After we've ordered our food from the menu, Greta looks out at the pool and shrieks, "Oh my God. Look! Isn't that the new teacher?"

We stand up to see as Greta says, "Let's watch her belly flop."

Ms Ray is on the diving board in a plain old black swimsuit and an ordinary white swim cap. She dives gracefully, and when Greta sees she's a good swimmer, she stops watching and tells us to sit down.

"Tell us about outside, Greta," says Ben. "Please."

We all want to know. But Greta makes us ask every time, and sometimes beg.

She tells us about the meals she's cooked. The TV programmes she's downloaded. That she received her first-ever wrong call on her cell phone. That it's still odd to pay for things in dollars and not tokens. How she went out to see a movie and came back to her apartment past eleven p.m. That she's having some blackout blinds made for her windows because she still hasn't got used to sleeping with such thin curtains.

I lean my head to one side and rub my neck where I have a pins-and-needles sensation. It's the third time I've had it. I've heard patients complaining about it too, but it can't be catching. Can it? Greta's boasting about the wifi in her apartment. That's far more irritating than the pins and needles.

"I. Cannot. Wait," mutters Drew.

"It's so great," says Greta. "But you've got to know how to handle it. People get obsessed with things like cell phones and social media." She shovels a forkful of bulgur wheat with edamame beans into her mouth and we have to wait for her to swallow it before she adds, "I'm lucky I was brought up here. I've seen people leave lectures because they've realized they left their cell phones at home."

43

Before she gets going on her usual rant about the other students being lazy with no routine to their day, I say, "Bet it's still exciting, living on the outside."

Greta nods.

"All that freedom," says Drew.

"Not being told what to do," says Zach.

"A phone," says Ben.

Luke, his brother, nods.

"It's cool," says Greta. "And I have so many friends." She turns to a passing waiter. "What's the fruit sorbet of the day?"

It's goals group after lunch and my chance to talk to Thet as everyone moves from the restaurant building to the therapy rooms on the ground floor of the main building. It's hard sometimes to find a moment when there's no one around to overhear us.

"How are you?" I ask when I catch up with her by the stairs.

"Six," she says. Six on a scale of zero to ten isn't too bad. "You?"

"Something odd happened," I say. I tell her about my uncle Frank, how it's unsettled me, how I want to know more about Mom's family but there's no way Mom or Dad are going to tell me.

"They want you to live in the present," says Thet. "They don't want you wasting energy on the past."

I sigh heavily.

"You need someone to do a search on the internet for you, I guess," says Thet.

"I tried already."

"No, the *real* internet."

There aren't any patients scheduled for a visit home at the moment. Perhaps Thet's thinking of Greta, but I know she won't do it. She'd say I was going behind my parents' backs. She might even tell her dad, who'd tell mine. I'd be accused of going against everything the Creek stands for. Punished.

"I can't ask Greta, but even if I could, I only have two first names. Frank and Vonnie. That's not going to get me very far in a search, is it?"

Thet shakes her head slowly. Her hair gleams where the sunlight catches it. "You need more clues."

We step outside, and the air is scented with the flowers in the densely planted borders. The pale rock sculpture on the lawn contrasts perfectly against the deep green of the expertly tended grass. Everyone else has gone via the covered walkway. It's just me and Thet here, and it's so peaceful, we can hear a bird hopping about in the undergrowth of a nearby bush. My uncle Frank can't live anywhere as beautiful as this. If he knew Mom lived here, he might have looked up the website, and become jealous. He might have a nasty ulterior motive for contacting her.

We linger outside for a few seconds, leaning against the cool brick of the main building to avoid the crowds inside. When we go inside, everyone is still bunched outside the therapy rooms, waiting for the doors to unlock automatically. We stand a bit apart so no one accidentally touches Thet, and I notice there's a new boy standing on his own. He's tall with pale skin and lots of dark blond hair. Gangly. Not many muscles under that orange shirt, and jeans that surely must be too hot in this weather.

Aha. He must be the patient from England.

He sees me looking, and steps closer. "Hi."

Beside me, Thet shrinks back. "Hi," I say.

"I'm Noah." His accent is definitely British, but soft. "I'm new," he adds unnecessarily. "Finding my feet."

"I'm Mae. I hope you settle in quickly."

"Thanks," says Noah. "This place looks amazing, but I wasn't expecting there to be so many rules. That Welcome Pack they give you is *huge*, isn't it? I skim-read the rules, so I probably didn't take them all in." He looks at his hands and decides to jam them into the front pockets of his jeans, out of the way.

"It's good to know the rules," I say. "They establish boundaries and make you feel secure. Don't worry. You'll learn them as you go along. I hope you have a great stay."

"Thanks. How long have you been here?" he asks.

I don't need to look at Thet to know she's smiling. "Nearly ten years," I say, and Noah's face is one of complete surprise and, I'm annoyed to see, horror.

Thet says, "She's a staff kid."

"Oh," says Noah. "You have to be tagged as well?"

"Tagged?"

Noah lifts up his arm to indicate his watch.

Everyone on Creek property wears a health-monitoring watch apart from day visitors or work people who come from outside. Mom had the very first Creek watch. Dad had it decorated with twelve diamonds round the edge, and when she has upgrades the diamonds are transferred.

"How else would you get such accurate data about your health?" I say. "Nowhere else in the world has such sophisticated monitoring as us."

There's a clacking noise coming down the corridor. Abigail, the head therapist, in her high heels, is heading our way with the other therapists. From where we're standing we can't hear the low clicking sound of the therapy rooms unlocking, but we see people push the doors open and go in. As Noah looks round, I say, "Do you know which room you're supposed to be in?"

"Room Three." He frowns. "I think that's right." He taps his watch and checks the screen. "Yes."

"See? The watches are useful for all sorts of things," I say. I wave goodbye to Thet and walk off towards Room Five.

My group is the one for staff kids. Joanie doesn't do goals group, but Greta is here, so that makes six of us, seven if you include Abigail, who's leading our group today. We sit on pale blue velvet armchairs in a small circle and stare at our knees or the white walls, hung with paintings that comprise part of the Creek's private collection of late twentieth-century art. We stare anywhere apart from each other because none of us finds this easy.

We begin by going round the circle, one by one, saying what our goal for the previous month was, how we managed, how we could have improved and what we learned. What we learned has to tie up with one of the Creek philosophies.

Ben is picked to start and he reminds us his goal was to eat a wider variety of fruit and vegetables. He lists what he's tried, and rambles on about what tasted better than he'd thought and what didn't. He says he knows that all the food at the Creek is part of a healthy diet and just because he thinks something is so gross it might make him throw-up, it probably won't. He has to respect his body and give it the best possible fuel. He has to trust the Creek chefs to make the fruit and vegetables taste as good as possible.

Abigail nods and smiles. As well as being the head therapist, she's also the youngest, and some patients have a crush on her. Because revealing tops aren't allowed she tends to go for something with a high neckline but some other distracting feature, such as a big bow or frill, or a lace overlay. Today she's wearing a yellow dress with short white sleeves and a massive white collar. She looks like an oversized daisy.

Drew's next. He only engages with goals group because if he achieves his goal he, like the rest of us, earns thirty tokens. Privately he says the real challenge is to set ourselves easily achievable goals. Today he tells us that he was aiming to beat his personal best for a ten-mile run, and he managed it. He grins when we applaud him loudly, and mutters something about sport helping his moods.

"Well done, Drew," says Abigail. "We need to keep working on those moods of yours, though, don't we?"

Drew nods. After he sees Abigail press submit on the online form to secure his thirty tokens, he slouches down in his chair.

I've achieved my goal too: I've spent more time with Zach, Ben, Luke and Joanie this month. I understand the importance of teamwork, and how we can all help each other flourish. It's one of the cornerstones of Creek life for everyone here, patients or not. We can all improve ourselves.

After we've each had our turn, we discuss new goals for ourselves. I fall back on my default option which is to keep a gratitude diary.

Abigail tips her head to one side. "I think you might want to consider something around your understanding of why we have certain rules here."

Everyone stares at me. Is she referring to me picking up the phone in reception? Dad must have told her. I wonder if that means every member of staff knows.

Drew wriggles in his seat. The others whisper. I don't know what to say.

"How about a diary entry each night for a month?" says Abigail. "Focus on a different rule every day and say why we have it." She smiles, waits for me to nod, then moves on to Luke.

I don't listen to anything else that's said in the group, although I look at each person who's talking as if I am. I think of Jenna and how she was the only member of staff I properly liked.

At the end Drew rushes off to practise some hoops. As I leave the room, I see Noah emerge from the room further along with Will, a patient who's been here nearly as long as Thet, and the boy who's been eating on his own. Noah glances back and sees me. He gives me a quick nod.

I go with Thet to the spa where we have facials, side by side, and I listen to her talk about her novel. It's set in a cruel land. The main character manages to run away to safety, but she later discovers every single member of her family has been killed apart from a baby sister, who has been captured and locked away. To rescue her, the main character must travel to an ancient forest where a rare snow-flower blooms once a year. If she tastes its pollen and survives its poison, she'll become a warrior and join a fierce tribe who will help her rescue her sister.

Despite the brutal storyline, Thet's voice calms me.

FIVE

"You didn't miss anything last night at my meal," says Drew as we walk towards the schoolhouse together the day after his birthday. "It was shit."

"Why?" I want him to say he missed me.

"It wasn't that cool having it at the cycle track. Joanie thinks getting dressed up means wearing her mermaid outfit, for God's sake. Greta was worse than usual, lecturing me about gratitude."

"The fireworks went on for ages," I say. I heard them from my room. The shutters were down, of course. I had to imagine the fizzingly vivid colours against the grey evening sky. "Were they good?"

"They were OK," says Drew. "But there are fireworks at every staff kid's birthday. I'd have liked something different." He sighs. "Like some time away from here."

All day yesterday I felt the weight of Jenna not being there. I'm sure Drew must have felt it too. I wish I could have seen him open the tennis racquet I'd spent a computer session designing, using the sports site's templates. I'll never know if his face lit up when he saw it. Did he see straight away that I'd had *To Drew Happy 16th Love Mae x* lasered on to the side? That kiss, I'm not sure if it was too much.

"Did Dad give—" I start. I'm embarrassed to ask. I'm not after a thank-you. It's occurred to me just now that Dad might not have handed over the present. Sometimes his punishments involve more than you first realize.

"Yes," says Drew. "Thanks. The racquet's cool."

All of a sudden I don't want to be here on the steps of the schoolhouse. I want to be in the long grass or the woodland gardens with Drew, rolling cigarettes, looking at the sky. We only do lessons for four hours a day – and I like schoolwork – but sometimes it feels much longer. And today I just want to get away.

"You free to meet after your afternoon exercise?" I ask. "Just us two?"

"Yeah."

"Woodland gardens. Third bench, seventh tree," I say.

"Got it," he says, and his smile almost winds me.

"Hello, you two," says Ms Ray. "Take your seats right away, please. We've got a lot to get through this morning." She's wearing a cross-over dress that has a rip on the sleeve. It's been sewn up neatly, but still. It's noticeable.

"From next week, anyone who's late will have to make up the time during morning break. And yes, I had my induction yesterday, thank you very much."

The announcements begin with a reminder about using the correct towels for the pool.

"Next we have an invitation to a swimming gala at Pattonville College," continues Ms Ray. The gasp in the schoolroom makes her look up.

"When?" asks Drew. The last time there was a trip outside was before Christmas, to the mall.

Ms Ray refers back to her laptop screen. "This weekend." She scans the information. "OK, it's for any boys in the area, aged nine and under." She looks up. "Luke. That must be for you."

The rest of us slump, except for Joanie who thumps her brother on the arm.

"No," he says in a small voice, then in a louder voice he says, "I don't want to go." He hugs his arms around himself and shrinks into his little body. He's always looked much more frail than his brother or sister, but he's surprisingly speedy at most sports.

"Loser," mutters Drew, and I kick him under the desk.

"You're an awesome swimmer," says Ben. "You could win a trophy for the Creek."

Luke slaps his hands over his eyes.

"It's OK, Luke," says Ms Ray. "No one's making you go." She looks round the room for someone to give her an explanation.

"He's only left the Creek once," I say. "It freaked him out."

She frowns and nods. "It's OK, Luke. I'll send a message back saying you're not going to enter it this time."

Ms Ray explains we're going to do a group project, involving material dyed with various household chemicals. First we have to learn about the chemicals.

We've never done anything like this before. Previously we went through work booklets at our own pace, had circle time where we discussed topics from the booklets and listened to audiobooks. Ms Ray teaches lessons that seem to work for all of us at different levels. She likes demonstrating things too. I hope she doesn't land herself in trouble for not doing things the Creek way.

After morning break, Drew, Zach and I each have a copy of the periodic table on our desks. We have to memorize as much as we can over the next week. Ms Ray holds up a fat chemistry book and one of us – Drew, Zach or I – are to read a chapter of it over the weekend for the purpose of doing a presentation on Monday on natural and synthetic dyes.

There's the longest silence before I crack and say, "I'll do it."

"Thank you, Mae," says Ms Ray, and it lands on my desk with a thump.

"We never have homework," says Ben. "How's Mae

going to have time to do it?" He looks at Zach who nods in agreement.

Ms Ray looks surprised. "There's this afternoon and the weekend. I know you have activities, Mae, but there should be enough time." She pauses. "What *is* your weekend schedule?"

"It's fine. I can do it," I say.

Drew says, "Six hours of sport on both Saturday and Sunday plus activities."

"Oh. I see," says Ms Ray. "Well, just do your best, Mae."

For the rest of the morning we do geography. Ben and Joanie act out being tectonic plates and somehow Ben treads on Joanie's hair, and in the ensuing meltdown, as I watch Ms Ray trying to sort it out, I wonder how long it'll be before she leaves this job. No teacher has ever lasted more than a year. As we're dismissed for lunch, she places a further book on my desk. A play to read "when you have time". It's by someone called William Shakespeare.

Zach notices and pulls a *What the hell's she doing* face. I give him a *I know right* shrug, but secretly I'm pleased that Ms Ray thinks I'm worth pushing.

It's humid today, but cooler in the Woodland Gardens. There's an assault course up here, built in the clearing. It's a neat hangout because the rope bridge can be used as a hammock, or you can swing from the top of the main frame into several trees.

The grounds of the Creek have been a paradise for Drew

and me since we were little. We've roamed every inch together. There were times when members of staff would be sent to round us up, on foot, or on a golf buggy. That was before we were given the watches with preset alarms. We made dens, played our own version of tennis, climbed trees and slithered on our stomachs while stalking the wildlife, as the Creek was built up around us, and then improved and upgraded. Sometimes we played with Greta and Zach, but mostly it was just us because they were too annoying.

As Drew's already unearthed our smoking gear, I walk straight to the third bench and turn off the path. The seventh tree I come to is big enough for us both to lean against and not be seen from the path, though Drew hears me coming.

"Following the rules didn't last long," says Drew, sticking his head out.

I sigh. The rules. I wish they were more . . . flexible. "I know I should have more self-control."

Drew holds his hands up, and a little piece of tobacco flies through the air. "Whoa. I'm not saying breaking rules is a bad thing, Mae." He reaches for the lighter and, with some difficulty because it's almost empty, lights a cigarette.

"I want to get unrestricted access to the internet," I say. "To find out more about Mom's side of the family. I know it's going against my dad, but I can't stop thinking about it." I roll a cigarette because I want to focus on something. I plan on merely holding it but when Drew leans forward for me to light it from his, I feel a strange sense of inevitability. As I draw the flame in, I see a tiny mark on his nose. A new freckle or a speck of dirt. "What's this?" I say and reach out with my spare hand to touch it.

He pulls away, and resettles himself between the tree roots.

I push down the disappointment. "It's gone," I say. "Don't worry."

"You want to track down mysterious Uncle Frank?"

I nod. I feel drawn to Mom's side of the family, intrigued by the possibility that I might have more in common with them than Dad's family, who rarely show any interest in me. "I'm going to ask if I can have a trip to the mall with Mom. See if I can somehow get into the computer store."

Drew nods. We spent a glorious quarter of an hour at the computer store before Christmas because we had a grad student as our chaperone who didn't know that we weren't allowed to be there. The thin laptops and tablets were things of gleaming beauty. Everything – good, bad, ugly and life-changing – was contained inside them.

"I have to come up with more keywords for the search," I say. "Right now I only have the first names of my uncle and grandmother."

"Have you looked for official documents?" asks Drew. "Papers. You know, the sort of crap you need on the outside."

Of course. He's right. I close my eyes. Picture myself sneaking round the apartment. *We work in a climate of trust.*

"The guys are working on smuggling in a phone or an

iPad," says Drew. He means Will and the tight group of patients who operate the black market. "Getting one in via a parent's car without the parent knowing is a possibility." When parents or guardians come on their occasional visits, their cars are checked, but not as thoroughly as staff cars.

"Imagine what it's going to be worth," muses Drew. His cigarette is down to its last millimetres. He inhales one last time and drops it into the powdery earth. Then he lingers on the words, "Because guess what," before adding, "the guys know the wifi code."

I'm stunned. "How?"

"Someone overheard Abigail tell the new receptionist."

The new receptionist is a man who arrives for his shifts in immaculate linen, expensive sunglasses and a mouth that never turns upwards.

Drew's still talking but I haven't been listening properly. Something about all he'd do if he had access to a phone or an iPad. "And I'd download one of those apps for meeting girls," he says.

Girls? "But you couldn't meet them," I say. There's a hollowing inside me, a making room for a strange sort of loneliness. "You wouldn't be allowed."

"I know," says Drew. He shrugs. "But it might help keep me sane until I get out of here."

SIX

The needle hurts some days more than others. It depends which nurse is taking my blood. This week it's Raoul, the head nurse. He finds a vein easily and he's relatively gentle. Despite having my blood taken in the medical suite every other week of my life since I was six, I still have a sensation of otherness when I see the dark liquid drawn into the syringe.

Raoul passes me a lump of cotton wool and I press it tight against the puncture mark in the crease of my elbow while he tears off a strip of surgical tape. Classical guitar music plays in the background, and I glance down at my watch to see that it's part of the Creek's latest playlist in the "Relaxing" category.

This room is gleaming white and sterile apart from a few sleek black items of Italian furniture. Raoul's *I've been to Disney World* mug and a wooden-framed photo of a boy in a grubby T-shirt with a cheeky grin and sticky-out ears, are the only personal possessions I've ever seen in here.

"You happy, little lady?" asks Raoul, as he sticks the tape over the cotton wool.

I nod. "Yes, sir," I say, because that's what I've been taught. Respect for medical staff above all others.

"You stay happy. It's the best way." Raoul turns back to the counter to place a printed label on my vial of blood.

"I'll try," I say. I'm suddenly overwhelmed with a longing to be seven or eight again, running around the grounds with Drew, not caring about anything other than being made to eat fish with bones in for dinner.

"You have a very nice life. A life I would be very proud to give my children."

I look at the photo of the little boy. I'm not supposed to ask about the private life of members of staff, but I risk it. "Is that your son, Raoul?"

Raoul shakes his head. "My little brother. He died. Poverty killed him. He got very sick and my family couldn't pay to save his life. That can never happen to you. You are lucky." He undoes my watch, and plugs it with a cable into the laptop. "And it will never happen to my children," I hear him murmur.

I sit up straighter in my chair. "Tell me about your brother," I say. I sound like a therapist.

"He's part of my previous life," says Raoul with his back to me. "Not part of this one."

I've overstepped the mark.

Within a few seconds, there's a ping, and Raoul reads

out loud the words that appear on the screen: "*Data received*." He hands back my watch, waits until I've strapped it on, then indicates that I should move from the chair. "Go on through to Dr Jesmond. And always be thankful that you have Dr Ballard as your father." He winks at me. "You promise me?" He holds my gaze.

"I promise, sir."

He nods. "Gratitude makes us beautiful."

Dr Jesmond, Greta and Zach's dad, prefers me to call him Dr J or Karl. With his big head, floppy cheeks and short legs, he resembles an overweight dog in a cartoon on Creek TV.

"Take a seat, Mae," he says. He has a folder on his desk, and a blank sheet of paper on top of it. We go through the questions while he jots down the answers with his large black fountain pen. Its gold-rimmed lid rests next to a small clock. I have a pen like it in my collection. It's worth a lot of tokens.

The medical questionnaire is usually the same, but you have to listen out for changes. They can catch you off guard if you don't concentrate.

"All your answers must refer to the period since I last saw you, yes?"

I nod and resist rolling my eyes. Why does he have to say that every single time?

"On a scale of very poor, poor, average, good and very good, how've you felt?"

"Good."

"How would you rate your sleep?"

"Good."

"Do you find it easy to fall asleep?"

"Yes."

"How would you rate your energy levels?"

"Average."

"Have you been taking your vitamins?"

"Yes."

"Any flu-like symptoms?"

"No."

"Problems with your eyes such as blurry vision?"

"No."

"Muscle pains?"

"No." *Not recently.*

"Headaches?"

"No."

"Racing heartbeat?"

"No."

"Any other unexplained aches or pains?"

"Not really."

Dr Jesmond stops. "Explain."

"Pins and needles in my neck," I say.

"Hmmm," says Dr Jesmond. "I'll have a look." He screws the lid on to his pen and washes his hands with the pink liquid soap in the dispenser above the sink.

When he touches me, I flinch. His hands are cold. They squash and probe all the way round my neck, up to my jawline, and down to my collarbone.

"How often has this happened?" he asks.

"Only once," I lie. I don't want to be pummelled any more. "It was at night. I'd probably been lying in an awkward position."

"Ah, OK," says Dr Jesmond. He returns to his desk and looks at something on his computer, but the screen is turned away from me. "That's all for today, then, Mae."

As I stand to go, he says, "How's the new teacher working out? Ms Ray, is it?"

"She's good," I say.

"Greta told me she's very . . . enthusiastic." He makes it sound like that's a questionable quality in a teacher.

I shrug. Greta needs to worry about her college course, not what happens in the schoolhouse. It sounds boastful, but I was always way ahead of Greta with lessons.

"You're a bright girl, Mae. As we're all too aware here, bright students can often be pushed too hard. I'm sure you've seen the distressing symptoms. I'd like to remind you to keep everything in perspective." He pushes his lips together in an approximation of a smile, one that doesn't quite reach his eyes. "Your overall health is what's important."

"OK," I say, though I have no idea what the point of that little speech was.

"See you in two weeks."

SEVEN

Saturdays start like every other weekday – with an alarm. I jolt awake. My heart is racing, but I think that's because I was in the middle of an action dream, running away from shadowy figures. It's pitch-black because of the shutters, and as I wait the two minutes until the next alarm and the lights, my eyes adjust slightly and my heart calms.

Getting out of bed is often the worst part of my day. But I'm Dr Ballard's daughter. I can't be lazy. This morning the first three things on my schedule are Exercise. Breakfast. Boot camp.

Boot camp is run by Mick, a former bodyguard who's been a fitness instructor at the Creek from the very beginning. It's non-stop exercise torture for one-and-a-half hours, which he says is a tough-love approach that celebrities pay big bucks for.

It takes place on the soccer pitch, in the far corner of the Creek. Mick cycles up there, and us staff kids take golf buggies. Drew and I take it in turns to pay the one token charge to release a buggy by inputting our account code, and we let Joanie hop in the back. The other boys usually go together, and somehow Zach always manages more driving time than the other two.

Whenever Zach's driving, Drew and I make sure to race him up to the soccer pitch, taking cross-country shortcuts whenever we can, even if it means running over the occasional flower bed.

This morning Drew's driving, swerving our buggy around because he wants to hear the whirring noise it makes when it's under strain. Ben, red-faced with determination and his blond hair sticking up with sweat at one side, is at the wheel of the other buggy and they're ahead. Zach leans out of the front passenger seat and yells at a group of patients who are running alongside the path. They're concentrating on the run, breathing with little puffs, some in sportswear they brought from home, but most wearing items from the new collection that's just become available online. "Pick up the pace, you losers." The grad student at the front of the patients makes a waving motion to tell him to shut up.

I notice the new patient, Noah, is lagging behind. I'm not surprised. It's hard for new people to keep up with the fitness regime at first. If he had to do our boot camp today he'd die.

Drew swerves so abruptly that my head slams sideways into the metal pole that holds up the roof, and I cry out in pain. He does an emergency brake and I'm flung forward. I yell, "Why did you do that?"

Noah stops running. "Hey, are you all right?" he shouts.

Joanie's crying in the back, and Drew turns to tell her I'm fine.

"How d'you know I'm fine?" I snap, as I rub my head.

Noah is beside the buggy now. "Are you all right?" he says again.

"I'm OK," I say. "It was more the shock."

"See?" Drew says to Joanie.

"That's good," says Noah. He places his hands on his waist and does an awkward bend from side to side, as if he's remembered he's supposed to be doing exercise. "It sounded like you'd really hurt yourself. I'll catch you later." He gives me a brief smile and jogs off slowly.

"He's one of the weirder ones," says Drew, not quietly enough. He starts the buggy again.

I give him a long hard stare which means when I look round to say thanks to Noah, the buggy has already whined past him and he's not looking at us any more.

"Clearly fancies you like craaazy," Drew adds. "Did you notice that?"

"What? How d'you know?" Is he being serious? Confused, I glance back at Joanie to see if she's listening. She is. "Forget it, Drew. Just get us there in one piece."

*

While we line up on the soccer pitch and wait for Mick to bark his orders, I go over what Drew said. It worries me how little I understand about relationships.

We begin with push-ups, jumping jacks and squats. We exercise in our own little worlds, dealing with the gruelling workout in our own ways. Mick shouts, swears and projects phlegm at me because I'm not fast enough. I run, I walk, I limp, and at one point I have to crouch because I feel so dizzy. But I don't cry. Mick loves it when people cry.

At the end of the session, I sit on a wooden bench to regain my breath and composure. It's the same style of bench as the ones in the Woodland Gardens. There are twenty of them dotted around the grounds, each with a metal plaque screwed to the top slat, all engraved with the same words: *"With thanks and gratitude to the Hummingbird Creek community from the Delaney family"*. When I asked Dad who the Delaney family were, he said their son was a patient but he couldn't remember the name of the kid or anything about him. Maybe he hadn't been someone who'd stood out.

Drew sags on to the bench next to me. I don't say anything to him, but I like having him next to me, even if he hasn't asked how my head is.

I drive the buggy back, so slowly that Joanie whinges all the way, but I find myself thinking about what I want to study at college. It's not just lack of knowledge about relationships that worries me; I don't know which college I'd like to apply to, or what I want to do after college. I suppose I've never properly thought about it because I've been too busy living in the moment. We reach the curve in the path where we can see the back of the main building. It's where Dad has his consulting room. There's a new thought in my head as I park up the buggy and connect it to the locking system: Dad is a world-renowned psychiatrist, yet neither he nor Mom have ever asked me what I want to study or do with my life at all.

As I open the door to our apartment, I sense Mom is there even though she's not scheduled to be. She plays tennis on Saturday mornings, and after we've had showers we eat lunch together on the terrace. This morning I see Mom's tennis shoes discarded on the living-room floor, rather than placed together in the shoe closet. She's abandoned her racquet on the sofa and the folding door to the terrace is closed.

"Mom?" I call. There's no reply. I'm stiff and my feet hurt, but I move quickly through the apartment. It's unlike Mom to deviate from her schedule. I find her lying on my parents' bed, on top of the white duvet cover, edged with apricot-coloured ribbon. She's on her side, facing away from the door, towards the window.

"Mom? What's up?"

She must have been dozing or lost in thought because she jumps. When she sees that it's me, her shoulders relax and she wriggles up the bed, against two apricot-edged pillows.

"Hi, honey." Her voice is croaky, and her face is pale. The skin under her eyes is darker than usual.

I sit on the edge of the bed. "Are you ill, Mom? D'you want to me to tell someone?"

"I'm tired, that's all," she says. "And so achy. Don't tell your father."

Napping during the day is laziness, and it breaks important routines. But she looks as if she has a temperature, so it's probably OK.

The room is airless. The only windows that open are the terrace doors because the apartment is temperature controlled. "Wouldn't you prefer to lie on the sofa?" I ask. "I'll open the doors and make a breeze for you."

She moves her head slowly, back and forth. "I can't face moving. I'm OK here. Can you water my plants for me?"

"Sure."

She attempts a smile. "When I feel up to it, I'll ask if we can go to the plant nursery together."

The plant nursery is off the highway. It stretches on and on as far as the eye can see. Rows and rows of plants. The Creek grounds staff order plants from the nursery, and Mom visits twice a year. I was allowed to go with her once. I loved how animated and happy she was there. She wandered up and down the rows, and entered the greenhouses. She touched leaves, snapped dead flower heads off, and eagerly read the labels on the pallets in the loading bays.

If the plant nursery had wifi, I could try to research Mom's family there. But I'd rather go to the mall where it's guaranteed.

"What about the mall, Mom? It's been ages since we've been there."

"You'd prefer that?" says Mom. She rubs one eye. "OK. I'll speak to your father." Everything has to go through Dad. Next to him she's like a piece of tissue paper, easily crushed. I'm sure she never used to be this bad. My vague memories of her playing games and laughing with me when we lived in England, while we waited long periods for Dad to come home from work, can't be made up. Whenever I've tried to speak to her about anything important, it's as if my words drift right through her. She has set phrases which she repeats whether they're relevant or not.

It's for the best.

Don't make life hard for yourself.

I'll speak to your father.

Unfortunately I don't make the rules.

You have so much here at the Creek, honey.

I can't change anything, but I love you, Mae. More than you'll ever know.

The plants on the terrace are Mom's pride and joy. Some hang heavy with large rich-coloured petals; others have buds in various stages of unfurling. One has no flowers at all, but leaves of multiple shades of green and burgundy. I water them, carrying the watering can from the kitchen through the living room five times. She's always wanted an outside water tap but Dad says it would look ugly. Even if there was a plant in front of it, hiding it from view, he says he'd know it was there.

After I've showered, I go back in and check on Mom. Her eyes are closed. I touch her hand. It's dry and cold. I open the linen closet to find something to cover her. Everything is neatly folded. Uncluttered and ordered. I find a cashmere blanket. As I drape it over Mom's legs and pull it up to her chest, she opens her eyes. "Tell Frank I'm sorry I didn't make the funeral," she says.

Her words bounce through my head. She's thinking about her family. "How do I contact Frank?" I whisper.

She closes her eyes again. "The back of my neck, it feels prickly. . ." She has it too. Is there a virus circulating?

I try something different. "Mom, what was your name before you got married? You were Louelle what?"

"I'm Louelle Ballard."

"I know. But before then."

I wait.

"Hill." She says it as if she's only just remembered, and then she says, "The Hills lived on a hill," as if she's reading one of Joanie's chapter books.

"You were Louelle Hill?"

She turns away from me and doesn't say any more.

71

Later, when I hear the soft sound of her sleep-breathing, I search the living room for anything that will tell me about Mom's family. There's nothing. I move into Dad's study and tug at the top drawer of his filing cabinet. It's locked. I stop when I hear movement from Mom. I look into the bedroom and see her easing herself off the bed. She smooths out the duvet cover and folds the cashmere blanket. By the time Dad comes home a few hours later, she's sitting on a chair on the terrace looking at a gardening magazine, her forehead shiny with sweat.

EIGHT

The following day, Mom seems a little better. She tells Dad at dinner that she and I need to go to the mall to buy key items of summer clothing. She's applied more make-up than usual, and she still hasn't the energy to water her plants, but Dad hasn't noticed. He's preoccupied with his patients, as usual.

"What about online shopping, Louelle?" he says.

I keep my face neutral. I haven't been able to search the apartment more thoroughly yet because Mom, Dad or the cleaners have been here. But if I can get to the computer store, at least I've got a last name now. *Hill.* Louelle Hill sounds strange, though. As if there are too many *l*s for it to be a real name. I imagine typing it into a keyboard.

"Hunter, Mae's body shape is changing and we need to work out what suits her. It's easier than ordering lots of sizes."

73

She looks at me and I say with some embarrassment, "I need more underwear."

Dad cuts up his grilled chicken. "All right," he says. "Mick can drive you to the mall at nine-fifteen a.m. tomorrow morning. Never let it be said I don't listen to sensible requests."

When I return from breakfast the next morning, Mom's still in bed.

"Why aren't you up?" I shriek when I walk into her bedroom. I was expecting her to be spraying herself with perfume or choosing which shoes to wear. My shouting startles the cleaner who stops her vacuum cleaner for a moment. In a quieter voice, I say, "We're supposed to be going to the mall today. Remember?"

"Yes. Yes, I'm sorry," says Mom.

I bite my lip. I want to step inside that computer store so badly, but she's not well. I can't do this to her. "Stay in bed, Mom," I say. "We'll go another time."

"No. I'm definitely coming shopping with you," says Mom, and she lifts the bedcover as if it's an effort, as if the sparkly watch on her arm is too heavy for her wrist.

"Are you sure?" I ask.

"I insist. I'm not going to miss a day out with you, Mae."

"Wait." I see she's still in her night clothes. "You didn't do your morning exercise or eat breakfast?"

She shakes her head. "I just . . . couldn't."

"Did you tell admin?" Mom wouldn't be fined for not going like I would, but a health team might come and assess her. Illness at the facility has to be carefully monitored to keep anything contagious under control.

"Oh," says Mom, standing up. "No. I forgot."

I run to fetch the phone in the hall. It has plenty of buttons but only one of them connects anywhere. I press the zero and hand the phone to Mom while it rings the reception switchboard.

She takes a deep breath, and makes her voice stronger. "Hello there," she says. "This is Louelle Ballard." She makes the usual chit-chat with the receptionist for a few seconds, then says, "Please would you put me through to Earl." After a couple of seconds, she says, "I'm going to the designer outlet mall with Mae today, so I needed extra time to get myself ready this morning. You know I don't like going out with my make-up not quite right. So that's why I was absent from my exercise class this morning... Thank you. Yes I'm having a quick breakfast on the terrace before we go." After finishing the call, she goes into the bathroom while I make her a cup of lemon-and-ginger tea.

It's only in the last week or so that I've seen how good Mom is at lying.

I think I'm being polite and doing the right thing when I call in at the schoolhouse at nine a.m. to say I won't be in class, but Ms Ray's face instantly shows annoyance.

"Why would you go to a shopping mall in the week when you'll miss important lessons?" she asks. "Why can't you go at the weekend?"

I don't know what to say. Doesn't she realize that I have no control over when I get to do things? She doesn't have the authority to tell me I can't go, but I wasn't expecting her to make me feel so bad.

"Whenever we go, we'd miss something," calls out Drew who's supposed to be ripping an old sheet into strips with the others for our chemistry project.

He gives one end of the sheet to Joanie and yanks her along the floor.

"And I guess you don't get vacations," says Ms Ray quietly.

I remember hearing a patient talk about vacations and having to ask what they were. "No."

Ms Ray sighs, and indicates that I should sit in a chair near her desk at the front of the room. "I won't hold you up for long, Mae." She lifts an ancient CD player from a battered shopping bag and plugs it into the wall. I see the others giggling at the low tech. Within seconds there's the shock of incredibly loud piano music filling the classroom. Joanie slaps her hands over her ears, and Ms Ray turns it down, but not by very much.

"Five minutes' creative writing, please, about how this music makes you feel," she says, then leans against the desk, next to me. The others won't be able to hear what she's saying.

"Mae, we have so much work for you to get through. You're behind most kids your age who'll be looking to get into a decent college."

My heart sinks. "I'm sorry. But I don't get the chance to be with my mom outside here very often."

"OK." She takes a sheet of paper from another bag. It's a long list in tiny type. "These are the books you need to read, fiction and non-fiction." She points behind her to the shelving unit that used to hold the art materials. Now there are piles of books, stacked on their sides so more can fit in. "Use these. Some of the textbooks are out of date. My school resource budget isn't big enough to buy the latest editions, even though you'd think..." She trails off. "I've got some books in my car which will be useful. You can't access the internet in your computer sessions, can you?"

"Some of it," I say. "At least one hundred websites, including an encyclopaedia. I can get access to even more, too. Like, I'm allowed on to pen collector sites."

"Right." There's a pause. Ms Ray clearly isn't a fan of pen collector sites. "Most schools block certain content, but this is extreme."

"It's because Dad's seen the damage the internet can do." I'm not sure why I feel I have to defend him. She must know the Creek philosophy. She must have covered this in her induction.

"Hmm."

This tiny utterance shocks me. All adults at the Creek

think Dad is inspiring, visionary and charismatic. I've never heard anyone question his views.

"We have a library," I say. "Have you seen it?" The library which is on the ground floor of the main building was recently upgraded. There are sofas in pastel colours, shelving with inspirational quotes carved into the wood, loads of books and a magazine stand, stacked mostly with fashion and home interior publications.

Ms Ray nods. "Have you ever been to a library outside Hummingbird Creek?"

"No."

"They can be incredible places – with up-to-date books and computers and space to study, and journals and newspapers." Her cheeks are flushed. She seems quite worked up.

"The people from the outside who saw ours on the last open day thought it was nice," I say in a stiff voice. I shouldn't let myself be wound up by Ms Ray. It doesn't matter what she thinks of the library. It's what the parents think that matters.

"It's very attractive," says Ms Ray. "And the books are all in great condition and you have magazines. But there are no important books there. Fiction about difficult subjects or decent scientific books or respected journals, and it doesn't have long enough opening hours. At first glance the library here looks amazing, but it's. . ." She stops abruptly. "Don't worry about your trip to the mall. I'll help you catch up."

Mick waits in the parking lot, standing next to one of the six silver Creek cars. He doesn't suit non-sports clothes. His big biceps and thigh muscles make his short-sleeve shirt and cargo shorts too tight in the arms and upper leg. He has a thick gold chain round his neck, and an immaculate pair of sneakers: super-expensive limited edition Nikes.

"Looking forward to your shopping day, ladies?" he says. He's chewing gum, making a sucking, saliva-y sound. "All set?"

I nod. He doesn't know how close Mom and I came to not being able to come on this trip.

He holds open the car door for us, first Mom, then me, and anyone watching would think it inconceivable that a few days ago he'd directed phlegm at my bare legs because he didn't think they were moving fast enough.

At the security building, Mick signs us out and picks up his cell phone, and as the gates open he whacks on some bass-heavy music. "This all right for you?" he asks.

Mom blinks.

"Yes, we're fine with it." I answer for us both, because I don't want him to notice that she's more spaced out than usual.

When he's growling along to the lyrics and thumping the steering wheel to the beat, I whisper. "How are you feeling?"

She pats my hand. I clamp it between both of mine for as long as I can before she tugs it away overdramatically, just how she used to years ago to make me laugh. I raise a smile.

"I'm happy to be with you," she says.

As we enter the underground parking lot for the mall, Mick quietens the music and I lean forward to say, "Mom's my chaperone today, right?"

"Yes. Why?" says Mick. He turns slightly.

Because you're harder to escape from than Mom.

"Because I want to buy some new bras and it would be embarrassing to have you hanging around."

Mick holds my gaze for a moment and then nods. Before we step out of the car, we arrange to meet him in four hours.

"Are you sure that's enough time for your shopping, ladies?" he asks with a sarcastic edge to his voice.

"Yes, thank you," I reply. I want to ask where he's planning to be for the next four hours. The perfect answer would be waiting in the car, but he's a Creek person. He'll probably be walking endless circuits round the corridors of the mall, timing himself and aiming for a personal best. As long as he doesn't spot me inside the computer store I should be OK.

Mom and I walk to the elevator and, as soon as I step inside and feel the upward whoosh, I'm excited. Stitched through the excitement is a thread of anxiety. It's not just about finding a way to leave Mom so I can go to the computer store. It's also about stepping into the strange world of the mall again: the noise, the brightness, the people, the overpowering smell of junk food, the choices. It's easy to see how life on the outside messes people up.

When we come out of the elevator, we have to think about which way to turn for the shops we want, and a woman with a buggy sighs loudly at us because we're blocking her way. I pull Mom to one side, and we stand for a moment, adjusting. Mom understands the outside world better than I do because she didn't grow up at the Creek, so she usually only needs a few moments, but today it's me who tugs her to say, *Let's go.*

We set off in the direction we remember, slowly because I want to look at the window displays, at the mini scenes that some of them depict: picnics, wedding guests, a kitchen with primary-colour gadgets. Slowly, too, because I sense Mom can't walk at her normal speed. When we walk past the computer store, I see that it's not as busy as it was before Christmas. There are two assistants in navy polo shirts with lanyards round their necks leaning against a wall, one chewing a fingernail while the other one is talking. I can't imagine being bored around real computers, tablets and phones. I wonder if that means I have the potential to be addicted to them.

Mom probably wouldn't mind if I begged to go in, but she might blurt it to Dad by mistake, so I keep walking. When we reach a clothes shop I like where Mom can sit in a leather armchair, I pick out some things that catch my eye – things that will make me look, and hopefully feel, more grown up. I aim for what the popular girls at the

Creek wear: tighter fitting tops and shorts, evening-ish trousers, a black dress with gold-zipped pockets and sexy underwear that's not so sexy that the Creek laundry will confiscate it. I picture Drew looking at me as I try on each item, trying to appraise myself through his eyes. Mom hands over her platinum credit card without asking how much anything is.

I persuade Mom to visit her favourite store, and we hold up garments on their hangers, inspect the quality and cut of the fabric, and murmur, "What d'you think?" I wait outside a cubicle while Mom tries on floaty clothes in peach and grey. She buys a couple of dresses, not watching as they're folded and wrapped in tissue paper. When the assistant suggests she buy a necklace that's new in that morning, Mom holds it in her hand for a brief moment before saying yes, as if that's the easiest option.

I keep checking my watch. My best bet for having time alone at the computer store is for us to eat lunch at the Oh My Goodness café nearby and, before Mom's finishes, tell her I need to go to the restroom.

I know Mom won't consider eating lunch until one o'clock, the time she has it at home. At precisely one minute past we sit down at a booth in the café, and I read through the menu. Even here, at the healthiest food outlet, there are dishes that are clearly laden with fat and sugar.

Mom doesn't need to remind me that our itemized bill will be looked at to see whether we can be trusted to come here again. She orders vegetable soup and a Vitamin C Boost smoothie. I order the same smoothie and ham on a seeded roll with no butter.

"You want salad or potato chips with that?" asks the waitress.

Across the restaurant, a little kid is crunching potato chips into his mouth like a machine. They look thinner and crunchier than Creek potato crisps. The waitress taps her pen against her notepad.

A "sss" sound is coming out of my lips, but it turns into "so. . ." instead of "salad". I clear my throat. "So I have a question. If I asked for potato chips, would you be able to put it down on the bill as salad?"

Mum makes an air-suck noise but I ignore her.

"Er. . ." The waitress screws up her face. "I suppose I *could*. . ."

I need to know for sure. "Please can you find out?"

"OK, I'll be right back." She goes off and before Mom says anything, I say, "Just this once, Mom. Please?"

"There are rules," says Mom. "And why would you want to harm your body with saturated fat and all sorts of additives?" Her words are wispy, almost half-remembered.

"A few potato chips aren't going to hurt us," I say. "Don't you want to taste them, Mom?"

"I have tasted them," she says. "A long time ago." She pushes the heel of her hand into her eye socket. "Oh. This headache of mine." She leans her elbows on to the table.

"Mae, my head hurts too much to argue. If the waitress can sort the bill, and you want them, have them." She lifts her head up. "But eat them quickly."

In case Mick sees us.

The waitress says it's possible, and Mom says nothing. The potato chips are salty, buttery and rough against the inside of my mouth. I love them. I offer one to Mom but she shakes her head once from side to side, as if it's still hurting, and returns her gaze to her soup.

I suck them until they dissolve, crunch them like the boy did, lick my finger and glue all the potato chip crumbs to them. I eat until there's no evidence left, and my stomach hurts from eating too quickly.

I've done one bad thing. And now I'm about to do another. I stand up. "Mom, I'm going to the restroom. Will you be all right for a moment?"

She's hardly touched her soup, just stirred it round and round her bowl. I shouldn't leave her, but I might not get another chance to do this, and desperation pushes aside my guilt.

"I'm fine, honey," says Mom in a fuzzy voice. The one that sounds like a drunk person in a movie. I know she has pills that she takes in the morning. Even though the Creek avoids giving out medication, Dad says her balancing pills are OK and she needs them to keep steady. She probably forgot to take them this morning.

I scrape my chair backwards and almost run, out of Oh My Goodness and along the shiny marble flooring.

It won't take long. If she's still bad when I get back, I'll contact Mick via the mall's public address system. I check around me before I enter the computer store, and then rush inside.

NINE

I make straight for the computers at the back. A navy-polo-shirted guy says, "Yo! You need help?"

"No . . . just looking . . . thanks." He'll think I'm crazy if I ask how to connect to the internet. I click furiously on icons. Boxes appear, but I can't see where to type in my keywords. Whole minutes go by. My underarms are damp and prickly. I picture Mom stirring her soup and I bite the inside of my lip, drawing blood.

"What are you doing?"

I turn and see a girl around ten years old staring at my screen of boxes. "Is this connected to the internet?" I ask. I take a step backwards and let the unspoken words jump between us. *Please help me*. A few clicks from her and I'm connected. "Thanks," I say, and suddenly I have unrestricted access to the world and no one can check what I search. There's a floating sensation in my body and the blood-taste of rebellion in my mouth.

I search *Vonnie Hill England*. There are a few listed but I can't find out much about them. One has run a marathon and raised over three thousand pounds. Another has a dog-walking business. There's no indication that any of them has recently died.

The store is filling up. There's another customer hovering behind me. I search *Frank Hill England* and there are heaps, but I don't know how to contact them. I think I might have to join a website and give an email address. I put *Vonnie Frank Louelle Hill UK* into the search bar and odd ancestry websites show up which don't help.

What was I expecting? I'm not sure, but something more. Perhaps a newspaper article about my grandmother's death, naming her children, Frank and Louelle. The English side of my family is just as much a mystery as they were to me before.

I should leave. I clear the screen and weave my way back through the store. When I reach the entrance, I glance across at the security guard and my lungs implode. He's talking to Mick.

Mick has his arms out in front of him. "Teenager. Dark brown hair. Tanned. Green top, maybe. Dunno. This height."

I turn back and vaguely attach myself to a group of three chatting women. I'm wearing a dark purple top and I'm taller than Mick thinks. I hope he keeps distracting the security guard. Fear fuses with nausea, and I force myself to move. Once outside the store, I speed-walk to the restaurant, my breath uneven and painful.

Mom is slumped back against the wall of the booth. Her eyes are closed. When I take her arm, she shudders, and then her eyes open. "Mae!" her voice is faint. "Mick went looking for you."

"I went to the bathroom, Mom," I say. "Did you tell him?"

She nods. "Need to go back. Not feeling well." She looks towards the purse on the table. "I paid the bill."

I've made her stressed, by ordering the potato chips and by disappearing for longer than she was expecting. And before that, by telling her about Frank's phone call. I think the news about her mom's death has hit her hard. "I'm sorry," I say softly, but I don't think she hears.

I gather up our bags and stand by the table to wait for Mick to return. It's something Thet taught me: standing makes you braver.

He calls across the restaurant when he sees me, so that most people turn to look at us. "Where've you been, Mae? Your mom's been on her own."

I refuse to speak until he's closer, but that might have been a mistake because his face is contorted with irritation by the time he reaches me. One of my legs is shaking. I don't know if having curious witnesses here will stop him behaving like he does at the Creek.

"The restroom," I say.

"I looked," he says. "You weren't there."

Coldness spreads through me. Mick went *into* the female bathroom to look for me?

"You must have missed me," I say. I work really hard on keeping my voice level. All I want is to get Mom home. "We should go. Mom's not well."

Mick stares at me. Is he going to yell and spit at me, boot-camp style? "You know the rules, Mae. You stay with your adult at all times."

"My *adult* wasn't well enough to come with me," I say, and that's it. Mom's saved me. It doesn't make me feel any better about myself though, and Mick's bound to make sure I'm never allowed her as my supervising adult again.

We help Mom to stand up and she leans against Mick all the way to the car. When he's helped her on to the back seat, I climb in next to her and fasten her seatbelt. Mick selects his music, and I scooch closer to her and whisper, "We shouldn't have come. I'm sorry." This time I make sure she hears.

"I want you to be happy," she says.

"We'll be home soon," I say, because I want it to be true. We're still driving circuits of the parking lot on the way to the exit.

"Your dad will run tests on me," she says in a flat voice.

"He'll make you better." I think of my conversation with Raoul. We're lucky to have world-class healthcare.

"You remember your appendicitis?" Mom murmurs, then sits up straighter. She's waiting for an answer. "When you had to go to hospital? Do you remember?"

"Not really," I say. It was back when we were in the UK. My memories are like snippets of blurry footage, each a few seconds long. Crying because I didn't want to wear the hospital gown. Mum lying on a bed with me. A Winnie the Pooh toy with a bandage round its stomach.

"D'you remember the horse?" asks Mom.

"Sorry?"

"The horse, Mae. The horse was there." She sounds distressed. Her face is very pale.

I nod. This conversation frightens me because I don't understand it and it seems to be important to her.

"In the hospital," says Mom. There are sweat beads on her nose and her body is hot. "It was the last time." Her eyelids flutter and her mind slides away someplace else.

Mick lowers the music volume.

"Mom?" I ask.

"Keep her awake," says Mick.

But I can't, however much I squeeze her arms and shake her shoulders.

"We have to take her to the hospital in Pattonville," I tell Mick.

He drives faster, towards the highway. "We're going back to the Creek," he says.

"Please," I say. Pattonville's hospital must be closer.

"No," says Mick. "We'll do as I say." He reaches for his cell phone. I listen to him call Creek reception, explaining we're going to need medical help when we arrive.

I shift Mom's body, trying to make her more comfortable, and I hold her hand so she knows I'm close. "Nearly there," I mutter, over and over as the journey goes on for ever.

Finally, I see the sign for the Creek. The gates are open. Raoul is there, and moments later he's checking Mom's pulse, then looking at her watch. Dad is running down the drive.

When Dad reaches us he barks at me, "What are her symptoms?"

"Muscle pain. Headache, no energy, not making sense," I say. "And pins and needles in her neck."

He nods. "You get out, Mae. Go through security clearance. Mick, I'll see you later."

I take the bags. Dad scoops up Mom as if she's a child and he's rescuing her. I watch him carry her up the steps to the main building, Raoul beside him. It's the quickest way to the medical suite.

In the security building I place my bags on the scanner, and a female security guard pats me down, then says, "Cleared to go." I mumble goodbye to Mick who's signing us back in and handing over his cell phone, and he grunts in reply.

I wait all afternoon in the apartment for someone to tell me what's happening with Mom. I tidy away my new clothes, watch TV, lean over the roof terrace to gaze at people walking around the grounds, and practise calligraphy with my newest pen. I write *Louelle Hill* in different styles and then block them out with a thick Sharpie before scrunching the paper and burying it in the kitchen trash. I pick up the phone and hover my finger over the zero, but even if reception puts me through to the medical suite, I won't be told anything because I'm being impatient. I have to be mindful. I have to trust.

The sun goes in and a breeze starts up. I sit on the terrace and pick a leaf off one of the plants. Tearing off tiny piece after tiny piece, I say in my head: *OK, not OK, OK, not OK.*

When the front door opens, I'm on my feet. It's Raoul with a couple of medical bags. I rush towards him. "How's Mom?"

"She'll be OK." He sees my face. "You doubted your father?" He holds up his bags. "She's coming back here soon, and I'm setting up my nursing station. Your mom will have gold-star care. Nothing to worry about, little lady."

I hate how he fobs me off. "She's really ill," I say.

"She has me," says Raoul. He pushes his wide chest outwards. "I'm the best nurse. In fact I'm more than the best nurse, I'm a biochemist."

"What does that mean?" I ask.

Raoul carries on through to Mom and Dad's bedroom. "It means I understand her illness," he says. "She's lucky to have me."

About an hour later, Dad brings Mom over in a

wheelchair. She's sleepy with a drip in her arm but her skin is a better colour. Dad and Raoul settle her in bed while I wait in the living room.

When Dad emerges for dinner he tells me I'm not allowed to see her until tomorrow afternoon. She needs complete rest.

"What's wrong with her?" I ask. It's strange eating at the table, just the two of us. Mom's always eaten dinner with me. Always.

"Not a lot," he says, as he hands me my vitamin. "She's run down."

No matter what he and Raoul say, I'm worried about Mom's condition. How can it be nothing serious if she wasn't making sense and has to be monitored twenty-four hours a day?

After dinner I go to my room to read one of the books on Ms Ray's list: *Animal Farm* by George Orwell. My mind keeps thinking of the bizarre image of a horse in the hospital. Mom was there when I had my appendix out. Dad wasn't there. He must have been working as usual.

Wait. There *was* someone else there before my operation when my stomach hurt so badly. An older woman with a lined face. Drawn-on eyebrows. She gave me sweets, which Mom said I wasn't allowed to eat, and the plastic horse. The one on my chest of drawers. I get up and go pick it up, and the memory becomes a little stronger. The woman hugged me and told me that soon the pain would be gone. Mom cried when she left.

We left England soon afterwards. Might that woman have been Mom's mom, my grandmother, meeting us without Dad knowing? Was that the last time Mom – and I – saw her?

TEN

I'm awake before my alarm. Unless it's an emergency, I'm not allowed out of my room until it goes off. Several times in the night I could hear Dad pacing around the living room. I couldn't tell whether Raoul was in the apartment too. Or if Mom's condition had become worse.

I lie in the dark, trying to forget about the severe ache in my thigh and the prickly sensations that come and go in my neck. Am I getting what Mom has? Although I can't override the lighting system, I could press the emergency lighting button which illuminates a glow-lamp on the wall. But if Dad was in the living room and saw the light, I'd be in trouble. So I grip my thigh and massage it, and I think about my English family. Mom's sad when she thinks about them, but she doesn't seem to hate them like Dad does. I know she wished she could have gone to her mom's funeral, and I'm pretty sure she was trying to get me to remember seeing my grandmother in the hospital before I had my appendix out.

Apart from possibly my plastic horse, I wonder if there's anything here in the apartment that links to Mom's former life. Where would she keep something she didn't want Dad to see?

I stop pressing down on my thigh. The two places she spends most of her time are the roof terrace and the grounds staff office where she has a desk. I should check out her desk when I can.

When my alarm finally goes off, I get dressed. The apartment is silent. The door to Mom and Dad's bedroom is closed. I want to creep in and check on Mom but I don't dare. I stand outside the door for a while, but I can't be late for my exercise class, so I give up after a few minutes. As I walk past Dad's study, I see his desk isn't as tidy as it usually is. There are pieces of paper all over it. Checking the bedroom door is still closed, I take a few steps into the study to see what they are.

They're covered with numbers – calculations – and what looks like science symbols, and medical-looking words. But mostly numbers, some with big lines through them, crossing them out. It's Dad's handwriting. Perhaps he was distracting himself with something medical while he was up in the night, worried about Mom. Or is this to do with Mom's illness?

There's a noise from the bedroom. I tread lightly and swiftly out of the room, then leave the apartment.

*

I'm the last one to arrive at the exercise session, and when Drew says, "How was the mall?" the tears spread across my eyes so fast that he's a blur. "Not successful?"

He thinks I didn't manage to get to the computer store. He probably doesn't know about Mom, and I don't have time to tell him because our instructor is here.

At breakfast I don't want to say anything in front of the others, and I'm desperate to get back to the apartment, so I eat a couple of mouthfuls of granola and scrape the rest into the waste while the supervisors aren't looking.

As I walk past Thet, I see she's partway through one of her tapping routines, one finger against the top part of her arm, so I don't stop to say hello or she'll have to start over.

I run across the lawn and input the door code in such a hurry that it doesn't register and I'm forced to do it again more slowly. The elevator takes ages to clank down to the ground floor, but I know the timings. Running up five flights will take longer, even allowing for the slowness of the elevator.

As I burst through the apartment door, I push it too heavily and it crashes into the wall.

"What d'you think you're doing, making so much noise?" Dad strides into view. "Your mother is sleeping."

I apologize. He's expecting me to go straight into my en-suite bathroom for a shower, and he's surprised when I walk towards him instead. "How is she?"

"I told you, Mae. There's nothing to be concerned

97

about," says Dad, but I've reached the living room and I don't take in what he's saying because there, sitting on the sofa, is Karl Jesmond. He rarely visits our apartment. My heart flings itself against my ribcage.

Instead of saying hello, I run towards the bedroom, push at the partially open door, and take a few steps towards the bed, where Mom is lying on her back, asleep. She looks peaceful but not herself. Her hair is dark with greasiness and her face is free of make-up, revealing sun spots and blemishes.

Her watch is attached via a wire to a laptop which is on the bedside table, and there's a very low regular bleeping noise. But there are no other wires. No drips or drains.

Dad is in the doorway. "Mae. Come away at once." He'd be more angry if Dr Jesmond wasn't here.

"What's wrong with her?"

"A virus." He grabs my arm, almost encircling it with his large, strong hand. "Now get ready for your lessons. Have you forgotten your manners with Karl?"

As we walk back into the living room, Dad drops my arm and I mumble hello to Karl.

Karl nods, a smile hovering on his lips. I expect he heard Dad talking to me. "Hello to you too, Miss Mae. What have you been learning recently in lessons?"

"Science... Geography..."

Dad interjects, "What sort of science?"

I fell easily into that trap, but now my brain is thinking fast. Ms Ray is only supposed to teach us topics that are in the work booklets. I try to remember topics that I've seen in the booklets. We used to skip the science questions with our last teacher.

It's easier to be vague and disinterested. "Er ... you know. Sciencey stuff."

Dr Jesmond chuckles.

Dad lets it pass. He tells me not to come back to the apartment before dinner so that Mom won't be disturbed. I nod and go to my room, but I don't click the door completely closed because I want to hear what's going on.

Dr Jesmond is telling Dad that he thinks Greta would make a useful teacher. I can't think of anyone who'd make a worse one.

I choose my clothes for the day, then before I have a shower I listen some more. Dad and Dr Jesmond are speaking quietly but I can hear snatches of their conversation. Dr Jesmond says, "We're agreed then, that going forward we reduce dosage?"

"It's the combination that's the problem. How they're interacting," says Dad. "So yes and no." He speaks more quietly so I can't hear what he says next.

"You're sure?" asks Dr Jesmond.

"I'm sure," says Dad.

On the way to the schoolhouse, after I've told Drew about Mom, I fill him in on what happened at the mall. He's impressed I was in the computer store on my own, and that I managed to get on the internet. He looks even more impressed when I tell him how I dodged Mick.

"He's a freaking nightmare. But you, Mae Ballard," he points at me, "did a good job. Next mall trip you'll have more information. Keep digging around." He's more confident than he should be. There might never be more clues, and I probably won't get to the computer store again, but I'm glad he thinks I did well.

"I'm going to search the grounds staff office," I say. "There might be something there." I'll wait until the gardeners' shifts are over for the day. Most staff have complicated shift patterns and also work at night, but gardeners and teachers only work in the daytime.

"Cool," says Drew.

I smile. I hope, finally, I've become a more interesting person in his eyes.

Ms Ray doesn't ask about the mall. She launches straight into lessons after announcements about the restaurant doing an Indonesian-themed buffet at lunchtime, and movie night tomorrow for those on full privileges.

There's no time to think about anything else because once she starts actual lessons, she pounces on us with questions to check we've been listening. At morning break, I remind her quietly that we're supposed to be using the work booklets that are stacked up in the closets in the entrance hall.

"You think that's important?" she asks.

"Yes," I say. *For a bit. Until Dad and Karl have forgotten about you.*

After break, she hands out a work booklet to each of us, and she sits at the front, and it's quiet unless one of us puts up our hand and she comes over to help.

I have mixed tennis in the afternoon: Drew and me against two new grad students. We win in straight sets and they can't believe it. They ask who coaches us and we tell them we have a different coach each summer.

"You two should totally play some serious tournaments," one of them says.

"Yeah," says Drew. He gives them a sarcastic thumbs-up. "Like we'd be allowed to take part."

"Oh. Right." The student is embarrassed. "I thought you guys got to go on lots of sporting trips."

"A few," says Drew. Neither of us can be bothered to explain, yet again, that we have to somehow know the event is taking place or be invited, it has to be approved and there has to be a member of staff available to take us.

Drew and I return the tennis balls and our racquets to the sports equipment room. We add a red sticker to the tubes that the balls came in so that the staff know when they've been used five times and need replacing, and we store our personal racquets in the staff kids' closet. We walk to the juice bar, and I sign for a Very Berry smoothie and wait for Drew on the patio, while he decides what to choose. We sit together for less than a minute before he sees Will walking over with a bunch of other patients.

"Gotta go. Things to discuss," says Drew. He winks, which means black market things.

"I'll come," I say.

"No." He almost shudders. He wants the negotiations to be his, not mine. "The less people involved the better."

I roll my eyes and go back inside to inspect the current jigsaw – a flamingo scene. And as I'm looking at all the pink pieces, I look up and see another load of pink: Thet in a silk dress the shade of my old ballet shoes. She's carrying the notebook that she's writing her novel in. The outside of it is raspberry-coloured dimpled leather with a woven elastic strap to keep it closed. Inside is the only place that Thet allows herself to scribble, change her mind and be untidy, and where her world isn't pink.

"How's it going?" I ask, nodding at her notebook.

"I'm writing the forest scene but the snow-flower won't bloom," says Thet. She hugs the notebook against her chest with folded arms. "Mae, I'm going home in six weeks. My grandmother's found a new school for me."

I'm supposed to say congratulations because it means she's worked hard at her treatment and done well at Hummingbird Creek, but I can't. This will be the second time I've said goodbye to Thet, not knowing if I'll ever see her again. I guess recently I'd been hoping that Thet's wealthy grandmother would keep her here until she was eighteen because she's so settled.

"I'm mostly better now," says Thet.

Six weeks, that's all. I can't help myself. "D'you have to go?"

Thet doesn't look at me. She mumbles, "It's been decided." She has no choice but to accept it.

"Maybe this time Dad will let us email or write to each other." I don't say it with much conviction but I feel the injustice. Patients can secretly tell each other how to contact them via email or social media once they've left. Staff kids can't do that.

"If he doesn't, find me on the internet when you're at college," says Thet. She pats her notebook. "You know the name of my main character. Search for her."

I'll have to wait two years before I can do that. I look beyond the lawn to the trees by the perimeter fence. All this land used to feel immense, but for the first time in my life it's closing in on me.

ELEVEN

I sit on the swing-chair on the schoolhouse veranda and wait for the last person to leave the grounds staff office next door. I don't have long until I need to be back in the apartment for dinner. When I walked past the office a few minutes ago I could see through the window that one of the gardeners was still there, writing a schedule for the following day on the big whiteboard.

A cleaner pushes a trolley slowly over the grass to Hibiscus instead of using the path. When she stops to key in the front door code, I almost miss the sound of the trolley's rattle. There's just the *thunk-thunk* of basketballs bouncing on the court the other side of the grounds staff office. From here I can see our roof terrace and glimpse Mom's plants through the tiny gaps in the marble railings, bright splodges of red, orange and pink against the white.

I don't like thinking of Mom up there, attached to the laptop, even less of herself than usual. To distract myself I get up and peer into the window of the schoolhouse. Ms Ray's been busy this afternoon – she's taken down the posters of inspirational quotes about how to live our lives and pinned up big pictures: strange buildings, purple-tinged mountains, a lake from above, a place where the dust is orangey-brown and people have pottery bowls laid out on squares of material. I'm staring so long at them that I forget to keep an eye on the grounds staff office.

As I walk across to see if the gardener's left, he comes out of the door and gives an upward thrust of his chin as a brief greeting. Gardeners aren't supposed to talk to patients or the staff kids, but he's known me for years. I used to visit Mom in this office all the time, but I haven't been here for months because I've wanted to spend all my spare time with Drew. In case he thinks it's odd that I'm calling in now when Mom's not around, I keep walking for a bit before doubling back.

I tap in the door code, which has never been changed. It's not as if there's confidential stuff in here, such as medical records.

The comforting wood, earth and metal smell of the office greets me as I walk in: stray seedling trays en route to the glasshouses by the vegetable garden, a few steel tools, although they're mostly kept in the attached shed, rain jackets hung by the door, boots, sprays to combat plant disease and piles of seed catalogues.

Mom does the gardening paperwork, inputting payments into the system and ordering plants and gardening equipment. Her desk is by a window that looks out on to curved flower beds. On it there's a pile of invoices in a wire tray. A mug of cold herbal tea. Pens. A highlighter without its lid snapped on tight enough.

I check through the drawers. There are envelopes and thick sheets of paper, engraved with a hummingbird. More pens, lengths of string, paper clips, plant labels and other bits and pieces. There are order books, and printed out emails from suppliers.

Emails… Does Mom have internet these days? I turn on her computer and enter the password that she's always had: *Daffodil*. I used to write pretend invoices for her, and I learned how to spell daffodil, her favourite flower, pretty quickly. There's a harp noise, and her desktop reveals itself. My eyes dart back and forth across the screen, which is cluttered with documents and folders. There's one that says: *Network*. I click on it and find a folder named: *Emails for sending*. Another: *Emails received*.

So Mom still isn't allowed internet either. She has to send her emails via admin. I click on other documents, but they're gardening schedules. A copy of a letter of polite complaint about a batch of diseased trees that were delivered. A shopping list. I recognize some of the items on it, clothes that she bought during the winter. There are photos of flowers that she must have taken on her own camera. The endless shots of unfurling petals make me sad for some reason.

I log off and carry on searching her desk, looking for

something – *anything* – personal. The shelf on the wall next to Mom's desk is crammed with gardening books. I stand to reach a couple of the books on the top shelf. Sitting back down, I flick through the biggest book, called *Shrubs for your Garden*. It has a few pieces of paper in it, but they're blank. Just bookmarks. The second book is on daffodils. As I flick through, a bit of paper drifts on to the floor like a pressed leaf.

When I pick it up I see it's not regular paper. It's a photo of a guy in his twenties, maybe younger. He's lounging against a gate, laughing. In pale jeans and a black leather jacket. Dark hair, black eyes, olive skin. In the field behind him are three horses. One is looking at the camera; the others are grazing. The colour in the photo has bleached out, as if it was kept in the sun too long. I turn it over. *F with Barney, Sunny and Rhonda.* And a date from seventeen years ago. Smudged biro. Curly handwriting. Mom's.

I study the person on the other side. Frank, my uncle. It's not a super-sharp image, but there's something about him that I recognize. His hair and eyes are darker than Mom's, his face rounder. The three names must be the horses.

Eager for more photos, I turn the pages of the daffodil book, faster and faster. I hold it by the front and back covers and shake it, but the photo of Frank is all that was there. Systematically, I reach up to the shelf and go through each gardening book. I fan through the seed catalogues in the corner of the room, and all the magazines.

There's only that one photo. It must either be hidden because it's precious, or she'd just forgotten about it. Her other photos were damaged in the basement flood. I place it back in the daffodil book, roughly in the centre, where I think it came from, and replace all the books back on the shelf.

I search through the rest of the office, including the other two desks. My watch beeps. Ten minutes to dinner. I leave the office, clicking the door gently behind me. Birds swoop in the sky. I hear the manic chirping of the hummingbirds, their song like someone snipping away with a sharp pair of scissors.

Dad's setting the table when I walk in.

"How's Mom?" I ask.

"Much improved," he says. "You may go and see her."

She's propped against two pillows. Her watch is still attached to the laptop on the bedside table.

"Hi, Mom," I say. "You feeling better?" Her skin looks brighter.

"Yes, thanks."

I look at the computer screen, then, glancing towards the door to check Dad's not there, I place my finger on the touchpad. Three graphs are on the screen. Heart rate, sleep pattern and temperature.

Mom coughs, and I catch her eye. *Don't do that with Dad so close by*, she's telling me. "Would you get me some more water," she says, pointing at the glass next to the laptop.

It's half-full, but she wants me away from the computer.

After I've tipped out Mom's water in the bathroom sink of the en suite and refilled the glass, I open her side of the cabinet. I've become sneaky. The cabinet is mostly filled with make-up, but on the bottom shelf there are two glass bottles of pills, one clear and one brown. The printed label on the clear bottle says: *Louelle Ballard. Take two every morning.* Someone – Dad, probably – has crossed it through and written: *1 only.* The brown glass bottle has a label saying: *Louelle Ballard. To be taken under supervision.* I think about the conversation I overheard this morning. Dad thinks Mom's illness is to do with the combination of these two drugs.

She wasn't making sense, had an intense headache, muscle pain and was lacking in energy. She had that strange neck-fizzing thing too. I've experienced some of those symptoms. Right now I have a painful ache in my thigh. I picture the muscle inside, bruised-black like an overripe banana. What if Dad's wrong? Could there be a disease sweeping through the Creek, and Mom has an extreme version of it?

I take the water back to her. She has a sip and asks me to tell her about my day.

I found the photo of your brother. I saw the horses. Barney, Sunny and Rhonda. Did the horses belong to your family? Frank looks handsome in the photo – what was he like in real life? Thet's leaving soon. But if I talk about it I might cry, and I don't want to upset you.

"Tennis was good," I say. "Drew and I beat the grad students."

She smiles.

"There's a movie night tomorrow," I say. We haven't had a movie night for ages. The movies are chosen by Dad, Dr Jesmond or Abigail and are mostly lame, but it's usually a fun evening.

"Nice," says Mom.

There's a knock on the door. Dinner. "I better go and help," I say.

Mom eats dinner on her own in the bedroom, her plate on a tray. Dad and I eat at the table. He tells me how pleased he is with how Greta is handling life outside the Creek, and asks me to make her feel more welcome on her trips back to see us. I don't mention how much my thigh is hurting, and we don't talk about Mom. I'd like to take my plate and sit on the bed next to her, but I don't dare ask.

In the morning, I have brain-training in place of exercise. Usually I quite enjoy it. Timed verbal and non-verbal reasoning tests make a change and most times I get enough of them right to earn ten tokens. But today Joanie is finding hers stressful and taps me on the leg to ask me to help her, so I end up doing two tests at the same time, and neither of us earns any tokens.

After breakfast, I enter the apartment and there's a cleaner wiping the doors to the roof terrace. Mom and Dad's bedroom door is open and I rush in.

Mom's not here. There are clean sheets on the bed. No laptop. The glass of water has been cleared away. I almost throw up.

"Please!" I call to the cleaner. "Where's my mom?"

The cleaner stares at me. "Exercise class," she says.

I release the breath stacked up in my body, and when I can speak, I say, "Thank you."

The movie for tonight is announced at lunchtime. As usual, I've never heard of it before, but none of the patients look wildly enthusiastic, and Will wanders over to the staff kids' table and tells us it's a crummy remake of an old film about mistaken identity. I don't care – I could watch any movie. I learn so much from them.

After dinner, I take the lift down to the basement level to the movie theatre. Will says we have one of the most advanced cinema systems in the world, with ultra-high definition and responsive surround sound. Possibly the most super-comfy adjustable chairs too.

Zach and Ben are sitting together at the front. Luke and Joanie aren't old enough to be here. I look round for Drew – he's sitting near the back next to Will and there are spare seats next to him.

I sit down and save the seat the other side of me for Thet, by placing my wrap-cardigan on it. She arrives as the orderlies start handing out popcorn and bottles of water.

The patient the other side of Will groans when he

sees the popcorn. He's Austin, the one with anger-management problems.

I say, "Don't you like popcorn?"

"Not this kind," he says. He picks up a piece. "Dry-popped. No butter. Salt-free. Tasteless. No, it's not my fave."

Will laughs. "After you've been here a few months, you'll come to terms with it." He takes a piece of Austin's popcorn, throws it up in the air and catches it in his mouth. "Just as you'll sit through the movie even though you'd rather die than let anyone know you watched it in real life."

Austin raises his eyebrows. "Thanks, dude. You're so reassuring."

An orderly comes round and checks that everyone's ready for the movie and warns a couple of people that they'll be asked to leave if they make inappropriate comments or spoil the movie for others. It looks as if he and a grad student are in charge tonight.

Drew grins at me. He's hoping for a silent popcorn fight as soon as the movie's underway. I want to tell him about the photo of Frank but I'll have to wait until a better time.

The lights dim and the music begins. "No trailers?" I hear Austin whisper loudly.

Drew throws his first bit of popcorn very high and sideways. It hits someone near Austin who chucks a couple of bits back. There are some sniggers, and the orderly who's sitting at the front says, "Settle down please, everyone."

"You want to move?" I ask Thet.

She shakes her head, but I know she's terrified of popcorn that's been on the floor landing on her. "Come on," I whisper. Even though I want to stay seated next to Drew, I can feel her anxiety levels rising. "We'll move a couple of rows further back." I point to two empty seats at the end of an aisle.

We leave our cartons of popcorn and crouch-run to the seats. As I sit down, I notice that my neighbour is Noah. The other side of him is one of the popular girls, Piper, who glares at me because I've interrupted their conversation.

"Hi, Mae," says Noah. He offers me some popcorn and whispers, "This stuff is utterly tasteless, isn't it?"

I nod but take a handful, and settle into a comfortable position.

After offering some to Thet, who declines, he turns to watch the film. He laughs in all the wrong places.

At the end of the movie, while the credits are rolling, I say, "What did you think?"

"Predictable plot. Terrible dialogue. But at least it was distracting. That scene on the train, though. The doors would be locked in-between stations, or is it different here?"

"Er…" Stupidly I hesitate, instead of agreeing with him.

Noah says the words I'm dreading. "Wait. Seriously? Have you never been on a train?"

Piper's talking to the person on her other side, so I shake my head and spit it out in one go. "I haven't been on a train. Or a bus or a boat." I've been on a plane, once, from England, and I've travelled in cars. That's it. I know this is odd for patients and grad students to hear. They've always done lots of travelling, so I don't usually tell them stuff like this.

"Have you ever seen the sea?" asks Noah. He says it gently, not in a mocking way.

"You mean the ocean?" I shake my head. I don't tell him I've never seen a lake either, unless I saw one in England that I can't remember. Embarrassment flickers underneath my cheeks. "But it doesn't matter. When I'm older, I can do all those things."

Something stings my cheek, then lands in my lap. Popcorn. "Excuse me," I say. I step past Thet and make my way to Drew's row, picking up stray pieces of popcorn on the way, and after I've reached him, I pull the neck of his T-shirt and stuff it all down his top.

Drew squeals and squirms, knocking Will's sweater off his lap, and I catch Will's eye and he knows I've seen what was underneath: him and Austin holding hands.

"Mae Ballard," calls the orderly. "Sit in your seat until the credits have finished."

TWELVE

"Drew – d'you ever have a prickly feeling in your neck, like pins and needles?" We're walking across to the schoolhouse on Monday morning.

"Occasionally," he replies. "Dr J told me it's a growing thing." He catches my puzzled face. "You know, your body growing a bit too fast. He says it happens a lot with teenagers."

"But Mom has it too sometimes," I say. "Even now she's officially better."

He considers this a moment before saying, "Maybe we're being poisoned?"

I can't tell if he's being serious. I've heard Dad talk about pesticide problems with Mom because he's instructed the gardeners to use organic products so we get some sort of certificate. But outside the perimeter fence are acres of crops that stretch so far the only thing beyond them is sky, and they're regularly sprayed with something.

Drew places his hand on top of my head, moving it back and forth really fast so that it messes up my hair, and runs ahead. "Another thing for my list of reasons to get the hell out of here!" he shouts.

I'd catch him up and do the same to him if I wasn't carrying a tote bag over my shoulder, weighed down with books from Ms Ray's car.

In lessons Ms Ray talks about the new pictures she's put up on the wall. It turns out she's been to all the places they show, but she isn't boasting, she's explaining little details that surprised her. I recognize the wavy feeling inside my stomach as excitement. One day I'm going to be someone who's seen breathtaking sights and trodden in dusty orange earth.

As we walk to the restaurant for lunch, Drew hangs back and says, "D'you want to meet up later and see if the lighter has anything left in it?"

I check my schedule on my watch and we agree a time after my three-monthly sight test, followed by swim technique clinic.

"Golf course?"

"Meet you by the buggies."

Will and Austin are sitting next to each other at lunch, engaged in deep conversation. Relationships between patients are forbidden. If caught, they'll find themselves separated for every activity, or even asked to leave. Will's been here for a long time and never been in trouble despite being so involved in the black market; as far as I know, admin has never discovered its existence. Punishments can be as severe for patients as they are for staff kids, but Will says it depends who your parents are, and how long they're prepared to keep paying for you to be here. I don't think this can be true. It's just he hasn't been caught.

Noah's sitting next to Thet on a different table. I wish I was with them, listening to their conversation instead of eating alongside Drew, Ben, Luke and Zach, the four of them bickering about which new PlayStation game in the games room is better.

I stare out of the window – at the brightness. It hasn't rained for a couple of weeks, but the lawns are still a vivid green because of the overnight sprinklers. I have to make the most of summer. It won't be so easy for Drew and me to smoke in winter. There'll be more rain, not just occasional showers. Cold winds. Storms. And by then Thet will be gone. I'm going to miss her.

I think back to Drew's comment about how we might be being poisoned and the weirdness in my stomach intensifies. We all take vitamins. What if the vitamins are poisoning us? What if they are interacting badly with Mom's other medication?

This thought whirls through my mind as I ace the sight test and swim fifty lengths of the indoor pool, working on my backstroke.

I walk out of the little gate in the pool area and collide with Noah.

"Sorry. Didn't see you," he says. His nose and the skin under his eyes are slightly sunburnt. He's dressed for tennis and is carrying a Creek-logoed tennis racquet. It might just be me misremembering, but he looks as if he's muscled up a bit in the last ten days or so. "Did I tread on your foot?"

"Yes, but I'm OK. It was probably my fault too. I was thinking about something."

"I was heading for . . . um, a place," says Noah. "A nice little hideaway that's not covered by the security cameras. You could come with me?"

I think of what I saw on his patient referral form when I was in reception with Jenna. *Noah Tinderman. Paranoia. Anxiety. In need of a calm, nurturing environment.* He's one of those patients who thinks everyone's out to get him. "It sounds very undercover. You've checked out the cameras?"

"Of course. But you must know where they all are."

There have always been cameras at the Creek, and new ones are installed all the time. Parents are reassured by them. They're there for everyone's protection. I've never gone round actually searching for them, though Drew and I always check before smoking in a new place. A few years ago Drew, Greta, Zach, Ben and I were taken to the security building by Earl, head of admin and security, and shown the huge display of monitors for the security cameras. We thought it was the coolest thing.

"Tell me where," I say.

"You're in?"

And I have some time until I meet Drew, so why not? "I'm in."

"OK. This might be a secret place that even you don't know about."

"You really think so?" I gaze around. Perhaps he's found a climbable tree by the perimeter fence that's not overlooked by a camera.

"OK," says Noah. "Meet me at the back of the security building, in the middle where the two corner cameras can't pick you up as they sweep round. Make it look as if you're heading for the sensory garden, then scoot off the path. I'll follow in a few minutes."

The two-storey brick security building is operational twenty-four hours a day. I used to find that comforting when we first moved here, and the security manager was a big teddy bear of a guy. Now it's Earl. He's either in admin or this building, and I avoid both places unless I have a very good reason to be there. He scares me with his unsmiling staring expression, as if he's waiting for me to step out of line, and his long fingers that may or may not have strangled someone.

I follow Noah's directions until I'm standing right up against the back wall of the security building, as if someone is about to throw knives round me. When Noah comes over, he points at the fire-escape ladder. "You ever been up here?"

"Nope." I would never have dared even if it had occurred to me.

Noah goes first, and I follow, copying the way he makes as little noise as possible on the metal structure, by taking more than one step at a time, and pulling himself up at an even speed, careful not to bash the tennis racquet on the rails.

I step on to the flat concrete at the top, and gasp at this new view of the Creek. It's like being on the roof terrace of Hibiscus but being able to look out in all directions. There's a waist-high brick wall, and a strange little fire-escape exit for the building which has its own overhanging tiled roof.

It's a forgotten place. There are weeds growing out of the concrete, little pieces of broken brick and dusty leaves that have blown in from the trees by the perimeter fence.

"Wow," I say softly. Noah really has found a secret place I didn't know about.

"A security building that doesn't have a camera trained on its fire escape. Ironic, don't you think?" says Noah. "Can't believe you never came up here."

"Neither can I," I say. This will be the hands-down most perfect smoking place for me and Drew if we can be sure the smoke can't be smelt from the ground. I won't tell Drew until Noah's gone home though, so we don't invade his private space.

Noah points at the fire-exit door structure and says, "If we sit over there, we're in the shade, and totally hidden from view."

I sit, and he settles next to me. Not too close, which is good. He's a Boy. And a Patient.

"So what shall we talk about?" asks Noah. "The 'something' you were thinking about earlier?"

I'm not going to talk about the vitamins. "I don't remember." I lean back against the brickwork.

"Tell me about you," Noah says. "Like, what d'you do when you don't have an exercise session or you're not doing those funny little booklets in the schoolhouse?"

"How d'you know about the booklets?"

"Your teacher came into my class at Larkspur and showed the teacher a few. She wanted his opinion on them."

"And?"

"He said if she wanted to change anything, she had to go through your dad." He shrugs. "She seemed nice, though, your teacher."

"She is."

"So," says Noah. "What d'you actually do here in your own time?"

"Watch TV... Spend tokens in the spa." I see he's expecting something more exciting. "Er... I hang out with Drew," I say. "You ever smoked?"

"Yeah. Weed a few times." He grins at my shock. "And no, my parents don't know. Mum found my stash of alcohol that I hid up the chimney in my room though. There was a bit of yelling about that. But mostly because my sister had bought it for me."

121

I'm appalled. But envious.

A light breeze judders a dried leaf across the roof towards us.

"What do you do when you're not at school – when you're back in England?" I ask.

"You don't want to know, it's too embarrassing," says Noah. "Computer games. Maths. That's math to you. But I like most subjects. I play the trumpet. Play in a rubbish band. Muck about composing stuff. Hang about with a small group of friends. Standard stuff. Not very interesting."

It's interesting to me.

He sighs. "But my head's a crowded place. My parents thought it would be good for me to get away for the summer. Do sport. Forget about exams." He places the racquet between us. "I'm involved in this human rights charity too."

Human rights?

"There's stuff I read about... Things that humans do to other humans, and not just in wars. It set something off in me... I went through a dark time. I got depressed and for a while I felt pretty paranoid." He picks up the racquet again. "I'm nearly out the other side. Being here," he says in a brighter voice, "is supposed to be a way of getting some distance from all that. Literally." He swipes at the air with the racquet as if he's reaching for a shot. "It was that or be shipped off to a family cottage in Ireland with all my cousins, who are either moaning about the weather, discussing captions for Instagram or bitching about celebrities. Doesn't seem so bad now, in retrospect, given how strict this place is. You know, what with the tracking device they call a watch, and all the cameras." He sees my face and frowns. "Sorry. I didn't mean to offend you. I was being sarcastic."

"Don't worry," I say. "Your world's different to mine, is all," I say.

He tells me more about the cottage and his cousins, making me laugh, though I'm conscious of keeping the noise down. After glancing at the time, I stand up. "I have to go and meet Drew."

"OK." He nods, then smiles. "Nice chatting to you."

"Yeah." I smile back and think how if he wasn't just here for the summer, he might turn into a good friend.

I descend the ladder as fast as I can and hurry across the parking lot towards the golf buggies. My mind's churning. Alcohol up chimneys, cigarettes, potato chips, pesticides, Irish cottages. Life outside frightens me. But I suddenly want it so badly.

THIRTEEN

I tap my four-digit pin code into the stand so that the front wheels of the buggy are released and my token is deducted. Drew appears from the side entrance of the main building. He's been to the sports-equipment room to pick up a couple of golf bags.

He slings the bags into the back and we set off.

At the Woodland Gardens, Drew jumps out and I wait while he unearths our smoking kit, then we drive on to the far side of the golf course, where I park the buggy behind a clump of bushes, in the shade. The place is deserted. The patients have a group activity, Joanie's gone home to watch Creek cartoons, and the other boys are probably wasting tokens in the games room.

We choreograph a pretend sword fight with our putters for about five minutes before sitting on one of the landscaped earth mounds, against a tree. The shade feels good. I'm thirsty but we forgot water. I'm not really in the mood for a cigarette, but I sniff the tobacco and the smell conjures up happiness and the touch of Drew's skin.

I kick off my flip-flops and we roll our cigarettes with pleasurable concentration. In a minute I'll ask him what he thinks about my vitamin theory, and I'll tell him about the photo of Frank. And how my mom must have been brought up with or near horses, which makes sense because when the riding school comes to the Creek, Mom's always the first one to sign up. She knows how to be around them. I've watched her sniff a horse's neck, closing her eyes as if it's the best smell in the world. Maybe she'd be like that with other animals too, but pets aren't allowed here because they smell and cause mess.

"Look! Still got a flame." Drew holds the lighter in front of me.

"Yay," I say as I light my cigarette.

As the smoke curls down my throat, I hear, "Mae! Drew!" It's too close. Too fierce. I peer round the tree and see him, maybe ten paces away.

Dad.

I cough. I can't stop. I choke, gasping for air.

"On your feet." Dad's in front of us.

We stand in a split second. I have bare feet. I can't drop my cigarette and grind it out, so I hold it behind my back, the incriminating smoke and smell coiling round me.

"Look at me," says Dad, each word over-pronounced.

It's impossible to misread the fury in his eyes. "Explain yourselves."

"We were curious, sir," says Drew. He speaks quickly. "We found a bag of supplies buried in the Woodland Gardens. Today we thought we'd see what smoking was like."

Dad's lips tighten. "Don't take me for a fool, Drew."

"He's right," I say. We would both rather live the rest of our lives in solitary than get anyone else into trouble over this. But I add, "We've tried it out a few times though," to make Dad think he's won more of a confession. That we don't take him for a fool.

Dad looks at the smoke and says, enunciating each word, "Put that cigarette out."

I crouch to the ground and he adds, "With your foot." There's spit at the corner of his mouth.

I'm barefoot. He wants me to *burn* myself? I grab my flip-flop and pound the glowing cigarette end, as if it were a poisonous insect. Ash flies up into my eyes and makes them water. I won't cry.

Dad swallows. It's one of the things they talk about in Coping Skills group, which I'm scheduled to attend once every couple of months. Swallowing helps you think before you speak, to regain control. "Maintaining optimal health is at the heart of everything Hummingbird Creek stands for," he says. "You both disgust me."

Smoking's bad, but this seems like a massive over-reaction. I push my feet into my flip-flops and flick a glance in Drew's direction. He's avoiding eye contact.

Dad's so close I can smell his sour breath. "Let me tell you, there will be consequences for this deceitful behaviour. To ensure this never ever happens again."

We look at the ground and nod.

"Now go home," says Dad. "I can't stand the sight of you any longer." He bends to pick up our plastic bag and smoking equipment.

We scramble to pick up our golf clubs and stuff them into the golf bags. I look round for his buggy. He's parked a little way away. That's why we didn't hear him coming.

Our buggy is behind the bushes. How did he know we were here? The golf course is huge and wooded, and we can't have been easy to spot. Is there a tracking device on the buggy? Or on our watches?

FOURTEEN

We don't talk much on the drive back to park the buggy.

"I hate him," says Drew when I've turned on to the main track. He slams his fist into the leather seat.

"I'm sorry," I say. I'm sorry this has happened to us, that my dad is so strict. He's probably not going to let us spend time on our own together for a while after this.

"I bet he was spying on us," says Drew. We've almost reached the buggy stands, and he leaps out early. He grabs one of the golf bags and he's gone, off to the sports equipment room in a rage.

I lock the buggy, and follow Drew with the second golf bag. He's leaving the room when I get there, and he makes a resigned I-told-you-this-place-is-the-pits face at me. He's slung his golf bag in the wrong place. There's a camera in here. He should be more careful. I position mine back in its slot then move Drew's, and trudge home to Hibiscus.

*

I've seen other people's bedrooms in movies and in magazines, but in real life I've only ever been in a handful: mine, my parents' and, one time, Greta's, when I had to go for a sleepover because Mom and Dad went to my grandparents' fiftieth wedding anniversary. I've also seen an empty patient room on an open day, when they bring parents of prospective patients through on tours. We live in a climate of trust with unlocked doors, and we share our lives with each other, but we need our own space too.

Drew's mom has never allowed me to go into Drew's bedroom because she says my dad wouldn't like it, but he took a few photos of it for me on his camera. It was clean and tidy, like mine, with a lot of basketball stuff and a poster of a cycle race through some mountains in France.

Thet's described her bedroom in her grandmother's house to me, all pink and grand.

My room has bright abstract artwork on the wall, which came from an auction in New York, a bed I helped design myself, and on it a patchwork quilt made using material from my clothes when I was little that Mom had made by the laundry staff. A couple of times I've found her in my room, touching the different fabrics, cottons and silks, stripy jersey cotton and soft cashmere from when I was little. "You've always had beautiful clothes," she once told me. She made it sound like she wasn't sure that was a good thing. I once asked her to tell me what memories each fabric brought back but she only muttered something about it being better to live in the moment.

There's a shelving unit by my bed, mostly filled with notebooks and pens. I've collected vintage pens ever since I saw an article about them in a magazine. I like calligraphy because it often absorbs me enough to block out every other feeling. I try it now, selecting a pen, some ink and a notebook. I write out the alphabet in different styles. Over and over.

I remember the times Drew and I planned to run away when we were little. Our plans didn't develop much beyond rattling the gates. It was around then that the games room was installed and we forgot why we were even thinking of running away.

The one time I almost managed to leave the Creek without permission was when I was ten, and it wasn't because I wanted to run away. It was because I was desperate to see what it was like outside the Creek at night-time. I wanted to see street lights and Pattonville nightlife, and Abigail's house. I thought it would be easy to hide in the car overnight. I knew I'd be punished for going missing but I did it anyway.

As Abigail was slowly leaving the parking lot, Dad knocked on her car window and she'd stopped, slid it down, and said, "Well, if it isn't my favourite doctor." I must have shifted in my hiding place, and he caught sight of the movement. I was pulled from the car within seconds.

As we grew older we realized, Drew and me, that

even if we left without being spotted, we didn't have any money, only tokens that were worth nothing outside, and we were in the middle of a flat, rural, empty landscape with nowhere to run to. By the time Drew was old enough to work on a proper way to leave, I was telling him not to. I said life wasn't so bad here. He should count his blessings.

I'm starting to think we should have tried harder back then.

I wait a long time for Dad at the apartment. He comes in, shutting the front door loudly. I hear him place his radio receiver on the table in the hallway, and then he comes into my room.

"Sit up, Mae." His face is unreadable. I'm not going to react if he sends me to a solitary room.

That was my punishment for hiding in the back of Abigail's car. The following morning Dad handed me to a nurse in the medical suite who told me to remove my shoes. As soon as I walked into the small empty white room, she slammed the door shut and bolted it.

I spent a long, long time in that room with bright strip lighting. With walls that were slightly soft so you couldn't hit your head against them.

Nobody came when I shouted. I had no idea of time; the display on my watch had been switched off remotely. Nothing happened when I banged on the door and said I was sorry, or when hunger came, or when the fear overtook me and I retched and cried hysterical tears.

When I was finally led out by the same nurse, and sent to Raoul for a medical check, I couldn't understand why I felt so ashamed of losing control in that room.

Dad paces in front of me in my bedroom. "You'll eat breakfast and lunch in your room until further notice. You'll exercise with Mick alone, and you'll do work booklets on your own in an office in the main building. You are to stay in your room for the rest of today. You are on zero privileges until Earl sends you a message via your watch to tell you otherwise. There will also be a further punishment."

"What will that be?"

He doesn't answer, he just leaves. I hear Mom outside my room later, asking to come in and see me, but Dad says, "It's out of the question, Louelle." After the shutters have come down, he returns with a dinner tray. There's a glass of water, my vitamin pill and a bowl of Tuscan bean soup. He watches me swallow the pill then goes out of the room. I can only eat two mouthfuls of soup and flush the rest down the toilet; I'm too full of worry.

I've never been on zero privileges. It means my tokens are frozen so I can't use them. Nor can I earn them, but I can still be fined. I'm not allowed to speak to anyone unless spoken to, and I'm excluded from all unscheduled activities.

It's hard to sleep. My room feels airless, and too hot, even though I can hear the faint hum of the air conditioning. Ben was once threatened with having to live in Larkspur with the most extreme patients when he'd done something wrong. If that's my punishment, I'll welcome it.

In the morning, I dress in my exercise clothes and as soon as I open my door, Dad appears with his silver laptop under his arm. "Mick's waiting for you in Studio 1A. After breakfast in your room, go to Room Twelve on the admin floor. Be there at nine-fifteen."

As I leave he says, "You were very stupid, Mae, to think I wouldn't find out you were breaking Creek rules."

I nod and let myself out of the apartment.

Studio 1A is the room used for individual, hard-core training. I wonder where Drew's doing his exercise – and if he has the same punishments as me. Mick sees me through the glass window and opens the door. "Let's get started," he says.

There's no equipment out. Mick quickly takes the readings from my watch, then points to the polished-wood sprung floor. "Fifty push-ups. Go."

As I'm doing lunges, Thet looks through the glass window and does a thing with her hand, pretending someone is dragging her away by the neck. It gets me through the rest of the session.

Afterwards, I go back to the apartment where breakfast is on a tray for me outside my room. The shutters are up and I can hear a cleaner sweeping the roof terrace. It's darkish outside. It's going to rain later. I eat everything on the tray in case I have to spend a long time in solitary.

Room Twelve is a side room that faces towards the grounds staff office, the non-veranda-ed side of the schoolhouse and, if I stand in the right place, some of Hibiscus. I watch the first heavy raindrops fall, shaking the leaves in the flower beds.

"Sit down." Dad is in the doorway. He nods towards the desk on which there's a work booklet, a pen, pencil and eraser. "Complete the booklet. When your watch alarm sounds, take the booklet to the schoolhouse and then go home for lunch. At two o'clock, you're scheduled to meet Mick in the lobby."

What's the rest of my punishment?

Dad leaves. I flip through the booklet. I've seen this one a couple of times before. Outside the rain is drumming down, but that's not the only sound I can hear. There's shouting coming from somewhere.

"It's time to get out of this hellhole... Screw you, Dr Hunter Ballard... I've been waiting for this moment."

Drew? I race to the window. I see him in his outside-sports cagoule, walking across the soaking lawn with a large plastic storage container in his arms, his hair stuck to his head from the rain. His parents are behind him, on the path with suitcases, their faces hidden by rain-jacket hoods.

It can't be. I'm paralysed while the breath has momentarily left my body, and then I run. Out of the room and down the staircase. Outside into the pouring rain. I can hardly feel the ground beneath my feet, only the thudding in my chest.

Drew shouts, "I'm not going quietly."

His parents tell him to shush, he's done enough damage. Two security guards are moving in. He notices me before they do, so they're not expecting him to break free. He drops the box to the ground and I run into his arms. Although he's drenched, he smells of every memory I've had of us together. Trees, grass, delicately scented breakfast fruit, sunshine on skin, sports kit and perhaps the faint waft of tobacco. "Your dad's thrown us out," he says. "I wanted to go, but not like this. My parents have lost everything."

"No." I clutch him more tightly. I shiver in my thin dress. I'm wetter and colder than I've ever been. "He needs your mom and dad. He can't."

"He has," Drew says. He pushes me back by my shoulders so I can see his face. "He sacked them. Because I smoked a few cigarettes."

"No." This is nightmarishly unfair. I look at his parents. They have grim expressions.

"I'll. . ." I start to say, but we both know there's nothing I can do. Nobody can sway Dad's decisions.

"Come on, Drew," snaps his mom. She doesn't acknowledge me as she walks past us with his dad. There's a silver car waiting at the exit of the parking lot. The engine's running.

"Where are you going?" I ask, my words tumbling together. I only have seconds left.

"As far away from this place as we can," says Drew. "A motel to start with." He sounds defiant but I detect a wobble in his voice.

I lunge myself at him again and hug him fiercely.

"Your dad's a bastard," he says.

"I know." My words are swamped by gasping tears. "Don't leave me," I choke.

"You've got to stay strong. Leave here as soon as you can, Mae. Then have a good life."

Don't go, I want to say. *Don't leave me.* But instead I stay silent.

He peels my arms away and I grab him again. A security guard pulls me away so fast that I stumble. I look up. Abigail is picking her way across the lawn with an umbrella towards me, slowed down by her heels. The rain is easing off, but the ground is saturated. The other security guard is leading Drew off towards the car. Mick is loading suitcases into the back.

This, I realize, is my further punishment. The worst I can imagine.

Lung-crushing pain grips me. I need Drew. How will I survive without him?

I fall to my knees and I'm pulled up again by the security guard.

Drew doesn't look back.

There are people watching now. A couple of gardeners.

Zach, Ben, Luke, Joanie and Ms Ray are on the steps of the schoolhouse. Admin staff including Earl are at the first-floor window, and there's someone looking out of the long window in reception. Is it Dad?

I scream. Loud and long. Until Abigail slaps me on the cheek.

"Stop it. You're hysterical," she says. "Are you going to walk away, or do you have to be dragged?"

Walking away is an impossibility. As the car doors bang shut, and the car moves down the driveway. I see Drew's shocked face as I'm dragged. I'm still being dragged when I hear the big wrought-iron gates clank shut, and my world folds in.

FIFTEEN

I'm taken to a treatment room. Raoul wipes my arm and injects me with something that's cold as it enters my bloodstream. As I swim out of consciousness, I hear Dad speaking.

"They contaminated the results. I can't forgive that."

Raoul murmurs his sympathies, and Dad says, "I'll drop by again later. Attach her to a monitor and tell me when she wakes up."

The words break into fragments in my brain. They swirl, change colour and disappear.

I'm chasing a silver car. Running even though I can't see it any more, because if I don't I'll die. And then I'm awake, but my eyelids are heavy and I don't want to open them.

I hear the door squeak. Dad's voice floats towards me: "How's the patient?"

I keep very still, even though I know I won't be fooling the monitor.

"Non-REM sleep, sir," says a nurse who isn't Raoul. She must have taken over from him, and hasn't looked at the screen in the last minute. She sounds like all the other members of staff when they have to interact with Dad. Flustered, flattered and eager to please.

A phone rings. My body jolts; I'm not used to the sound. Surely they must know I'm awake now?

"Hello?" I hear Dad say. "Right. Yes, put him through. Hi, Peter." *Peter. . . Who's Peter?*

"Excuse me for a moment will you?" He clears his throat. "I'll take over here with Mae. You can get back to your other duties. Thank you."

"You're welcome, sir," says the nurse.

He waits until the door closes – then he says, "OK, fire away."

There's mmming and uh-huhing, then, "You saw the latest data report? Yes, all the research is going in the right direction. Minor hiccups here and there, of course. As always." He pauses. "You think we should push it that far? . . . I don't see why not. Yes, it's been a while since you saw the set-up. Come and visit."

I'm lying down but I'm dizzy. I'm still a little sedated. Wooooozy. I have to catch each thought as it spins round my head. They keep flying away from me in unpredictable directions, like bats. My arm hurts where Raoul injected me. It feels as if someone trod on it.

A couple of minutes after Dad ends the call, I move my sore arm. Then my leg.

"Mae?" Dad places a hand on my forehead, and I fight the instinct to push it away, opening my eyes slowly. The light is bright, so I close them again.

"Sit up slowly. Take your time. You might feel dizzy," says Dad.

I don't want to face him but the alternative is to lie on this bed for the rest of the day attached to a monitor. After a few minutes I sit up. I feel OK but weakened, and there's an unpleasant taste in my mouth.

Dad reaches over to detach the cable from my watch, and the smell of the anti-bacterial soap from his hands is overwhelming. "Good," he says, as he winds up the cable. "I'm pleased we've reached the point where we can discuss what happened calmly. I should have been more aware of what was going on. Drew was clearly a bad influence on you, so your punishment also serves as a way of protecting you. You must remember that I know what's best for you."

Drew is never coming back.

"OK," continues Dad. "You may go to Hibiscus. I've cancelled your afternoon exercise. You'll start again with Mick tomorrow morning. I'll review your behaviour in a week's time. I need to see evidence that you are in tune with all the Creek values if you are to regain any privileges. Perhaps a therapy session on coping with change will help; I'll set one up." He gives me a smile, and I let it pass through me.

My throat tightens as I recall Drew's shocked face as he left. I push down the shuddering sobs that are rising up.

Dad holds out his hand to help me down from the trolley-bed. I refuse it by pretending not to notice.

"I'll have lunch sent up to you soon. Your blood-sugar levels are low." He turns away to the laptop on the counter.

I walk unsteadily out of the medical suite and the main building. I need a friendly face. I look out for pink clothes, but I don't see Thet. I want Mom, but she'll be in the grounds staff office.

Once I've stumbled into my room, I curl up under my covers, and I don't answer when there's a knock at the door. Someone says, "Mae? Your lunch is outside." A while later, there's another knock, and a different voice says, "I'm going to have to log that you didn't eat any lunch."

Time passes. I hear Mom's voice. "Honey, are you awake?"

I lift my head a fraction and see her hovering.

"Can I sit?" she says.

I nod and she perches on the end of my bed and clenches her hands together. "I heard about Drew," she says quietly. "I'm so sorry."

His name stabs me. "How could Dad do that?" I whisper.

She shakes her head. There's a long pause before she says, "He's doing it for the best. It's important to separate ourselves from negative influences. Drew was a negative influence."

Her words don't surprise me because she never criticises Dad, but they still hurt me. "You really think that?"

She says, "You have Greta."

"Greta?" How can she think my friendship with Drew is in any way comparable to the barely functional relationship I have with Greta.

"You should try harder with Greta," says Mom.

I'm about to shout at her. But I notice Mom's squeezing her neck. "Does your neck hurt?" I ask.

"Just a fizzing feeling," she says. "Raoul says it'll pass."

"What was wrong with you when you were ill?"

"A problem with my meds," says Mom. "Nothing to worry about."

"What meds are you on?"

Her face is blank. She doesn't know. "I let your father take charge of that. He's the doctor."

I think about the bottles of pills in her bathroom. "But don't you want to know?"

"I have to trust him," says Mom. She looks back at the door. "I don't have any choice."

I know I'm pushing her in a direction she doesn't want to go. She stands up. "Come and watch TV with me," she says. "I'll fix you a sunset."

By the time Dad's home, I'm watching Mom's favourite soap, a red and orange fruit mocktail half-drunk on the table beside me.

"Everything OK?" he says.

I don't answer but Mom says, "We're fine, Hunter, thank you."

At the dinner table, I pour the water, and Dad fetches the vitamin tablets. I bet Drew is eating a hamburger and fries in his motel tonight. Is he thinking of me?

"I'm upping both your vitamin doses," says Dad. He looks from Mom to me. "Your bodies have been under a lot of strain, and I'm worried you aren't fortified enough to recover properly – especially after you skipped lunch, Mae. For the next few weeks, you'll have two each."

He watches us swallow them. I resolve to stop taking them as soon as I can find a way. To see if it makes any difference to how I feel. Dad crunches his sweet pepper salad and talks about the bicycles that have been ordered for the cycle track. As if that's the most eventful thing that's happened today. As if my heart isn't in pieces.

SIXTEEN

I can't get out of bed. I don't feel anything.

Mom pleads. An orderly snaps at me. Hauls me to my feet. I sway a little. All I want to do is sleep and never wake up. I disintegrate slowly and gracefully, like sand through a timer.

Dad speaks into his radio. His voice is icy cold.

Raoul is in my room, talking to Dad. Has the double dose of vitamins done this to me? Everything feels heavy, especially my bones. Raoul takes my blood and hooks me up to a laptop.

"Nothing wrong," I hear Raoul say. "Hysterical reaction."

I'm left to sleep the rest of the day, but Mom wakes me for dinner. For vitamins and vegetable chilli.

Dad frowns at me. "We need order back in this home. You will get up tomorrow and you will do as you're told."

I go through my morning exercise without once speaking

to Mick. "You're not even going to ask where I took Drew and his parents?" he taunts in my ear.

I might have been tempted to ask, except I know he's too scared of Dad to ever tell me.

"Too bad. Anyway, they've probably moved on by now to somewhere else."

There's something different about the booklet on the desk in the empty office. When I pick it up, I see it's thicker than usual. Extra pages have been stapled into the middle. Harder questions, in Ms Ray's spiky handwriting.

I let my body sag on to the chair, and sink my head into my hands. I have no energy, and it feels as if my brain has been coated with something thick. I stay like that for a long time until loud birdsong jolts me. I go and stand against the window frame, watching a gardener neatening the edging along the path. Everything is still and calm. Unchanged. Apart from me.

Eventually I start the booklet. It takes me much longer than usual because of the extra questions. There are a couple of math problems I don't understand. While I wait for my watch alarm to go off, I practise calligraphy even though I only have a regular pen. I feel my breathing become slow and regular, and I imagine Drew coming to rescue me. He'd storm the gates with a heavy vehicle of some sort, and while he turned it round to face the other way, I'd come running. I wouldn't waste time grabbing possessions, and I'd outrun everyone.

I plan to leave my booklet inside the door of the schoolhouse but Ms Ray must have been looking out for me because she's there waiting in the entrance area. Chunks of hair have escaped from her ponytail and mascara has smudged below one eye. I'm not allowed to speak unless spoken to, so I hand her the booklet without saying anything.

"Mae, come in. Close the door." She takes a big breath. "I'm so sorry to hear what happened. Not that I condone smoking. Not at all. But I wouldn't expect such a ... severe outcome."

"It was my punishment," I say flatly. "Dad says Drew was a bad influence on me."

Ms Ray steps back. "Do *you* think Drew was a bad influence on you?"

There's a muddle in my head. "I don't know," I whisper.

"This is my first teaching job, Mae," says Ms Ray. "I took it because there's time for me to work on my own studies, and because I split up with the person I was seeing and a fresh start seemed like a good thing. But, to be honest, I feel pretty exhausted by it."

She shouldn't be telling me this stuff. She should be professional. Embarrassed for her, I gaze at my manicured toenails.

"I was unprepared for Creek life," she says. "It's very strict and controlled. The way I'm expected to teach is ... strange. And there are so many ordinary things that you haven't done,

146

and it's not because your parents can't afford it."

I look up.

"From what you kids say, you've never been to a museum, or an art gallery, a concert or the theatre. Not even the cinema. You've never been to a supermarket, a place of worship or ... I don't know ... walked a dog on a lead." She sounds exasperated. I find myself thinking of England, of a family I never got to know.

"The outside makes people unhappy. That's why they have to come here," I say, but I know I'm only repeating what I've been told.

"Happiness. Unhappiness. They're both part of life. *Real* life. Being stuck here, for years? Sorry, but I think it's wrong. And the intense focus on health and exercise is, in my view, obsessional."

Even after all that's happened, it's hard to hear her criticize the Creek. "Greta can do whatever she wants," I say. "The rest of us have to wait our turn. I'm only here for another couple of years."

Ms Ray sighs. "Greta's not been encouraged to spread her wings. She's still tethered here."

There's a flicker of movement by the glass door that leads to the schoolroom.

Ms Ray says, "I thought it might be helpful to know an outsider's views. One who isn't as much of a fan of your father as other people."

How does she know I won't tell Dad what she's just said?

Joanie opens the glass door. "Ms Ray. . .?" She catches sight of me and grips me round the waist.

"When are you coming back, Mae?"

"Soon, Joanie."

"When's Drew back?"

"Never," I say, because I can't protect her from that.

SEVENTEEN

As I do my morning exercise, while my muscles burn, and sweat drips down my top, I imagine Drew beside me telling me to be strong. I concentrate on the thought that in two years I'll be able to find him.

I gasp for air. It's hot in this little studio. "Need to cool down," I tell Mick.

He shouts at me for wanting to quit. "On the floor now. Twenty push-ups."

I'm slow and my eyes hurt. My vision is blurring. Are my eyeballs sweating along with the rest of me?

While Mick inputs my end-of-session readings, I hold my neck. The pins-and-needles feeling has enclosed my entire neck.

"What's up?" asks Mick.

"I'm tired," I say.

He prods my leg with his sports shoe. "You're weak. That's your problem."

After the weekend, I have even more pages stapled into my work booklet. One is the step-by-step method to solve the math questions I couldn't do before. On the facing page there's another similar question for me to tackle. I want to concentrate, but I can't. All I can think about is Drew being gone. Tears fall on to the booklet and I don't wipe them away. I lay my head on the table on top of my arms, and let the sadness out in muffled sobs.

I'm gradually aware of more chatter than usual on the admin floor. Is someone coming to check on me? I need to blow my nose and wipe my sore eyes. I wait a moment, but nobody enters. Carefully, I open the door. There's no one in the corridor, so I slip along to the ladies' toilets, noticing the massive flower arrangement on the window sill, the type that's only done on days when important visitors are expected. As I splash water on my face, I hear someone say, "He's on his way."

People are coming down the corridor. I open the door a crack. Dad's walking towards the glass door that you need a swipe card for, with a man who's wearing military uniform. Earl is walking behind them, glancing around. I stand back and when I hear they've gone past, I look again. Earl, one of the top people in the Creek, is acting like some sort of bodyguard for the man in the military uniform. Could that man be "Peter", who Dad was on the phone to when I was in the medical suite?

*

After lunch in my room, I sit on the roof terrace and practise some meditation techniques. I'm interrupted by the sound of a truck. It lumbers up to the cycle track. Behind it is the minibus of builders. The Creek has a tranquillity manifesto. It employs a lot of builders to do a few hours' work from midday rather than less of them working all day.

My next exercise session is tennis. To reach the courts, I walk between the schoolhouse and grounds staff office. Ms Ray is sitting on the swing-chair on the veranda with a pile of paper in her lap and a pen sticking out of her mouth. She waves and calls "Hello!" I nod back. I don't think she should attract so much attention to herself. No other staff member would shout across the lawn like that.

I look for Mom through the window of the grounds staff office. She must be out gardening because there's no one there, but something catches my eye as I walk past the door. A security camera. I don't remember seeing it before. How long has it been there? Did it – I'm hot with panic – catch me going in the other day? It's OK, I tell myself, there'd be nothing out of the ordinary about me going in there.

But what if there's a camera *inside* the office? I push away the thought; there's nothing I can do about it now. I'll just have to be more alert in future.

A flash of neon pink running shoes on the basketball court distracts me: Thet and a few other patients, including

Piper and Austin, are doing star jumps. The instructor counts them down from ten, but when he reaches one, Austin keeps going. He springs extra-high, flinging his arms and legs wide, on and on in a steady mesmerizing rhythm. He's hardly out of breath.

"Wow, Austin," calls the instructor. "That's awesome."

Thet raises her eyes at me through the fence. It's becoming more freaky than awesome.

Austin's jumps finally become slower and then he stops. "No," he shouts to the instructor. "You mustn't."

"Mustn't what?" asks the instructor.

"Keep away from me!" Austin walks backwards, away from the group.

"Easy there, buddy. What's wrong?" asks the instructor.

Backing slowly into the wire fencing, Austin holds his arms up, as if someone's pulled a gun on him. "Don't kill me." He drops to the ground, cowering behind his hands. "Please. No!" He screams over and over. *Please. No! Please.*

The instructor shouts. "I'm not going to hurt you. I'm not going to *touch* you." He turns round and sees me outside the court. "Go to the medical suite. Get help."

I run to the nurse at the front desk who stands up from her chair. "What's wrong?"

"A patient. Austin. He's flipped out on the basketball court."

She presses the button on her desk and Raoul appears from the door that leads to the treatment rooms. "Code one. Basketball court," the front-desk nurse says.

Raoul nods, and pats the pocket of his white tunic. "I'll let you know if I need assistance."

I follow him as he breaks into a run towards the screaming. Ms Ray and a gardener are also running. Mick is already on the court with the instructor. He's a few metres away from Austin who's making horrible squealing noises.

"No one's going to kill you, man," says Mick.

A second later, Raoul grabs hold of Austin's arms. "You're safe, bro."

Austin kicks out. "You're hurting me." He screams again. "My eyes. What have you done to my eyes?"

"You can't see?" asks Raoul.

He's crying now. "I can't see. Why can't I see? And my neck. What's happening to my neck?"

Mick jogs forward, and without seeming to consult with Raoul, he takes over, pinning Austin down so that Raoul is free to take a syringe from his pocket and inject him in the arm. The shriek as the syringe goes in is high-pitched and terrified. It stops abruptly, replaced by silence as Austin goes limp.

Thet has her hand over her mouth. Most people are crying. Piper looks as if she might be having a panic attack.

"What's going on?" asks the instructor.

"We've administered a sedative," says Raoul. "Go get a wheelchair from the medical suite."

Ms Ray picks up the syringe which Raoul has dropped

153

on the ground. "What's wrong with him? It looked like he was hallucinating."

"As I'm sure you understand, ma'am," says Raoul, "Austin's medical history is confidential." He holds out an official disposal bag for the syringe. "Be careful with that. You shouldn't have picked it up."

Ms Ray straightens up, but she's clearly upset. The instructor comes back with a wheelchair, and Mick and Raoul lift Austin into it. Austin's big, but they move him easily. Raoul pushes the wheelchair towards the medical suite, and Mick shouts, "Mae. Stop gawping."

When Mom says it's just her and me for dinner, I'm grateful. "Your father has an important colleague visiting," says Mom. She turns down the volume on the TV. "There's a special dinner for the senior team in the private dining room." She looks at me. I wait for her to ask me how I am but she doesn't. I think she's frightened of the answer.

"Did you hear about Austin?" I ask as I sit on the second sofa.

Mom rubs one eye. Is she crying? "Poor kid. It's easy to forget, living here, how troubled a lot of these kids are."

Noah's face flashes in my mind, and I find myself wondering once again about how paranoid and troubled he really is. I'd like to talk to Mom about what's happened with Austin, but I couldn't bear it if she brushed it off and told me to trust the medical staff to make him better. Instead, I ask, "Who's in the senior team?"

She scrunches her face as she thinks. "Your father, of course. Karl. That therapist – Abigail. Mick, and Raoul."

I try to tread carefully, so I don't scare her off answering. "What does he do, this colleague?" I ask.

"Oh, I don't know, honey. Nobody tells me these things." Mom seems clearer-headed today but still as out of touch as ever.

"What's his name?" *Is it Peter? Does he have a military title?*

"I don't know," says Mom. "But I heard an extra chef was brought in by helicopter."

There's a landing pad a couple of miles along the road to Pattonville. Extra-rich or important people land there, but I've never heard of a chef arriving that way.

Mom's made a special request for pizza for the two of us tonight. I'm surprised I'm allowed it because I'm on zero privileges, but perhaps the kitchen staff are distracted by the visitor. The base is speckled with wholewheat flour and piled high with green vegetables.

I fetch the vitamins from the sideboard and I know this is it: the first time I'm going to pretend to take them. The bottle is labelled with our names, but no other identification. I shake out two for Mom. Then, as the image of Austin's face, contorted with panic, flashes through my mind, I fake-swallow mine.

It feels like a victory.

*

I'm woken in the night by laughter. It confuses me because Mom and Dad never laugh together. I sit up. There are two male voices.

"I'll override the shutter system so you can see the whole place floodlit from the roof terrace, Peter," I hear Dad say. "Not many people get to see it for obvious reasons. Hang on. I'll locate my whisky."

Nobody from outside has been invited back to our apartment before. Alcohol is banned. What's going on? I creep towards my door so I can hear better.

"Sounds good to me," says Peter. He sounds jovial and relaxed. A couple of minutes later, he says, "You're running everything very well, Hunter. I'm pleased, and the data is looking promising. That boy today. It was extremely interesting, I thought. Didn't you?"

"Yes," says Dad. "Fascinating."

EIGHTEEN

Is denying your talents ever justified? Discuss.

I read the essay title that's been handwritten at the top of a sheet of blank paper and placed in the middle of my booklet.

If Dad knew Ms Ray had crossed out all the printed questions and written out this one, he'd fire her for sure. She must know that. It's hard to believe that encouraging me to write more challenging essays is worth the risk. That title though – it's aimed at me. She thinks I'm not making the most of my talents or working hard enough, and maybe she's right, but it's not my fault the lessons I've had up until now have been rubbish, apparently. I chuck the booklet back on the desk and go to stand by the window.

I watch the sun emerge through a gap in a large puffy cloud and wish I'd understood more of Dad and Peter's conversation last night. But I heard enough to feel uneasy.

At the desk, I rub my eyes and think about how I can churn out a few paragraphs about talents and denial. I'm tired and hungry, and I just don't feel like doing this. But once I start writing, my hand and brain work together, forming an argument, explaining the risks of pushing people too hard and idolizing talents. Well-being is more important than anything. And I've heard patients say that denial isn't always a bad thing – that it can protect people against pain and anxiety. As I write faster and my handwriting becomes messier, it comes to me that it depends on who is doing the denying and the reasons for justifying it. Maybe the balance between physical and academic doesn't have to be the same for everyone.

The door handle makes a clunking sound. "Mae?"

I don't turn round. I have a sentence in my head that I need to write down and I don't want to engage with anyone right now.

"So. I heard you were caught smoking."

Spinning round on my chair, I see Greta. Hands on hips. She's had her hair highlighted since I last saw her. It makes her look older. Harsher.

"How are you managing without Drew?" Greta walks across to the window and leans against the window sill. There's mockery in her tone.

"I miss him," I say, surprised by my candour. But I'm too sad to care what she thinks about it.

Greta tilts her head. "Aw, that's sweet of you."

"For someone who's supposed to be in Pattonville for a

summer session, you drop by a lot," I say.

"I don't drop by, Mae. I book my visits in advance with admin," says Greta.

This is news to me. "Why?"

Greta pulls her head back as if I know nothing. "So they can update my schedule. Tell the kitchen to cater for me. That sort of thing. If you want to know when I'm going to be around, all you have to do is ask them for my schedule." She twists her mouth into a half-smile. "I expect you have to be on full privileges though."

"If I was here so often, I'd be worried about failing my summer session as well as my first year exams," I say pointedly.

"Oh, whatever. The Creek paid for a new sports building a couple of years ago, so I'm going to get a degree whatever I do." She laughs at my surprised face. "What are you so shocked about? I told you that when I first got in."

"Oh," I say slowly. I remember her telling me about a Hummingbird Sports Hall, kitted out with the same top-of-the-range equipment as our fitness complex, but I didn't really think about the name.

Dad believes in supporting health and fitness in the wider community. It says so in the prospectus. It's why we're very occasionally allowed to go on sports trips outside the Creek. Who knew that it could buy you a place in a college?

"So you don't need to worry too much about your

lessons," says Greta. She glances over at my booklet and I snap it shut. She leans towards me dramatically so that her dress gapes at the top. It reveals the silver hummingbird at the end of her necklace that was a leaving present from her parents when she went to college. "D'you want to know the real reason I'm here?" she whispers.

"You hate college?"

"I've just had a meeting with your dad," she says. She watches my face to see if I knew anything about it and, satisfied that I didn't, she continues. "He's offering me vacation work after my summer session finishes and said that he'll give me a full-time position when I leave college." She waits for a reaction.

"You're coming back here – *permanently*?"

Greta smiles. "Yes. I'll be given my own apartment in Hibiscus." The thought, which obviously excites her, depresses me beyond anything I've ever imagined for myself post-college.

"Which department will you be in?" I ask.

"Admin." Greta walks to the door. "But I've said I'm more interested in teaching if a slot becomes available."

I hand Ms Ray the essay, sandwiched in the middle of the booklet. The others have all gone to lunch. "I probably haven't written what I'm supposed to," I say as she scans the first paragraph. I'm starving, so I'm eager just to drop it off and move on to lunch.

Alongside the posters on the walls in the schoolroom

are big tatty sheets of paper with words I don't recognize written out in different coloured felt-tips. There's foreign music coming from her antique CD player. I think it might be Spanish.

"The criteria I'll be assessing it on is how well you've written it," says Ms Ray. "Whether you can back up your argument. How convincing you are. Not the actual content."

"Oh." It hadn't occurred to me that she might give it a good mark even if she disagreed with what I wrote.

"What d'you think of the solar system we made today?" She points to a mobile hanging above the sink, made from different-sized balls.

"It's great. You're still doing the booklets though, aren't you?" I check. "In case anyone asks."

"Of course," she says. "I'm just adding in extra things here and there."

I picture Greta in here, enforcing rules, sticking rigidly to the booklets. Teaching kids things she doesn't understand herself, with no room for persuasive arguing. The wall displays would be schedules and charts. She wouldn't be able to stand anyone being too smart, but she'd be hard on anyone failing to make progress.

Why do I care, though? By the time she gets to be a teacher – if it ever happens – I'll be long gone from here and it won't make any difference to me.

Right now, all I can think about is lunch.

"Here," says Ms Ray. She hands me a math textbook

and a play called *The Crucible*. "Read the first six chapters of the textbook by tomorrow. Make sure you understand it. Read the play and write an essay for me explaining the impact of fear on Salem society." She yawns, then apologizes. "Please forgive me. I've been studying too. It's tiring."

I'm at the door of the schoolroom when she calls out, "By the way, Mae. Have you had trouble with blurry vision lately?"

What are you going to do if I say yes? "Er..."

"Ben and Luke have been complaining of it, and I noticed Zach rubbing his eyes today."

"It could be the air conditioning," I say.

"Or allergies," says Ms Ray. "I was just worried. You know, what with that patient suddenly not being able to see. Austin was his name, wasn't it?"

"Yes. Austin." For a moment it's as if the room sways. I steady myself by reaching for the wall. Are we getting what Austin had?

"Do you know if he's OK, if he's back yet?" I ask.

"No, I haven't heard anything. At least everyone's health is so closely monitored here," says Ms Ray. "That's something."

At lunch, I wolf down my order too quickly, and it isn't enough. But somehow it fuels me through an excruciating afternoon exercise session with Mick, and when it's finally over and I've taken a shower, I lie on my bed, wrapped in a towel, and work my way through the first chapter in the math book. After a bit I chuck it on the floor and lie on my bed, aching more from missing Drew than the day's exercise. Nothing will ever be the same without him.

I'll never forgive Dad for firing Drew's parents. I think about his conversation with Peter. Were they experimenting on Austin? How – and why – would they do that?

I get dressed in shorts and a T-shirt and go on to the roof terrace, where I lean over the railings. I want to find out more, to make sense of what little I already know, but I feel so helpless, just going through my usual routine. Exercise and living in the now. Not talking, not questioning, not reacting to the terrible thing that's just happened.

It's not wellness; it's torture.

From here, I can see someone jogging near the perimeter close to the security building. Noah. I bet I know where he's heading. Sure enough, he seems to disappear. I glance at my watch. Dad and Mom will be busy. I go back into my room and change into clean sportswear. No one will look at me twice if they think I'm going to do exercise. It's risky, still being on zero privileges, but I think I'll get away with it. At the last minute, I stuff my math book into a backpack.

I scale the fire-escape ladder as stealthily as I can. The Creek is quiet. Work on the cycle track has finished for the day. There's just the occasional shout from the outdoor swimming pool, and the squawks of the jays in the trees by the fence.

The second to top rung of the ladder clanks, and I say softly, "It's only me, Noah," as I step on to the roof.

Noah is standing by the fire-escape exit, hands over his mouth. "Oh my God, Mae. You almost sent me into cardiac arrest." He drops his hands, and sits down. "We need to get a system sorted. A series of three taps on the handrail or something."

I nod. "I'm sorry." I go over and sit next to him, wincing as I lower myself down.

There's a long but comforting silence, then Noah says, "I heard about Drew. It must be tough."

"It is," I say. "All these years I thought we'd leave the Creek together but now I don't even know where he is." I tell him how frustrated Drew was. How I always stood up for Dad and now – well, now I hate him.

Then I tell him about Thet, how she's going to leave too. I'll be left with Joanie and Greta. I'm so sick of my life. But as soon as I say that I feel guilty because I remember Austin, and my stomach lurches at the memory of yesterday. I ask Noah if he knows anything.

"He's been released from the medical suite. He's much quieter than before, but he can see again."

"That's good," I murmur. I think of the word Dad used to describe what happened: *fascinating*. It's cold and mean.

"I'm not going to lie," says Noah. "The Creek's weirder

than I was expecting, and believe me, I was expecting weirdness. I thought at first it was because patients were here so long but now I think it's just a very odd place."

I open my mouth to argue but instead I say, "I've had nothing to compare it with."

Noah gives me a half-smile. The sunburn on his nose is peeling. It distracts from the fact that he has very long eyelashes, and interesting curvy creases either side of his mouth when he smiles. To stop myself staring, I open my backpack and pull out my math textbook.

"Would you mind talking me through some of this stuff?" I ask. "Ms Ray says I'm behind on maths, and I've got five more chapters to understand before tomorrow."

Noah takes the textbook. "Sure." The curvy creases shoot outwards.

He's good at explaining, though he's frustrated at not having paper and a pen to make his points. We storm through three more chapters before I mock-collapse sideways away from him, on to the concrete. I am so tired.

"We need some cushions," I say, righting myself again. "I might take a couple from the juice bar. They won't be missed."

Noah flips the textbook shut, and stretches out his legs.

"You have such pale skin," I say.

"This is pretty tanned for me," he says.

I manoeuvre into a cross-legged position. "Tell me more about your life."

He talks about his family. Parents who he mostly gets

on with, an older sister, a dog. Endless cousins who come and crash at their house in London.

I tell him about my English past, learning about my relatives there, and finding the photo of Frank and the horses.

He explains what it's like to do exams in a hall, and how he had to force himself to do them, not because they were hard, because he actually found them easy, but rather because he was bunched up with anxiety. He says he has a love-hate relationship with his brain. "I like to have places where I feel safe and calm," he says. "Like up here."

It's strange that an ugly strip of broken concrete and weeds above a security building can be that place. Noah stands up, but I notice he stays in the middle of the roof so he's less likely to be seen. "I came up here last night to get away from it all," he says. "The main building was floodlit. It looked dramatic, like an abandoned movie set. And kind of creepy."

I blink. I've seen the main building floodlit on birthdays and last night it must have been in honour of Peter. It's not about the floodlighting. It's how Noah succeeded in not being caught. "How'd you manage that?" I ask.

"I'm not locked in – that's all part of the Creek trust thing, right? Though yeah, there are orderlies, cameras and security guards. No one checks up on me in the night. I'm not high-risk. The orderly on duty was that dopey one with the gelled hair."

"But Larkspur has cameras at the entrances, doesn't it?"

Noah nods. "Most of the entrances have two cameras, but the entrance opposite the main building only has one, and it swivels. I timed it right, and dodged the other cameras on the way here. Perhaps I was just lucky and the security guys weren't checking the monitors very carefully, or they were out on patrols. They can't be expecting anyone. Staff would use the underground walkway at night, wouldn't they?"

I'm speechless at Noah's nonchalance. His bravery. Drew and I thought we were brave, but we never even thought to try anything at night.

"You should come up here with me one night to experience it. If you can escape. It's worth it. It makes you feel alive and free."

"Really?" I say. "I'd love that." Excitement zigzags through me. I'm not sure if it's only the thought of being up here at night illicitly, or if it's also because he'd be here with me.

But I'm also worried about getting him sent away. Everyone I grow close to gets sent away.

"How hard d'you think it would be for you?" asks Noah.

I chew my lip. "Don't know. The doors aren't locked in Hibiscus but. . ."

"We'll make a plan sometime," says Noah. He glances at his watch. "I've got a group session in a minute." He scoots across to me. "Mae? You might think I'm being paranoid..." He pauses. "It's occurred to you that we can be located by our watches, yeah?"

I think about how Dad found me and Drew smoking. "Mmm," I say, playing for time. I don't know how much I should feed his paranoia.

"I've been thinking that leaving my watch off when I come up here might be a good idea," says Noah. "But then how would I know how much time has gone by?"

"You shouldn't risk setting off the alarm by removing it," I say.

"Who gets notified by the alarm?" asks Noah. "Is it the medical staff or security?"

My dad? Dr Jesmond? "I don't know. You get into huge trouble, I know that. I mean huge."

"Has it ever happened to you?"

I shake my head. "It's the biggest rule. Patients have been sent to solitary for it."

"You're too scared to take your watch off?"

"It's about missing out on data. Health data can literally save lives."

"Right," says Noah.

"And I'd be frightened to, yes."

NINETEEN

When I wake up I have a message from Earl to say I've been moved up to quarter privileges, which means I'm allowed to initiate conversations and have lessons and do sport with others, but I'm still banned from unscheduled activities. I can now earn tokens, though I still can't spend them.

I move from being semi-oblivious about security cameras to looking for them. I want to be just as aware of them as Noah is. For days, I've perfected a technique of pretending to swallow my pills then transferring them into my pocket to dispose of down the toilet.

At morning exercise the grad student taking our session bursts in through the door with her laptop and bottle of water, and says, "You'll have to bear with me today, guys. We've got new software. It might take a bit longer than usual until I get the hang of it." She sits cross-legged at the front of the studio. "Form an orderly line, please."

I'm nearest to her so I'm there first, and I crouch next to her. Technology's not her thing. She's logged on but her cursor is all over the place. The home screen has changed. She finally opens something called Health Data, looks up and says, "Mmm, Mae Ballard. Let's find the *b*s." With the previous software, the instructor typed in a name.

She scrolls fast but I see there are hundreds of names before mine. My name is near the beginning of the alphabet. Does that mean there are thousands of names on this list – including people who aren't at the Creek any more?

"Okaaay." Before she selects my name, I see a menu bar at the top. That's new. There are headings: *Detailed Medical Records. Groups. Schedules. Data Graphs.* I also see Mom's name above mine, but not Dad's.

"Soooo, let's have your heart-monitor reading."

I show her my watch and she squints at the figure, then inputs it into the box.

There's another box below it. The wording next to it says: *Appearance of subject using the Energy Scale (rate from one to ten).*

I want to see what rating she gives me. But she swivels the laptop round. "You lot aren't allowed to see this. It's confidential medical data."

"But it's my data."

She shrugs. "I don't make the rules round here. Next, please. We need to speed this along." She stands up and balances the laptop on one arm, and uses her free hand to input data, so that Zach who's behind me can't see what she's doing.

I see Austin as soon as I walk into the breakfast café. He's sitting next to Will, subdued and pale, as if he's been made to get out of bed too early. Will is chatting to him but I can tell by the way he's watching Austin mash a banana repeatedly with his fork that he's concerned.

Noah isn't there, but Thet is. I want to talk to her about Austin, the vitamins, about Peter, the cameras, the watches. All of it. She knows this place from the patient side. She's known it far longer than Noah. And I can trust her completely. "Wait for me when you've finished?" I murmur as I walk past her with my breakfast tray.

I time eating my slices of multigrain toast and honey with Thet and her sugar-free strawberry-oat muffin. We leave a few seconds apart, and meet outside.

"I'll walk with you to Larkspur, but via the tennis courts," I say.

"Are you OK?" she asks.

I start with the vitamins and my worries about them.

"But we all take them," says Thet. "Vitamins are one of the building blocks of health."

"What if they're not actually vitamins?"

"What else would they be?" She looks at me. "You sound like one of the paranoid patients. You know I'm supposed to report paranoid behaviour?"

My gut twists.

"Of course I wouldn't report you," says Thet when

she sees my expression. "I'd never do that." Thet's grandmother taught her loyalty and silence. When Thet's parents were killed for being on the wrong side of the war, her grandmother brought her to the States as a baby, where she changed their names and built up a massively successful hair product business.

"There was a visitor in military uniform the day Austin went crazy. Was he linked to any of the patients? Did anyone say anything about him?"

Thet shakes her head slowly. "Military? No. Are you sure?"

"I'm sure," I say, but I don't add anything more. Am I leaping to the wrong conclusions – seeing conspiracies that aren't there? I rub my eyes, fighting back drowsiness.

"I hate that you're not allowed to spend tokens," says Thet. "Facials aren't the same without you."

We walk slowly, and I listen to her talk about her novel, and I wish that I knew how to help her with the ending.

Every so often, the cleaners do a deep clean of the apartment. Everything's inspected – my clothes, my books, my stationery, my toiletries – and I have to rescue the second-hand pens in worn-out cases from the throwing-away pile, along with notebooks that are more than half full. Soft furnishings are steam-cleaned, furniture is moved, and everything scrubbed, polished, vacuumed and assessed for replacement.

Several years ago, a cleaner discovered a half-eaten packet of Haribo that I'd hidden under the T-shirts in my chest of drawers. I'd forgotten they were there.

I'd found the packet on the ground at an athletics tournament. It was only the second time I'd left the Creek. They were already half-eaten when I found them. Looking back, I'm not sure why I never ate any myself. I think I liked the bright colours and the squashy texture, and just having them.

The cleaner handed them to Dad and that evening for my punishment he gave me a pink drink that made me throw up within minutes. He never asked me how many I'd eaten, and I never told him because he would have thought I was lying anyway. And lying was worse than eating refined sugar that hadn't been measured out by the Creek kitchen.

Usually there are signs that a deep clean is about to take place: a pile of extra cleaning products and bin liners the day before or steam-cleaning equipment delivered by the maintenance department. But not this time. I come back from breakfast a few days after moving up to quarter privileges and see that a deep clean's already begun.

I struggle for breath, and the room spins. *The textbooks. My extra lessons. Homework I'm part way through. Essays I've had marked.* I don't know if they'd be a problem, but I haven't even hidden them properly; I don't want to get Ms Ray in trouble. I've kept them on my shelves with my notebooks. I walk into my bedroom as steadily as I can, and out of the corner of my eye see that they haven't been touched yet.

The mattress is on its side against a wall, and the cleaner's checking all round the cherry wood bed frame.

After saying hello I tell her I need to get changed.

"Use the bathroom," she says. "That's already done."

I can't argue or plead. She'll think I have something to hide. So I nod, select some clothes from the chest of drawers and take them into the bathroom. I scan the small room, circling once before snatching a jar of bath salts from the side of the bath. I drop it from above my head on to the floor. It cracks but doesn't break so I have to tread on it with my sneaker to break it enough that the salts spill out. If I scream it'll be too obvious so I make an *agggh* noise, loud enough for the cleaner to hear, then I come out and say, "I'm sorry. I've knocked a jar off the bath and made a mess."

She rolls her eyes, walks into the bathroom to check, then without a word, goes to find a dustpan and brush.

I grab my lesson books and essays from the shelves and hide them in my backpack.

"Why do you have to do a deep clean so regularly?" I ask the cleaner when she returns.

She frowns. "This is a psychiatric facility, miss. We have to look for banned substances."

"But I'm not a patient," I say.

She shrugs. "I do as I'm told."

*

In the schoolhouse I work solidly through the extra questions Ms Ray's sneaked into the middle of my booklet. Each time I look up and see Drew's empty chair and desk, the loss inside me expands. I just want to lay down my head on the table and cry. But I don't.

At lunch my salmon nicoise looks pitifully small, and my stomach grumbles for more. I wonder if someone is screwing up my calorie allocation. I don't notice Noah follow me out of the restaurant until he's actually hissed my name, and I turn on the third step down to see him.

He walks down past me while murmuring, "I've checked the cameras outside Hibiscus. There aren't any above the fire-exit door. I'll let you know when the incompetent orderly's back on night duty. By the way, a good place to have a private conversation is the indoor pool. Sound will be hard to pick up and there's only one camera, at the shallow end, which you can turn your back on." He's gone before I can say anything.

I don't know what to think of his clandestine behaviour, but a couple of hours later when I'm in the juice bar, I note that there are three cameras inside and one outside covering the patio. When Thet comes in and says she overheard an admin assistant whisper something about the military visitor during her computer session, I tell her I'm on my way for a swim in the indoor pool.

"Come with me," I say. *It's important. Please trust me.* "Get your swimsuit. I'll meet you there."

I've done ten lengths before Thet appears. She's twisted her hair into an intricate braid, and she's wearing a new pink-and-white marbled-effect swimming costume, teamed with the pink glitter plastic shoes which she keeps exclusively for trips to the swimming pools.

"Since you've been in isolation, I've been rethinking my allegiance to pink," says Thet, crouching down by the ladder into the pool, which I'm hanging off by my feet. "I might branch out into orange. Shake things up."

"Cool," I say, smiling, and I move away from the ladder. Thet doesn't leap into anything, especially water. It takes a while for her inch down the ladder.

When she's fully in the water and we're swimming side by side up to the deep end, I tell her about the rooftop. I say I'm going to ask Noah if he'd mind if she joins us up there before she leaves.

"There's a great view – and it's a really neat place to be," I say.

"You know I hate heights," says Thet. "And, I mean. The *security building*. Hello? What are you thinking?"

"It sounds strange, but it feels safe up there," I say.

We've reached the end of the pool and she holds on to the rail with one hand and spreads her other hand on the water. Her nails are beautifully manicured with a pearlized colour called shell pink. They make me long to see shells along a seashore.

"Four weeks until I leave," says Thet. "My schedule's already been changed to give me a chance to relax and reflect on what I've learned here." She chews her lip. "I don't want to leave, but Gran says I have to."

This is the second time Thet's left. I know it's unlikely she'll be coming back.

"Have they stopped your vitamins?" I ask.

"I'm on three-quarters of a tablet."

"From two tablets?"

"No, I used to take one."

That means I'm on *double* her dose. "D'you feel any different?" I ask.

She thinks. "No. I don't think so. I'm stressed, but that's because I'm leaving. Mae, the doctors know what they're doing." She turns to swim back to the shallow end, but I stop her.

"Wait. There's a camera that end. Let's stay here a moment." I wait until we're both facing the other way again before I say, "I've stopped taking my vitamins."

Thet shakes her head. "You shouldn't have done that. Vitamin supplements are good for you! I mean, people on the outside are always taking multivitamins. You can't be sure you're getting everything you need from food."

"I wanted to see how I felt."

Thet frowns. "I'm worried you're getting paranoid."

"Listen," I say, desperate for her to hear me out. "D'you think the amount of cameras here is excessive?"

"It's for protection, isn't it? The more there are, the better we're protected. My grandmother has cameras installed everywhere at home."

Is that because she's still looking over her shoulder? Worried for her safety? I guess Thet is the wrong person to ask about cameras.

We swim another couple of lengths. My eyes ache but I don't think it's from the chlorine. When we're back in the deep end, I ask Thet if she knows anything about the new software on the Creek laptops. She doesn't, and she's never heard of the Energy Scale either.

"We're always being measured for something," she says.

"But I'm not a patient," I say. "I don't want to be rated." I regret my words as soon as I've said them. We never really talk about it, the patient non-patient thing.

"Don't you mind it, Thet?" I ask gently. "Being tested, watched and rated?"

She sighs. "Not really. I'm scared of what it'll be like when I'm not."

TWENTY

We're doing the warm-down when my heart races and sweat breaks out all over my body. I don't want Joanie, who's beside me, to notice, so I keep going, doing a weaker version of the stretches, scared of the creeping blurriness in one eye. I wonder if my watch might set off an alarm when it detects my heart has gone into double-time. If Raoul's going to come running with a syringe.

The moment passes. I stumble to my feet, stack my mat on top of the others. I eat half a blueberry wheat pancake at breakfast and feel slightly better. Perhaps it was a panic attack, or maybe my heart's malfunctioning because of Drew being gone.

Today for the first time I notice a tiny camera, the same pinkish colour as the walls, on top of a framed print of a group of hummingbirds in the schoolroom. It's a big drawing I've looked at many times. In big lettering at the top it says *A Group of Hummingbirds Is Called a Charm*. I guess I've always been too taken by the fact they're called a charm, and by the illustrations of the hibiscus and larkspur plants that hummingbirds love, to notice the camera.

I think it's lucky Ms Ray hardly ever sits at her desk, which is where it's pointing to. She likes to move about.

Later, when I listen to Joanie reading on the swing-chair on the veranda, I notice she's rubbing her neck.

"Is your neck OK?" I ask.

Her hand springs back to her lap.

"Does it fizz a bit?"

She bites her thumbnail. "Like fireworks," she mumbles.

I smile even though I'm worried. "Did you tell Dr Jesmond?"

She shakes her head.

I swing the chair back and forth by bending and straightening my legs. Even up to a year ago, I could make her fall asleep by doing this if I did it long enough. It relaxes her.

"I don't want more injections," she says. "They hurt."

"I understand," I say.

"Time to come in, girls," calls Ms Ray through the window.

The sun is hot but not fierce as Luke and I trudge across the lawn for lunch. He's grown in the last couple of months which makes him look even more skinny. He tells me he wants to go fishing so much he's prepared to leave the Creek for it. His dad says that one day there might be a lake at the Creek. "But it'll be a fake lake, won't it, Mae?" he says. "Fish dumped in there for me to catch. Like, on purpose."

"Maybe it's better than nothing," I say. I can't imagine a lake at the Creek. I remember when they drained a small pond years ago; there were too many safety issues. "But you can learn about fishing while you wait until you're old enough to go to a real river." I've never taken much notice of Luke. I guess I've always been too wrapped up in Drew, to think about him, but I realize that while Zach and Ben are buddies, and Joanie kind of has me to talk to, Luke doesn't really have anyone.

In the restaurant, the glass doors have been folded right back, and tables and thick white sunshades have been placed on the terrace above the outdoor pool area. A member of kitchen staff stands discreetly in the corner of the terrace, to stop anyone attempting to jump off the marble railings on to the patio below, even though they'd land in carefully positioned soft vegetation. The pool water sparkles, and there's a slow-motion quality to the day. I am doing everything I can to keep from nodding off.

I smile at Noah as I sit at the staff kids' table. He's at the next table, but the seat he's chosen means he's almost sitting next to me. He acknowledges me with a smile which lights up his whole face, and makes his eyes scrunch. They're a golden-brown colour with green flecks, and even though they're fairly closed right now, I can picture the exact shades. I smile back before he carries on talking to Will, and I'm ashamed at the elevator whoosh in my stomach. Drew has been gone less than two weeks. Thet is on the table beyond that, surreptitiously cleaning her cutlery with an anti-bacterial wipe.

The inside of the restaurant area is dark and shadowy because we're out in the bright sunshine, so when a figure staggers towards us, it takes us a few seconds to recognize that it's Austin.

Will lifts his sunglasses. "Over here, buddy."

Austin's not walking in a straight line, and then he stumbles. Will says, "Oh my God."

Everyone looks as Austin lurches on to the terrace, as if he's been shoved from behind.

"Something's wrong," says Will.

Austin is between our tables now. He grabs hold of Zach's chair. His eyes are red-rimmed and glazed over, and he doesn't seem to be focusing on anything.

"S . . . slorry," he slurs.

"Oi," says Zach. "Are you drunk?" He shouts to the member of staff in the corner. "Hey, over here! I think this guy's drunk."

Austin sways. He picks up a glass of water. I think he's going to drink it, but he swings round and throws it. It flies sideways, in the direction of Thet's table, but it goes over the terrace and smashes on the white stone slabs below.

Thet screams. She's on her feet, water on the sleeve of her top. Piper shouts a string of swear words at Austin.

The member of the kitchen staff runs towards him, her hair net slipping down her head. Austin shouts words at her that don't mean anything: "You vile… Can't contain… No… Bitch!" He slumps, twitching, to the floor and she's frozen to the spot, blinking.

"Ben, get help," I say.

Ben shoves through the crowd that's gathering, and Will drops to the ground next to Austin. Austin's eyes have rolled back and his face is grey; I'm not sure he's breathing.

"Put him in the recovery position," Noah says. "Mae, help us."

The three of us roll him on to his side.

"You're OK, Austin," says Will. "You're going to be OK." His tone tells me that he's as scared as I am.

The member of staff shouts, "Step back. Step back. That guy needs some air."

"Call an ambulance," someone shouts. But we have no phones.

The crowd parts and Karl Jesmond is there, a few paces ahead of Dad. He has a bag of instruments. A stethoscope. Needles. Dad checks Austin's pulse, then uses a pair of surgical scissors to cut Austin's T-shirt from the bottom to the round neckline. Then he grabs a defibrillator from the bag and I realize that Austin's heart must have stopped.

"Stand back," calls Dad. "Karl, clear the restaurant."

Austin's body jerks as Dad shocks him, and I can't help but watch. Thet is beside me, sobbing, but I'm numb. Dr Jesmond pushes us. "Everyone leave. You" – he points at the member of kitchen staff – "take them outside."

We walk down the stairs in stunned silence. Will is the last one on to the lawn where his shocked composure gives way to huge, horrible howls.

Mick appears and shouts for quiet. We're told to go to our rooms for a while. Our schedules will resume at four p.m. There's nothing to worry about. Austin's getting the best possible care. Snacks will be available in the juice bar later for those who didn't finish their lunch.

The patients walk towards Larkspur, while Zach, Ben, Luke and I head towards Hibiscus. Zach is in a state of excitement about the defibrillator.

"Did you see that guy's body leap?" He jolts his own body in demonstration.

"Shut up," I say. "And his name is Austin. Of course he wasn't drunk. He's ill."

"You're an expert on alcohol, are you?" says Zach. "I bet he smuggled some in."

I tut with disgust but Zach's looking past me, towards the ambulance slowly rolling through the gates.

At four p.m., us staff kids have our monthly art therapy group. Kacey, who heads up the department, asks us to bring a stool into a circle. I'm not in the mood for one of her visualize-yourself-as-an-animal-to-unlock-creativity sessions, and wrap my ankles round the legs of the stool to prevent myself tapping my feet impatiently and being fined.

"So," says Kacey, pulling up a stool herself, her Creek laptop under her arm. "Dr Ballard tells me that you experienced a distressing incident at lunchtime. I'm sure you're still processing it, hmm?" She looks round. We nod. I hope we don't have to discuss it. As it is, my heart is beating like crazy, and I feel like the walls are closing in on us.

"Anyone want to share what they're feeling?" Kacey swivels her head, like a bird looking for movement from its prey.

"Sad," says Joanie.

Kacey nods. "I'm going to read you a statement about Austin, from Dr Ballard." She opens up her laptop, and peers at her screen. After a quick cough she reads.

"*I know everyone will be thinking of Austin today. It is with great sadness that I have to tell you that he died this afternoon in the hospital. We don't know the exact cause, but he had complex medical needs, so the definitive reason may never be known. Dr Jesmond and I, and all the therapists at Hummingbird Creek, are here to support you through this difficult time and will do our best to answer any questions you have. Hummingbird Creek will be looking at ways we can best remember a fine young man who had much to give.*"

Kacey looks up. I'm dimly aware of Luke sniffing. I hear him as if I'm the other side of a glass wall. I can't believe Austin is dead. The phrase *Complex medical needs* echoes in my head. I remember what Peter said to Dad the day Austin had his first attack: *That boy today. It was extremely interesting, I thought.*

The ambulance I saw coming up the driveway wasn't in a hurry. Does that mean they'd been told Austin was already dead? If that was the case, I don't know why Dad would say he'd died in the hospital.

"I'd like to go to Austin's funeral or memorial service," I tell Dad at dinner. He arrived late and snapped at Mom for not having the vitamins out.

He prods at his Pad Thai with chopsticks. "It's been a very difficult day, Mae. Please don't make it worse. Austin's family live too far away – it's a ridiculous idea."

"That poor boy," murmurs Mom.

"We'll send flowers, of course," he says. "Louelle, you can be in charge of that."

"Sure," Mom says.

"Make it big. Classy. Let me write the message. I'm thinking of naming the cycle track after Austin. Or setting up a fund in his name for research into anger-management techniques."

Mom nods.

For the first time in a while, I can't eat. I hide as much as I can under my cutlery, and prepare to say I feel sick, which is true, but Dad doesn't say anything when Mom clears away my plate.

When I go to bed, it's impossible to sleep. I close my eyes and the images of Austin stumbling, his arching body on the floor and his grey, unresponsive face frighten me. I want more air than is in this room. If I could open a window or sit on the roof terrace I might feel calmer, but I can't. Everything in this apartment is controlled, including me.

I'm aware of the low growl of someone speaking, of the floor being paced in the living room. I climb out of bed without a sound to listen.

"I know all that, Peter," Dad says. "If we could have avoided it, we would have."

He's on the phone to the man who was here in our apartment.

Dad's voice becomes a rumble instead of distinct words, and then I hear, "I've told you. The cause of death will be inconclusive."

My head pulsates in the silence while Peter is saying something back to Dad. They must be talking about Austin.

"His watch?" Dad says, his voice rising as if Peter's being ridiculous. "Of course we have it. Yes. Perfect data." He finishes the conversation and I creep back to bed.

I'm not being paranoid.

TWENTY-ONE

"You can't stop thinking about Austin, right?" asks Noah in a low voice, as I pretend to scrape the remains of my granola into the waste bin. But I've eaten every last bit of it, of course, and hunger still gnaws at me.

"Right," I say. I can't stop thinking about the phone call either. Dad's cold response to Austin's death. The mention of data on the watch.

The supervisors aren't looking at us, and we're in a camera blind spot, but I need to be very careful that we're not overheard. I'm frightened of Dad. It's the first time I've properly admitted it to myself.

"Did you hear Will had to be sedated, he was so traumatized?" asks Noah.

I shake my head.

"I don't want to be here any more," says Noah. "They probably won't let me leave early, but I'm going to ask anyway."

"Please don't," I say.

"Why?" asks Noah. He turns his plastic cup of water round and round.

"You'll sabotage your wellness plan and ... and I don't want you to go. I'm scared about what's going on."

He tips his water away into the spill tray and fills up the cup again, which seems odd until I realize that a supervisor is nearby. I shouldn't be so public about being friends with Noah; I'm still on quarter privileges, and I don't want him on Dad's radar.

"You two!" shouts a supervisor. "Move along."

I'm called to a therapy room to give a witness statement about Austin. Abigail is there with her laptop open. She looks me up and down when I walk in. There's something about me that she's never liked, even before that time I hid in her car.

After a brief how-are-you–please–sit–down, she starts firing off questions. Was I fearful that Austin was going to be violent when he walked to my table? Did I witness Thet scream because she thought the glass might hit her? How quickly did the member of kitchen staff react?

If I try to explain things more fully, she says, "Don't stray off-topic, Mae. We've got a lot to cover. Your father is doing his best to get to the bottom of what happened."

The more detailed questioning is about how Austin was after he collapsed, before Dad and Dr Jesmond arrived, and he became unresponsive. What colour was his face? Did I touch him? What temperature would I say his skin was? Did it look as if he could see anything? Was he sweating? Foaming at the mouth? Clutching any part of his body? Gasping for breath?

I see Austin on the floor again. Noah is giving Will and me instructions. We move Austin on to his side, and I can feel the dread in my veins again. The wringing-out of my gut. Panic.

"I can't tell you any more," I sob. "It was horrible."

Abigail stops typing, and finds a box of tissues from under her chair. "Blow your nose, Mae. I know this is hard, but this session isn't about you. It's about Austin. There will be other sessions for you to process your feelings, but for now you need to set them aside."

She tugs the corners of her short-sleeved cardigan and does up the top button. I blow my nose and answer the rest of her questions in an emotionless voice.

Dad hands me my two vitamins at dinner and I pick up my glass of water. I gaze at the beige tablets in my palm. I hate the way I've been feeling the last few days – tired and hungry, and a terrible mix of depression and panic – and it's only getting worse. Is it because of what's been happening, or is it because I'm no longer taking these pills? If I swallow them, will I feel better?

"How's everyone feeling?" Dad asks.

I try to compose my face into a blank expression, but my mind is racing. *Has he noticed anything?*

"What was the mood like at breakfast and lunchtime?" he clarifies.

He's referring to Austin.

"Sad," I say, and I fake swallow my pills.

He nods. "Only to be expected." I watch him press down on his salmon with the side of his fork. It widens, then chunks apart.

"His poor mother," Mom mutters.

For several long moments the only noise is the clanking of silver cutlery against the white china dishes. I clench my hand round the vitamins, so the round edges push into my palm.

TWENTY-TWO

After a week on quarter-privileges I'm moved up to half-privileges. I'm still unable to spend tokens, but I'm allowed to do some unscheduled activities.

At morning exercise, our instructor has left his laptop open at the front. I'm barely able to keep up during our aerobic routine, but I edge forward to look at the screen, and see an endlessly spiralling screen saver. If I jiggled the cursor and interrupted those spirals I'd be able to see what's really on the screen. With one or two clicks I might be able to see my data and what it's being used for.

"Take a few steps back, folks." The instructor is right next to me. He flaps his arms as if we're scavenging birds that have come too close. When he goes back to the front again, he flips the lid of the laptop down with his foot.

The laptop is never out of his sight. I need someone who's more flaky.

Kacey. She's always popping in and out of the art room.

She doesn't use her laptop to input readings from our watches before or after art sessions, but she writes notes in it, or reads out messages, and she leaves it open on the large desk at the front.

I wait for my chance. I tell Kacey I'm making a couple of mugs for Thet as a leaving present, and I'd like to practise until I've made two that I'm completely happy with. Drop-in art sessions for staff kids and adults are an unscheduled activity, but she grants me permission to attend.

Unfortunately there always seem to be people in the art room. Zach is working on a project spray-painting dead beetles, and he notices me eyeing up the laptop as I prepare fresh clay.

"My sister's getting one of those laptops when she starts her work here."

"She already has a laptop," I say.

Zach sprays a beetle which is still alive. "She's going to be a research assistant. You need a silver laptop for that."

I fight the urge to close my eyes. Since I've stopped taking the vitamins, my eyelids have become too heavy. "What's she going to research?"

"Stuff," says Zach. "Important stuff. That's what my dad says. He says she's an asset to the Creek because she does what she's told to, unlike some people." He makes it clear who "some people" are by holding my gaze longer than he needs to.

My opportunity finally comes when someone spills a pot of paint that splatters over the table, floor and a chair.

"I'll find a cleaner at the end of the session," says Kacey. There are no phones in the art room to call anyone, only the red panic buttons if anything kicks off with the patients.

When the session's over, I make sure I'm in the art closet, selecting a glaze so Kacey thinks the room's empty. After I hear her leave, I take a deep breath and stride towards the front desk, swiftly moving the laptop to the end of the desk where the camera won't see me. I hope that if anyone saw that movement on a monitor, they'd think it was Kacey's arms not mine.

Ten minutes is probably all I've got, at most.

I place my finger on the touchpad. The screen wakes up, and it's a page on a patient who must have been here earlier. My head throbs, but adrenaline pulses through me and I try to stay focused.

The patient's calorie intake/expenditure is red. I don't know if that's because he's eaten too much or too little. His heart monitor reading is green. There are descriptions of him throughout the day.

Pale. That's from Mick.

Lacking in energy. From a grad student.

Motivated for first half of session, not for second. From Abigail.

Fine motor skills poorer than usual. That's from Kacey. Harsh.

There's a box that says *Symptoms patient has complained of in your session.* Kacey has written *Headache. Says he thinks it's the glue. (He's making a mosaic tile.)*

I click on the x in the corner. The page shrivels to his

name in a list. It's in alphabetical order. My heart speeds up as I scroll up to mine and click on it.

Mae Ballard.

Both my calorie intake and heart rate readings are green. In the comments section it says:

Rubbed eyes a lot.

Angry demeanour – poss to do with Austin?

Quieter than usual.

There's a link in blue that says: *Latest Test Results.* I click on it. Each line on this page has something that has been measured in my body, including different hormone levels, blood oxygen level, blood pressure, pupil dilation and brainwave pattern.

The date for my brainwave pattern is last year. I remember going into a scanner that had been rented by the Creek for a month. All patients were scanned. I remember the words Dad used: *Standard practice.*

"It's standard practice, Mae, to check that everything is as it should be."

We took our watches off and placed them on a tray. I had to work hard not to panic in the scanner. I thought about doing my favourite trampoline routine. What helped, too, was realizing that my watch couldn't record the excessive pounding of my heart and the increase in sweat. Panicking in private was a luxury.

When I click on "brainwave pattern" it says *Access Denied. Level 2 Clearance Required.*

My eyes go to the menu bar at the top. Detailed

Medical Records. Groups. Schedules. Data Graphs. I click on Detailed Medical Records. A small box appears saying *Level 3 Clearance Required.* I try *Groups.* Same thing. Each section at the top requires Level 3 clearance.

Kacey must only have Level 1 clearance.

There's a noise from outside the room. *Kacey.* I fumble back to the long list of names. I can't remember the name of that patient. I might throw up right over the keyboard. What was his name? My brain stalls.

Snap – I shut the lid down. Shove – I slide it along the desk.

The door opens.

"Mae? I didn't know you were still here." She eyes the laptop, lid down, in a different position on the desk.

"I was choosing a glaze," I say weakly.

"I see." Kacey shouldn't have left her laptop unattended. If she reports me she'll be in trouble too.

"I'm just going," I say.

"I don't ever want you alone in the art room again," says Kacey. She points at the door. "Get out."

I nod. The number of staff who dislike me is growing. But I've learned what my next step needs to be: find someone with Level 3 clearance. And I know who's going to have it: Dad.

TWENTY-THREE

Noah is standing by the breakfast fruit platter, trying to get his allotted portion but having trouble with the tongs.

"Mango too slippery?" I say.

"Oh my God, Mae," says Noah in a whisper. His breath touches my cheek and it tingles. "I've been waiting here for *ages* for you. It's safer than the water cooler. *Don't look round.*" He blows out the breath from his puffed cheeks as he pretends a slice of mango has slipped out of the tongs, and I can't help smiling at his antics. "I've got nothing on from three to three-thirty. You want to come up to the rooftop and tell me what's going on round here?"

I tap discreetly on my watch and scroll through my day's schedule to double-check. I try to make it look as if I'm doing it because I'm impatient waiting for Noah to finish up with the fruit. I'm on half privileges, so we don't have to lay as low, but ... still. "Yes. I'm free then too."

He looks up and my insides melt as our eyes lock. Noah feels differently about me than Drew did. I can feel it.

Ms Ray rattles on about the food groups as if we know nothing about nutrition. We've filled in our work booklets for the morning and she's talking to us as she goes round the room collecting them. I struggle to keep my eyes from closing. I know I'm at constant risk of falling asleep in a therapy session or not trying hard enough during a workout. My body feels weak and I swing between being too hot or too cold. I have a new sort of headache; it's as if my whole head is muffled, and it's hard to concentrate or manage complicated thoughts.

How much of this is to do with not taking my vitamins? Is it worry? Grief at Drew being gone, mixed in with confused feelings about Noah?

"Sit up, Mae," snaps Ms Ray. She flicks her eyes over the extra work that was in the centre of my booklet: a print-out about a parasite that lives in dogs, and a comprehension exercise based on it, followed by handwritten math questions so incomprehensible it's as if they were written in a different language. The comprehension started off quite fun, but it required serious knowledge of biology. My brain was so fuzzy that I abandoned the work and practised writing my name around the paper with the vintage Montegrappa pen I brought to the schoolroom.

"Disappointing," says Ms Ray quietly.

I'm disappointing. Disappointed. Not myself. That's

why I ask her the question in front of everyone: "Do you know anything about the vitamin tablets we take here?"

"What's to know?" says Zach. "Vitamins are the building blocks of good health."

"You all take multivitamins, do you?" asks Ms Ray.

"Yes," says Ben. Luke and Joanie nod.

Ms Ray shrugs. "If you have a balanced diet, which you certainly do, there should be no need to take supplements," she says. "In fact studies have shown that multivitamins can sometimes do you more harm than good."

We're silent for a moment, shocked.

"You're talking nonsense," Zach finally says. He scrapes his chair back by pushing against his desk, stretches out his legs, and folds his arms. "You don't know what you're talking about. There's a work booklet about vitamins. That has all the facts."

Ms Ray's face reddens. "OK. I'll have a look for that booklet, Zach." She consults her Creek watch. "Ten minutes left. Let's draw self-portraits."

But what if we're not really taking vitamins at all? If we're taking something else, which hasn't been fully tested, I wonder what harm it might be doing to us. I think back over how I've been feeling for the past few days: the tiredness, the anxiety, the incredible hunger. If I'm feeling this bad from not taking the pretend-vitamin, what does it mean? That I need it, or that I'm having severe withdrawal symptoms after being on it for so long?

*

199

After lunch I have my medical check-up. Raoul isn't there, so another nurse takes my blood and stares at the readings from my watch. I wonder what sort of clearance she has.

"You taking your multivitamins?" she says.

I nod. "My dad gives them to me at dinner."

"How are you feeling right now?" she asks.

"OK," I lie with a shrug. I don't want more tests, or questions.

She studies my face closely. "Are you feeling light-headed? Tired? Weepy?"

Can she see my huge, heavy tiredness? Has it shown up in my readings? "Stop interrogating me," I say.

"I'm just doing my job," she says through tight lips.

Did you see Austin's watch readings after he died? I wonder. I'm guessing Level 3 clearance was required for that. She'll probably mark down that I'm being combative.

Dr Jesmond leans back in his chair when I'm shown into his room. "There seems to be a few irregularities with your results today, Mae," he says. "Nothing to worry about." He laces his hands together as he speaks, and I focus on his perfect nails, the white tips all the exact same size. He talks about keeping an eye on things and reviewing the results again in two weeks. I wonder if by then he will be able to tell that I've stopped taking the so-called multivitamins?

There's a faint ruffly breeze on the rooftop, and the clouds are tinged with grey.

I arrive with a towel for us to sit on. I've kept my watch

on – it'll be worse if the alarm goes off. I just have to pray that no one has any reason to want to track me down.

A faint clicking sound has me on my feet, alert for danger. It's OK: it's the three-tap signal. Noah appears. "Hey, Mae." He's wearing sunglasses and his sunburn is now more brown than red. He looks good. More solid, somehow – probably from all the exercise. More confident, but with a shyness that tugs at me.

We sit awkwardly on the towel and he says, "Spill the beans," which I guess means *What's going on?*

I tell him that since I've stopped taking the vitamins it feels as if I'm losing my mind. "Perhaps I've had something wrong with me for years that I didn't know about," I say.

Noah bites his thumb. On anyone else it would probably be super-annoying, but on him it looks endearing. "Thing is," he says at last. "There are a few of us patients who are given a white vitamin tablet, not the beige one."

The one Dad takes.

"When I asked why I didn't have the same as other people," says Noah, "I was told my blood test showed I needed a different combination of vitamins. But the thing is, I've only seen two colours. White and beige. If everything is so individualized, why are there only two types?"

"How many people are on the white ones?" I ask.

"I don't know," says Noah. "But Piper's one of them. I've noticed that she and I have a similar sports schedule. It's not as full-on as other people's. I mean, it's still

201

loads, but it's not the hours and hours other people do. I thought it was because I was new, but Piper's been here a while."

"You haven't experienced muscle aches, blurry vision or a prickly neck?"

Noah gives a sort-of laugh. "Muscle aches, yes. God, muscle-*burn* after those hideous workouts. But it doesn't sound quite the same as the deep aches some of you talk about, and I've never had blurry vision or a prickly neck."

"D'you know what vitamins or drugs Austin was on?" I ask. I think of his *complex medical issues*. The Creek tries to be drug-free wherever possible but, perhaps he was on something else too.

Noah shakes his head.

I tell him about the conversations I've overheard between Dad and Peter, and he's shocked. "There's something bad going on, isn't there?" I ask.

He nods. "I think so. I don't think it's us being paranoid." I can't help but wonder if Noah's history with paranoia makes him better or worse at identifying it.

"I have to figure it out, and the only way I can do that is to break into the medical suite to see if I can find some sort of clues, or hack into Dad's computer." I hug my knees. "Both of them are impossible."

"Not impossible," says Noah. "You could distract your dad somehow once he's logged into his computer."

My feeling of hopelessness grows. "He's not the type to be distracted," I say. I thud my head into my open hands.

There has to be something wrong with me; my mind has thickened so much I can't think of a single way I can get to Dad's laptop. And even if I managed it, would I even understand what's written there?

I can't hold the tears back any more. It's a relief to let go, to give into the exhaustion. I sense Noah crouch closer, and I long for him to hold me tight.

"Mae? Start taking those pills again. They can't be vitamins, and it might be dangerous for you to stop."

I nod, pathetically grateful that Noah's made the decision for me. My symptoms frighten me; I feel as if I've lost control of my body.

"Take this." Noah's off the towel and handing me a corner of it to wipe my tears.

"I just want to sleep," I say.

"Have a power nap," says Noah. "I'll keep watch."

He indicates that I should curl up on the towel, and I wordlessly do as he says. My body jolts once, then I relax and close my eyes.

TWENTY-FOUR

While I watch TV with Mom, Dad's in his study on his laptop. I fantasize about spiking his mint tea with a sedative, so that he slumps in his chair long enough for me to go on his laptop and search through my medical files.

Mom leans across from her sofa to pat my leg. "I'm so happy that you're watching this programme with me, Mae."

I let what's on the TV screen come into focus, and see that the soap opera we were watching has changed to a gardening programme. Some guy is raking up leaves with ridiculous enthusiasm, and talking about building a rockery. What the hell is a rockery?

I imagine the two pills that I swallowed earlier slowly dissolving in my stomach, making me well again. I think about being on the rooftop with Noah, of feeling safe and believed.

When Greta strolls into the classroom, I'm trying to decipher *Macbeth*. My head is still woolly and I have to rub my eyes when the words blur, but I'm feeling slightly better.

"What's that you're reading?" she asks me, bypassing a hello. She looks like an old-fashioned teacher with her low, neat bun and that thick cotton skirt that bunches round her waist – and no doubt cost a fortune because Greta only buys her designer clothes at full-price.

Ms Ray scurries over. "Hi, Greta, can I help?"

"It's more the other way round," says Greta. "I've finished my summer sessions now. I've got a job in admin but I have a few extra hours to help out here. I could start now, if you like?"

"Ah," says Ms Ray. "Let's have a chat after lunch, when I'm not busy. Just so you know for the future, I'd prefer it if you told me when you'll be coming to the schoolhouse." She glances round at us, frowning, and we return to the books we're supposed to be reading.

Greta stands up straighter, so that she's taller than Ms Ray. "Just so *you* know, my dad and Dr Ballard are keen for me to support your teaching when I have time."

"I see," says Ms Ray. "Well, thanks for coming by. I'll see you later."

Greta turns the cover of my book over and screws her face up. "Since when did we read plays?" she asks.

"Things have moved on since you left," I say.

The corners of Greta's mouth turn down. "By the way,

Mae, you're invited to our apartment for dinner tonight." She glances up at Ms Ray in a dismissive gesture. To tell her that this is a private conversation and she has no business listening in.

Eating at someone else's apartment is such a big thing she must have already gained permission from our dads.

"Why?" I say. The others are curious too – they stare from Greta to me.

She shrugs. "Your dad thought it would be nice," she says.

"But I'm only on half-privileges," I say. We both know that eating dinner somewhere other than your usual place is something you have to be on full-privileges for.

"I was only told to pass on the message, Mae," says Greta.

Mid-afternoon and I find Thet writing her novel in the juice bar with a cucumber cooler and no straw. "I'm working on the lips on glass thing," she says.

"Will you come to the sensory garden with me?" I ask.

As we walk across the lawn, I notice that her toenails are painted with bright pink nail varnish apart from the second one of each foot, which is painted her new colour, orange. We sit on a safe bench, one that's not covered by a security camera, and I ask her about her vitamin dose and colour. She's down to quarter of a beige tablet and has no side effects.

"Are you sure?" I can't quite believe it.

She nods.

"Don't you feel tired?"

"I'm not doing so much exercise, so no." She studies my face. "You know the exercise schedule is reduced alongside the vitamins? It's to get you ready for real life again."

I sit up. "Noah and Piper are on different sports schedules. Whatever is in the so-called vitamins must be linked to exercise." That's it. I feel so much more energetic now that I'm back taking my tablets. I've always been scheduled for huge amounts of physical activities.

Thet plays with the elastic on her notebook. "Are you sure you're OK, Mae?" she asks. "You seem hyper. I'm worried about you."

I tip my head back so I can only see the sky. "Maybe it's a good thing you're leaving, Thet," I say quietly. "For you, I mean. It might be better to be away from all this."

She doesn't say anything, but I feel her there beside me. Her feelings of being torn between two worlds. Mine, and her life waiting for her back home.

Into the silence, a message beeps on my watch. It's from Earl: I've been moved straight from half-privileges to full.

Three o'clock feels more like five as I climb the ladder to the rooftop, hoping that Noah will be there. The temperature's dropped and the brightness of the day has softened.

He's hiding behind the fire-escape structure, even though I tapped on my way up. When he emerges, I think for an exhilarating moment that he's going to hug me, but he doesn't. Maybe he's distracted by my backpack which I thump to the ground.

"Textbooks," I say. I brought them in case he wasn't here.

"You know how to make someone feel good about their conversation skills," says Noah. He sits down on the towel, and I sit close. So close, our shoulders might touch if one of us tilted ever so slightly sideways. "Show me what you've got in there, then."

He tests me on cell biology, reading out chunks from the book that has Ms Ray's pencil notes scrawled in margins from when she was a student. He pauses now and again for me to fill in the missing words. I mumble them into my folded arms. "Course, this is just a memory test, Mae. I should be making you apply this knowledge to something." He flips to the front of the book. "This was published ten years ago. You need something more up to date." Seeing my stricken face he says, "But in the absence of that, this is good."

We discuss poetry from the anthology Ms Ray gave me. It's toe-curlingly awkward when it comes to the sexual references. Noah blushes a little as he tries to explain things.

"Don't you know anything about sex?" he asks.

It's shameful how little I know about life. About how

my own body works and sex. "There's a book in the schoolhouse about it," I say. It's about eggs and seeds, and saving yourself. It's a scruffy book because we've all looked at it so much and tried to make sense of the vague drawings. I used to try to talk to Drew about sex but he never wanted to. Perhaps it was because he didn't want me pulling him out of the friend zone into something else.

"I'll explain anything you want," says Noah. "But some things are more embarrassing than others." He pulls a freaked-out face which involves a double chin, then flops back against the brick structure to flick through the anthology. When his face is back to normal, I study it more closely.

"Your skin looks nice," I say without thinking, and immediately cringe at myself.

He touches his cheek. "I'm trying to hang out more at the spa. I gather it's where you hear the best gossip." He grins and goes back to the poetry.

His face comes alive when he speaks, eyes sparkling, and his smile pushing laughter lines out all over the place, but when he's concentrating, like now, it's alive in a different way. "Any faves in here?" he says, shutting it and waving it in my face.

"Not yet," I say. "I'm only just getting into it."

He places it on the concrete.

"I've been thinking. I'm going to smuggle out one of the so-called multivitamins, one of the beige ones, when I leave," he says. "But I'm going to stay until the end of the summer."

He's staying for now, but the thought of him leaving at the end of the summer hollows me. No Drew. No Thet. No Noah.

"My sister has access to a chemistry lab. She's doing a masters. I'm going to ask her to analyse it."

"Really?" Excitement drops to dismay. "But you won't be able to tell me the results."

"Aha." Noah looks super-pleased with himself. "Will's having an iPad smuggled in very soon. One of the mini ones. Drew was first in line, then someone else, but I've outbid them. It's for you. For when Thet and I've gone, so we can keep in touch."

I can't speak. I never completely believed Drew when he spoke about the iPad. I thought it was more of a fantasy. Noah's prepared to pay goodness knows what above the market price for an iPad for me? His generosity lightens my limbs and brightens the mess in my head. I find my voice. "Thank you. I'll pay you back one day," I say.

Noah blinks away my thanks. "No need. We're big on good causes, my family. You've made my stay here better. You've made me feel. . ."

"More paranoid than you were when you arrived?"

He laughs. "Maybe."

I admit to him that I saw that his referral letter mentioned paranoia.

He chews his bottom lip. "I've got it under control," he says. "But I reckon I'm just more watchful now. More aware of things that other people choose not to see."

I'd like to hug him or squeeze his arm but the moment passes because he says, "I think you should still work on accessing your medical records."

"I can't see a way."

Noah bites on his thumb, then removes it to say, "How about I cause a massive disturbance sometime when your dad's on his laptop, so he has to visit me on call-out."

"No!" I'm shocked Noah would even consider that. "Dad would log out before he left his laptop, and he only does a call-out if someone's way out of control. You'd be sedated. Maybe punished." I twist my watch strap. The smoothness of it no longer pleases me. I've worn different versions of the same watch for nearly ten years. That means Dad's received ten years' worth of data from me.

"Some of the patients are talking about a protest," says Noah. "About Austin and the lack of answers."

"What sort of protest?" Nothing like that has ever happened before.

"I don't know. A strike. Maybe spray paint or banners. Will's behind it. He thinks the Creek let Austin down. He says they knew something was wrong and didn't do enough about it. Says Austin should have been sent to a proper hospital after what happened in the basketball court."

I admire Will, but I'm worried for him.

The Jesmonds' apartment is a back-to-front version of

ours. The equivalent of Dad's study in our apartment is Zach's room in theirs. Greta's room makes my head spin; it's like a flipped-over version of mine, with fake book wallpaper and a disturbing amount of cuddly toys for a nineteen-year-old. Their living room looks towards the fields outside the perimeter fence. I step out on to the small balcony that they have instead of our big roof terrace. There's one plant out here. It looks exactly the same as when I was here for the sleepover five years ago. I reach out and feel a leaf between my fingers; as I suspected, it's plastic.

Dr Jesmond has a desk in the corner of the living room. It's tidy, like Dad's. No sign of a silver laptop. I wonder if Greta has hers yet, and if she'll ever let me look at it.

Greta's mom, Everleigh, ushers me to the table along with the others, who are shadowing me but not exactly making conversation. She lifts the lid off a dish of summer vegetable risotto, the same food I'd be eating if I was in my own apartment.

Zach stares at me so hard across the table that I discreetly touch my nostrils to check if there's anything dangling.

I wait to find out the reason I'm here.

"So, we thought it would be nice if you two girls hung out together a bit more," says Everleigh with a smile that alarms me. She's not usually a smiler.

Dr Jesmond – Karl – hands round vitamins. I already had mine before I came.

Greta gulps hers down then shovels risotto into her mouth and speaks before it's empty. "You've really grown since Drew left. It's had a positive effect on you. You've become so much more mature, so much nicer."

I open my mouth but I can't formulate the right words. Nicer? I'm not nicer, just shocked and wary. Probably quieter.

"In the fall, we thought you might like to visit Greta for a day at her apartment?" says Karl. He looks at me expectantly, wanting a sign that I consider this the most exciting thing ever to have been offered to me. This is what they want – to push me together with Greta. To get me back on track.

"Would I get to see Pattonville College?"

Karl smiles. "We might be able to arrange that. Are you looking forward to college?"

I nod. "But I haven't decided which one I'd like to go to yet."

Everleigh says, "Zach, would you pass Mae the salad, please," and as Zach hands it to me, the silver salad servers slide down into the bowl to become covered in the fat-free dressing. There's a good deal of tutting, and fetching of another linen napkin to wipe the handles.

Conversation turns to the weekend. Greta and Zach appear to know that it's the annual Creek kids' barbecue on Saturday night, something which hasn't been formally announced yet.

"I love the Creek barbecue," says Greta. "Don't you, Mae?"

I used to – none of the top-ranking adults ever attend,

and it's a treat to be outside after the shutters come down. One year Drew and I threw bits of bread roll at another table and had an epic silent battle for about five minutes before a supervisor came by. "Yes," I say.

Karl watches me. His teeth have been whitened since I last saw them. They gleam like a shiny car hood. "I'll be at a boring old conference while you kids are having fun."

"And I'll be here home alone, probably working on my charity newsletter, which I still haven't finished," says Everleigh. She rubs Karl's arm. "Nice for the patients to have a good time after what's happened."

She means Austin.

"I'm glad you're being sensible about Drew, Mae." says Karl. "There's nothing to be gained from moping. We've had enough trouble lately with the patients, with silly hysteria over certain events." He doesn't mention Austin's name either. Maybe he thinks we don't care about Austin because he was a patient we hardly knew.

I reach for my glass of water, so that I can avoid eye-contact with him. A few uneasy silent moments later, Zach tells his dad about Ms Ray turning Greta away this morning.

Karl frowns.

"She's not what we need, Dad," says Greta. "She's not a Creek person. Not at all."

I push my remaining risotto to one side of my plate; my appetite has definitely gone down since I started taking the vitamins again. "She's actually quite disorganized, isn't she, Zach? She's always losing her glasses," I say. It suddenly seems important that Karl doesn't know how good or enthusiastic Ms Ray is.

Zach laughs. "She can hardly work that CD player of hers. Greta, have you seen it? It's like something you'd see in an old movie."

"Fruit kebabs next!" sing-songs Everleigh. She collects my plate first. "As you're our guest, Mae, I won't insist you finish your meal."

I don't understand why she'd bring it to Karl's attention like that. Nobody else clears up. They leave it all to Everleigh. When I stand up to help, Karl pats the air, meaning for me to stay seated.

I'd rather help than listen to Zach go through his personal best times and scores in every single sport, followed by Ben's scores, which are naturally lower than his, as Zach is so much bigger. As I look out of the window at the plastic plant, there's a scream.

Karl is on his feet. "What now, Everleigh?"

"There's a beetle in the hall." Everleigh runs into the living room. "Karl, there's a *beetle*." She's trembling and breathing heavily.

"For heaven's sake. We've worked on this," snaps Karl. "Ignore the damn beetle."

Greta and Zach look uncomfortable. The relationship between Everleigh and Karl doesn't seem so different to the one between my own parents.

"Please," says Everleigh.

Karl sighs so loudly I can picture his lungs flattening to the width of a wholewheat pancake. "Oh, for God's sake," he says. He pushes down on the dining table with his soft white hands as he stands, then strides out of the room towards the trolley. A few seconds later I hear the sound of his polished shoe coming down heavily on the beetle.

TWENTY-FIVE

Some of the weeds have flowered on the rooftop. Their tiny yellow flowers are startling against the mottled grey of the concrete. I tell Noah my idea before he tests me on some equations.

"Risky," he says, "but genius. Count me in."

"You can help with the first bit," I say, "and tell Thet about it when you have the chance, so she doesn't wonder what's up when it happens."

On Saturday afternoon, three hours before the barbecue, I pierce the lid of a plastic tub from our kitchen with a sharp knife and take it in a small backpack to the woodland gardens where Noah's already waiting.

"I used to love bug collecting when I was little," says Noah. He kicks over a stone. The ground is teaming with huge ants. I lift up a few with a leaf. The bigger bugs are harder to find. We peer in the undergrowth, and lift up fallen branches. Scuff up the dry leaves. Each time we spot a decent-sized one, it scuttles away from our clumsy scooping method and we don't have anything to trap it with.

Noah walks further into the wooded area and lies on his stomach.

"Aren't you worried they'll climb on to you?" I ask.

"Shush," he says. "I'm trying to blend in. Get the box ready."

So I position myself next to him, as if I'm waiting to start a race, and with a quick movement he cups something in his hands, then pushes himself up to a kneeling position.

I lift the lid of the box and he opens his hands into it. Our faces are close, just a couple of inches apart. I've never been this close to a patient before. I imagine closing the gap, my lips on his, pushing him back down into the soft earth, lying on top of him so that I fit against his body like a curved jigsaw. I blink away the image.

"Look," says Noah, pointing.

Two beetles with iridescent armour.

"You want a turn while I hold the box?" he asks. He follows me to one of the big tree trunks and waits next to me as I hover, scanning the ground, super-aware of him next to me. My neck feels sensitive, as if it's about to get the pins and needles sensation, but I don't touch it. I stay motionless. I want this moment to stretch.

*

Coloured lights hang outside the juice bar and in the trees opposite. It's not quite dark yet, but it still looks pretty. Tonight we're allowed to stay outside for an hour after the shutters come down. Staff have set up extra tables on the patio with pale blue tablecloths and linen napkins. The smell of the barbecue curls around us as the chefs grill, sauté and flambé the meat and vegetarian alternatives. Two long tables hold platters of salads and artisan breads. A string quartet, brought in from Pattonville, is playing on the temporary stage. Earl is walking round the area with his radio, checking arrangements with the security staff and the grad students.

Five extra cameras have been attached to the lighting stands borrowed from the drama studio. The lighting is soft in an attempt to create a relaxed ambience. I have to be careful not to show the anxiety that's squirming in my stomach. We staff kids have drinks on the juice-bar patio, and are keeping our distance from the patients there. Greta is wearing a sequinned dress and shoes that remind me of iridescent beetles.

"Interesting outfit choice," she says to me.

I look down at my short, stretchy Calvin Klein dress and patterned running shoes, chosen so I can move quickly later. There are scratches on my bare legs from kneeling in the woodland garden earlier. "Urban casual," I say. I saw the term in a magazine.

"We're as out of town as it's possible to be," says Greta. She frowns as Will comes towards us. He's lost weight and his eyes are sunken.

"Hello, Mae," he says, ignoring Greta. "Do you know any more about what happened to Austin?"

I shake my head. Does he really think I'd know more than him?

"Austin had a complicated medical history," butts in Greta. It's the official line, the explanation that Will must have heard a thousand times.

"I want to go to his funeral, but your dads are being asses."

Greta's face tightens. "I'd like to inform you that I'm now a member of staff," she says. "That sort of language is unacceptable. Our dads are doing pioneering work in the field of holistic medicine and it's an honour to be treated by them." She turns away, and I look at Will and mouth, *Sorry.*

"Nobody knew Austin like me," says Will. "The staff had him down as aggressive and angry, but he wasn't. Really. He was just unhappy."

Is Will right? I wish I could say something useful.

He looks down at the patio. "I should have done more for him. Pushed them to get him proper medication. All they cared about was their bullshit vitamin therapy."

I want to ask more. I'd particularly like to know if he was taking the same multivitamins as me and how many, but there are cameras and Greta's still here, even though she has her back to us, sipping her Paradise cocktail.

Will looks up, expecting me to continue the conversation, but I drop my eyes to my elderflower cordial. I want to say I know how precious Austin was to him, and I understand his anger, but I don't. I daren't.

"It's not just me," mutters Will. "Other patients are starting to ask questions. People are getting angry." He walks away, shoulders hunched, as a supervisor calls for hush and announces that the barbecue is ready.

At the staff kids' table the boys discuss a computer game while Greta talks me through proposed changes to her apartment. All her kitchen appliances are being upgraded to the latest models, and she's having new curtains for the living room. Silk with star shapes woven into it, imported from Thailand. I'm not required to participate, only listen. At one point she grimaces and clutches her upper arm. "Growing pains," she says.

And then the eating part is over, and we move to the seats that have been set out for us to watch a concert, put on by some of the patients. A grad student is ready to film it, to send each segment back to the appropriate parents to show how well their child is doing and how much the Creek is broadening their horizons.

The floodlights have been switched on. Everyone is ooo-ing. I make sure that I sit on the end of the back row with Noah and Thet. Greta and Zach gravitate towards the front as usual, where they think they belong.

Thet says, "Good luck, my brave."

"Abort the mission if anything feels off," says Noah.

."See you on the rooftop tomorrow morning for a debrief."

The first person comes on to the small stage and everyone claps. We decided I'd leave during the second song, but I'm itching to be on my feet, and walking briskly across the grass to Hibiscus.

As soon as the second song begins my leg muscles tense, and I wait for Noah to indicate when the camera is rotating the other way.

As he tugs on his ear, I stand and walk away, avoiding the sweep of the camera.

I'm almost at the parking lot when a stern-looking grad student steps out from a shadow and says, "Where are you going?"

Zach once told me how little animals can die of fright. I never believed him until now, as my heart simultaneously squeezes and catapults against my ribcage.

"Home," I say. "I don't feel well." I touch my forehead with shaky hands. The shaking's for real.

"Did you tell a supervisor at the barbecue?"

I shake my head. "I just want to get home," I say. "My dad's there," I add. I feel like Greta, using my dad like that to make the grad student back off.

The grad student nods. He's inexperienced enough not to know that my dad would be furious that I hadn't told a supervisor I was leaving.

I run.

Dinner will be over for Mom, Dad and Everleigh in

the two separate apartments. If this plan's going to work, Everleigh has to notice the bugs I'm about to drop into her hallway, and Dad has to be working on his laptop. Greta and Zach have to still be at the concert.

I don't want to draw attention to myself when I'm supposed to be at the concert, so I tap in the entry code and push open the door at the right moment in the camera's rotation. The bug box is where I left it. I pull out the leaves and discard them in the trash can, then I go up to the Jesmond floor, pressing flat against the wall on the stairs in two places to avoid being picked up by the cameras while I'm holding the box.

I visualize the plan in my head one last time before I do it: remove the lid, open the door slowly, hold on to the box tightly and fling the bugs into the hallway. If Everleigh sees me, I have a story about how the bugs are for Zach's spray-paint art project. I feel bad for the bugs, but I can't think of any other way to do this.

I open the door. I hear the TV. Everleigh's watching the soap that Mom likes. With an underarm bowling action, I hurl the insects forward, scattering them across the marble floor.

I close the door and run upstairs to our apartment, slowing myself down as I walk through the hallway, and call, "Hi. I'm back," as I open the door to my room and throw the box on my bed.

"But the concert's still going," calls Mom. She's on the roof terrace with her plants, listening before the shutters come down. Did she see me cross the lawn and notice that I was longer than usual coming up the stairs?

"What's up?" calls Dad from the study. "Why are you back early?"

"Stomach ache," I say. I walk to the study doorway and place my hand on my stomach. Yes! He's on his laptop. "Too much meat. I'll watch TV until it passes."

Dad grunts. He believes me because who would give up the treat of being in the grounds after the shutters come down?

Everleigh's screams bounce through our apartment as I flip through the movie selection. Mom rushes in from the terrace. "Hunter! That's Everleigh!"

Dad runs for the door, and Mom follows.

I scoot to the study. *Don't think about this. Do it.* It takes several agonizing moments to find my way round Dad's computer, to minimize the document he's working on – something to do with payments – and to locate what I need: the *Detailed Medical Records* drive on the network.

Quick. Quick. The network is mind-alteringly slow. Downstairs Everleigh is still screaming; I imagine Dad speaking to her in his deep, calming professional voice.

I click on *Detailed Medical Records* and ... I'm stuck: I need a password. I slump back on Dad's chair. Defeated. But then a row of *x*s appear in the box. Dad's set the password to be saved. I hit enter and I'm in.

Scrambling down the list, I find my name. I double-click it and skim past my date of birth, blood group, percentile chart for height and weight and my vaccination records. I skip to information about illnesses.

I had bronchitis as a baby, gastro-enteritis twice and I've had my appendix removed. But I knew all that.

Medication: it says that for most of my life I've been on something called HB. That must be an abbreviation, but I've never heard anyone talk about HB. My dose was doubled recently and, according to my records, I've had very few side effects, though at my last check Dr Jesmond was concerned about something called "breakthrough symptoms". Was that when I stopped taking the vitamins?

There's no sound from downstairs. How long have I got before Mom and Dad come back? Minutes? Seconds? My eyes hurt. I fight the urge to lose time by rubbing them.

I flick my eyes up to the top of the document again. *Mother: Louelle Ballard. Father: Unknown.*

I stare at the screen, hardly able to process what I've just read. But then I hear noises outside the apartment, on the stairs. There's no time to look at anything else. I log out of the network, find the payment document and maximize it. My hands are quick, steady. They only tremble as I step away from the desk, sprint out of the study, and lie on the sofa and say it inside my head: *Father: Unknown.*

Dr Hunter Ballard isn't my dad.

TWENTY-SIX

Dad – or rather, the person pretending to be my dad – walks into the living room. I stare at him, which he interprets as me wanting to know what happened downstairs. "It's OK. Just Everleigh taking fright at some insects."

How come my father is *unknown*? If I asked Mom for the truth, would she tell me? There are photos of Dad – Hunter Ballard – with me on the day I was born, so Mom must have been with him then.

I remember how she reacted when I asked about Frank, and her mom. I can't risk her reacting to this.

"I feel for Everleigh," says Mom.

If I'd had more time on the laptop I'd have read Mom's medical notes next. More than ever, I want to understand who she is, where she's from.

I hold my breath as Dad – no, not Dad, *Hunter* – goes back into the study. Will he notice I've been on his laptop? After a few excruciating moments, I hear him start typing again, and I think I'm in the clear. As I sink against the sofa cushions, I feel nauseous.

I dream that Dr Jesmond is my real father, but that he didn't want me because he preferred Greta and Zach.

I wake up disoriented for a moment. It's Sunday. No morning exercise. The basement cafeteria is closed. Most members of staff have the morning off. Patients eat breakfast in Larkspur and staff kids eat in their apartments, which means I'm free until eight a.m.

I pull on my favourite zebra-print sportswear, then I grab one of my calligraphy pens and write a pleasing-looking note to say I've gone running, which I leave on the dining table. As if I could be anywhere other than within the grounds of the Creek.

It's humid outside. Greyness overlays feeble blue sky. Rain's likely. I run on the track next to the perimeter fence. As I pick up the pace, one thought pounds in my head: *Will I ever know who my real dad was?*

I stop at the gates. Resting my forehead against the bumpy metal that looks so smooth from a distance, I imagine myself running on that long flat road to Pattonville, and far beyond.

A red car appears on the horizon. The sound of its engine takes longer to reach me. It's Abigail's car. She's the only member of staff who has a button she can press to open the gates without having to wait for security to do it.

I hear the lock click, and I know she's activated

the gates. If I carry on standing here, this side of the gate will push me back as it opens inwards. It's thick, metal and strong. But if Abigail wasn't paying attention and if security staff weren't watching the monitor that the gate cameras feed into, I could slip out unnoticed. I wonder how far along the road I'd get before the alarm was raised. Two miles? I'd still be alongside fields.

I run on, to the sensory garden where I make sure I'm picked up on camera doing stretches in the drizzle, then I sneak back to the security building, tapping my nails on the rail as I sprint up the ladder.

Noah's already on the roof, wearing an enormous khaki-coloured rain jacket, and I love how his face brightens when he sees me. He holds his hand up as if my just being there is a minor miracle.

"Thank God you're OK," he says. "Sit down and tell me what happened."

The towel is gritty. The wind must have blown bits all over it. I take a deep breath and say out loud that Hunter isn't my father. I have a sense of spinning away while still being attached, like a yo-yo.

"Whoa. Seriously? That's got to be messing with your head," says Noah. "You're living with someone pretending to be your father and he's been giving you some nameless drug for years." He takes a packet of sugar-free chewing gum from the pocket of his oversized jacket, and hands me a tab. "Want to talk about it?"

I shake my head. "Not yet." I crunch down on the

228

outer shell of the chewing gum pellet and chew for a moment. "The drug I'm on does have a name. It's called HB. I didn't get a chance to see anyone else's records, but it must be the vitamins."

"What's HB?"

"No clue." I look up at the sky. The drizzle is turning into proper rain.

Noah shakes his arms out of his hoodless jacket and lifts it over his head. "Come under here until the rain stops. There's clear sky over there. It shouldn't last long." He holds up the side of his jacket.

I wish I'd studied myself longer in the mirror before leaving, to check my waterproof mascara and lip gloss were as good as they could be. It's gloomy and damp-smelling inside the jacket-tent, but cosy. Weirdly intimate. The rain patters down hard on my trainers and ankles, but I don't care.

Something occurs to me. "Noah, do you think maybe" – it's hard to say this – "I'm given HB because I have a rare disease, one which Mom has too because we're both given the same pills? Maybe everyone else on the beige pills has the disease too. Perhaps Thet's been cured. Maybe that's why she can go home?"

"Of course you don't have a rare disease," says Noah. "You'd know. And how would all these other kids have the same rare disease?"

"But if nobody ever told me, I wouldn't know, would I? What if I do and I'm never able to leave the Creek?"

Noah shakes his head. "Mae, the world doesn't just end outside that gate, I promise you. Whatever medication you're on, you can get it outside the Creek. If you even need it, which you don't."

The raincoat slips down and Noah has to grab it. His bare arm brushes against mine, and I want the shivery feeling to be replicated all over my body. Noah moves, but not away. He places his arm round my shoulder, and the weight of it anchors me to a new sensation: a flare of joy. I don't want to risk looking at him and breaking the spell. We watch the rain pool in puddles on the rooftop, and wobble the yellow flower heads.

"Whatever Dr Ballard's doing is wrong," says Noah eventually. "It's probably illegal but it's definitely unethical. You have to get the hell away from here."

Rain seeps through the towel to my shorts and underpants, and with it a coldness. I shiver. "I'm being kept away from real life for some reason."

Noah adjusts his raincoat again. It's no longer much protection against the driving rain. "I'm really sorry, but I'm going to have to go in a minute," he says. "If I'm not there for breakfast, I'll be in trouble."

He goes down the ladder first, and I watch him run towards Larkspur, his enormous jacket flapping. He looks like a large bird trying to fly.

I wait until he's no longer visible before I go down the ladder. As I walk, dripping, through the apartment door, Dad – Hunter – calls out, "Mae? We need to talk."

TWENTY-SEVEN

"Look at you. You should have run on a treadmill in the gym." Hunter's dressed in his weekend on-call clothes. Long trousers, a short-sleeved, open-necked shirt and brown brogues imported direct from Italy.

"Yeah." The water is dripping down, starting to pool on the marble entryway floor. What does he want to talk to me about? Can he tell I've been on his laptop? I bend down to undo my laces and ease off my running shoes, so he can't see my guilty face.

"You were seen loitering by the gates. You must be careful. Those gates are heavy."

I peel off my socks. They're so wet I could wring them out. Who saw me? Was I on CCTV, or was it a gardener, or the receptionist? Did they contact Hunter especially to tell him?

Did they see me go up the ladder, too?

"Grab a towel, then we need to talk" he says.

I hear noises from the kitchen – Mom making Sunday breakfast – as I go into my room to take a towel from my en suite. When I come out, Hunter is leaning against the door frame to my room. Is he ever planning to tell me that he's not my dad?

"You're agitating for a life outside the Creek. We need to talk about it," he says.

Even though relief makes me want to collapse, I keep my expression neutral, nod and wrap the big fluffy towel round my shoulders, over my wet running clothes.

"You're probably looking ahead to when you leave this place." His tone is friendly.

I nod. "I'd like to aim for the best college I can."

He leans forward slightly, as if he's not sure he heard correctly. "You'll be going to Pattonville," he says. "But I thought you might like to know the details."

The battle of keeping emotion from my face is lost. "Pattonville? But I don't want to go to Pattonville." I sit abruptly on my bed.

Hunter walks further into my room, pushes back some of my things on top of the chest of drawers, and props himself against it. "There's absolutely no need for you to go further afield. Pattonville is a fine college, and you'll enjoy the many, varied opportunities it has to offer. And you'll be close enough that I can help you adjust to the world outside Hummingbird Creek. You'll live with Greta in her apartment there, and the two of you will come home for vacations or whenever you want, as long as you let admin know in advance. I'll buy you a car, of course. And then you'll have Zach with you when he's old enough to go. And by then, Greta will have graduated and be living back here."

So he wants Greta to continue to tell me what to do and report back to Hummingbird Creek, and when she's finally gone, I'll have Zach breathing down my neck.

"I don't like how you've been obsessing over your lessons." He frowns and I'm acutely aware of all the textbooks I have on my shelves and the bag of books under my bed. "You're a smart-enough girl. . ." The way he says smart-*enough* breaks something inside me. "There's no worry about you not getting into Pattonville College."

Because you've donated that building. You've bought me a place.

"Nor is there any worry about you finding employment afterwards. You'll have work for you here in the Hummingbird community." He gazes at me, and I think how small and mean his eyes are. Not handsome at all. "I hope that puts your mind at rest."

During his speech, my small world has shrunk to the narrowest of dark corridors which leads to a blocked exit. "But I don't want to go to Pattonville," I repeat. "I definitely don't want to live in an apartment with Greta, or Zach."

"You and Greta are going to get on." He lifts his chin,

a backwards nod. It means it's been decided. "Pattonville is the right place for you. You have to trust me on this, Mae."

I don't trust you on this or anything else.

The dinner at the Jesmonds' apartment. It was about forcing me and Greta together.

"And if I say I'm not doing that?" My ribs are pressing in on my chest, threatening to take my breath away.

Hunter frowns. It's as though this possibility has never occurred to him. "In that case, I'd say you were on your own. I wouldn't be funding you any longer. It's a harsh world out there, Mae, and you wouldn't last five minutes."

The blocked exit is bolted from the outside. I have no money of my own – not even a few dollars in a savings account. Not even ten dollars in cash. I operate with tokens, which are meaningless outside the Creek.

He stands up and places his hands in his pockets. I've seen him do that when he's talking to patients' parents. It's his I'm-a-down-to-earth-guy-but-I-know-what-I'm-talking-about pose. "When you've thought about this properly, it will make sense. Let go of those wild thoughts of moving far away." He walks towards the doorway. "This is where you belong."

I am never ever going to be able to escape this place.

When Hunter's gone, I crawl under my comforter and pull it tight around me. Why doesn't he want me to have my own life? I'm not even his daughter. The patients will keep cycling through, staying a few months, while I stay for years, growing old here. I'll become too old to make friends with patients, or too bitter. I think about Drew, and Thet. I think about Noah.

Eventually I have a shower. I am a zombie at lunch, then I go back to lie on my bed afterwards. I'm prepared to be punished for laziness. At some point in the late afternoon there's a knock at the door. Mom walks in with a mug of herbal tea and says, "Your dad's gone to the gym." She places the mug on my bedside table, then sits on the bed next to me, and runs her fingers over my patchwork quilt. "I love you so much, Mae."

I hate her for accepting everything without question. I hate her for lying to me about Hunter being my father, but most of all I hate her because I know she wouldn't be brave enough to tell me about my biological dad if I risked asking her. "Do you seriously want me to be stuck here for the rest of my life, Mom?"

"You'll go to Pattonville. You'll have a nice time." Her voice is soap-opera bright.

"I don't want to be watched over."

She nods slightly and looks down at the stupid quilt. "You don't understand how hard and cruel the world can be."

"Tell me."

Mom picks at a patch of rough skin on the side of her finger. She whispers, "When I was a child there were days when I didn't have enough to eat. When we had to hide because my parents owed money."

I hold my breath.

She says, "I wanted a different life for you. It wasn't much of a choice."

Does she mean hooking up with Hunter when she was pregnant with me? "What choice?" I ask. *Tell me about my real dad.*

"It was a difficult time," says Mom. She's clamped up.

"Where did you even meet Hun— Dad?" I ask. Their meeting story has always been a vague "through friends". Friends who didn't have names.

Mom looks round, as if Hunter's going to materialize in the doorway. "He came to my clinic," she says. "In England."

"What clinic? What were you doing there?"

"He came for research."

I bite back my frustration. "Research?"

She nods, and I urge her on with my expression. *Tell me about the research.* But again she veers off in a different direction.

"I had a best friend when I was growing up," she says. "I don't see her any more. That's how I know how hard it is for you, honey, not seeing Drew."

I'd like to talk to her about missing Drew, but I know I need to keep her focused. "What was your best friend's name?" I say it slowly, in the voice that Abigail might use. Firm. Expecting an answer.

"We used to go to the field with the horses. We shared our dreams. Had a laugh. Tiny little thing, she was, with a big mouth on her."

"What was her name?" I repeat.

Mom closes her eyes. "Callie Ridgeway," she mutters.

It's not the name of my dad, but it's something. I'll take it.

TWENTY-EIGHT

Greta and Ms Ray are standing at the front of the schoolroom in silence. We sit in our seats while keeping our eyes on them. Something is up.

"May I make the announcement?" Greta asks Ms Ray in her open-day voice.

Ms Ray nods.

Greta gives a little cough. "It's my pleasure to tell you that I'll be teaching you alongside Ms Ray this summer."

"I thought you had another job," I say. "In admin."

"Yes, I do," says Greta. "That's in the afternoons. I'll be in the schoolhouse in the mornings." She looks at the others. "Any more questions?"

"Why do we need two teachers?" I ask.

Ms Ray steps forward. "I'm sure Greta will be a helpful addition to the schoolroom." She doesn't look at me as she says it. Her face tells me she doesn't believe it.

Greta picks up the pile of work booklets on the front desk and hands them round. "Do a few pages," she says, "and then we'll have a circle time."

I open the booklet and colour in all the middles of letters a, e, o, b, d, g, p and q, then I write my name in a super-curly script. *Mae Ballard*. Except I'm not a real Ballard. I don't know who I am or what's being done to me here, but I'm going to find out.

Callie Ridgeway could know who my biological father is and she might not have anything to lose by telling me. I picture all the different spellings of her name in super-curly script. I'm too afraid of the little camera on top of the hummingbird picture behind me to write them down. But they are scorched into my brain, waiting for the time I have access to the proper internet.

Ms Ray and Greta sit at the front, waiting for us to put up our hands for help. In circle time Greta tells us to discuss Creek values. I say precisely nothing and she uses her new authority to fine me five tokens. Joanie becomes upset and tells Greta that it's because I'm still sad about Drew. Luke tries to intervene too, his quiet voice shaky as he says he thinks Greta's being unfair. She shuts them down quickly. I want to hug them both, but I look at my feet. Pedicured feet in sandals that are worth three hundred dollars.

At morning break, Ms Ray busies herself with marking the booklets, but I see her rub her forehead, as if she's too weary to concentrate. When I walk past her, she places a history textbook on the desk and indicates that I should take it. She says nothing, but I understand what she's telling me: *keep going.*

It may or may not be deliberate, but in the afternoon Mick takes Zach, Ben and me on a run that goes past the outdoor pool. There's an inflatable session going on. Patients sliding in off the plastic rafts and throwing around a huge stripy ball. Shrieks and laughter. One guy holds up a girl on his outstretched palms as if she weighs hardly anything. I watch her spring upwards and double-somersault gracefully into the water. The grad student life-guard stares at them and jots something down in a notebook, but spectacular sports feats are the norm here when you train as much as we do.

Mick stops for us to do some stretching. It's one of the glorious cloudless sunny days that feature in Hummingbird Creek's brochures. Thet is in the pool, standing in the shallow end, watching, her pink glitter plastic shoes are lined up on the side. Noah's there too, clambering on to one of the rafts. His swim shorts have chemical symbols printed on them. He's not as all-over ripped as a lot of the other boys our age. I guess he hasn't being working out as much as them. But I like his tall, slim build.

I've sat in group therapy sessions for years. I understand the concept of living in the moment. Being mindful. My friends deserve to be happy, they absolutely do, but right now their happiness is hard to see.

We carry on with our run. Mick takes us up by the cycle track. There's already a plaque up in memory of Austin.

Later, in my trampoline skills session with Joanie, we go through an easy routine a few times, and then she stops and asks me what's wrong. I say I'm fine, but we lie on the trampoline for an extended cool-down and after a bit she takes my sweaty hand and says, "I don't like Greta."

"Me neither," I say. "But we have to do our best not to let her know that, OK?"

"OK." She pulls away her hand and flips over on to her stomach. "I miss Drew. Were you in love with him?"

I play for time. "What are you talking about?"

"Ben and Luke say you were. But that you'll never see him again."

I cover my eyes with my forearm to block out her and the sun. My own smell, of warm skin and lavender soap, soothes me. "I thought I was, Joanie. But maybe it turns out I was just clinging to him."

"We saw you clinging to him," says Joanie in a solemn voice. "When they took him away."

One day, it's going to be down to me to explain to Joanie that how we live isn't normal.

Our trampoline time is up, and there's a trio of patients waiting to use it. I walk with Joanie back to Hibiscus, but I don't feel like going home myself. There are patients in the sensory garden, which means there's a risk I might be

241

seen going up to the roof, so I go to the spa instead for a pedicure, to pass the time.

Noah's there, having a haircut. "Posh-boy haircut suit me?"

I nod. "You look . . . like somebody different." Perhaps even someone I'd be too shy to talk to, if I'd just met him. I select the nail-varnish colours I'd like for my toenails from the stand.

The therapist finishes Noah's hair and runs warm water into the foot bath for me. Suddenly Noah's sitting beside me in the other pedicure chair, asking for one too.

"Wait until the toenail tools come out," I say. "You're going to regret this."

"This bit's nice though," says Noah, as he slips his feet into the soapy water. "Mm. How often d'you get this done?"

I shrug. "When I feel like it. If I have enough tokens. Thet and I love the facials best."

The therapist disappears for another clean towel, and Noah scans the room. I know exactly what he's looking for. "Just one pointing to the desk," I say. "I already checked."

He smiles. "Good work, Agent Ballard." He lifts his feet out of the water to look at them, and says in a low voice. "I've got the iPad for you."

The magic key. "Oh my God. How?"

"It's better if we don't know. That way we can't leak it."

I'm 47 per cent worried and 53 per cent completely and utterly excited.

"One thing, though." Noah's face is still serious. "It's fully charged but there's no charger. Will doesn't know when he can get hold of one. So you'll have to go easy on the battery. The dozy orderly is on duty at Larkspur tomorrow night. You want me to give you the iPad on the rooftop then? If I just leave it there, I'm worried it might rain, and anyway I can show you how to use it."

I imagine myself sneaking out of Hibiscus at night for the first time, then typing in Callie Ridgeway's name. Tomorrow night I might find her. Her name is more unusual than the names I searched previously, and I could try it in combination with Mom's or Frank's. Surely that gives me more of a chance?

My throat is dry. "Yes," I whisper. "But I'm scared of being caught." I think of orderlies, security guards, other staff on night shifts, cameras, Mom or Dad waking up and noticing me gone. "It would be solitary confinement for sure." Or worse.

"We'll be very careful. I know what to look out for. Come out of the fire-exit door in Hibiscus," says Noah. "Five to midnight? I'll meet you."

The therapist is coming back, and we stop speaking.

The next day passes slowly. I'm in a constant state of observation and alertness, watching for signs that it will or won't be safe to leave Hibiscus at night, but everything follows familiar patterns. The worries I had about falling asleep by mistake were misguided. I'm far too jittery and I have a deep muscle ache in my thigh. When my watch shows 23.45, I sneak out of the apartment.

I'm wearing pyjama shorts, a T-shirt and Converse. The stairwell is dimly lit with night lights, which give off a faint humming sound. I walk in a sort of ghost-like glide, in stark contrast to my heart's panicky rhythm.

At the back-door fire exit I push the shiny metal bar with both hands, holding my breath in case an alarm goes off. The door opens with a loud jolt. Noah startles me: he's right there, holding a large stone the size of a brick.

"What's—"

"Shhh," he whispers. "I'm going to wedge the door open so you can get back in later." He's wearing long shorts, a hoodie with a distorted pocket, which must be where the iPad is, and sneakers; I'm dramatically underdressed. The sky is the dark of blueberries, the half-moon white-bright against it. The stars are like pinpricks of light showing through from another universe. My skin goosebumps, but not just because the air is cooler than I expected. I'm alert like I've never been before, fuelled by terror and anticipation.

We dodge the gate cameras by ducking and crouching. There's no light coming from any buildings except for the security building. Yellow light shines from the window at the front. Nothing's floodlit tonight. After the gates, we stay down, and keep to the shadows near the fence, but not so close that we're picked up by any of the cameras. We sprint and catch our breath at the ladder.

I climb up first, faster and faster, and at the top I can't stop myself gasping at the 360 degree view. It's familiar and unfamiliar at the same time. On the occasions I've been allowed outside at night-time, there have been people around. Noise and bustle. This evening the Creek is showing me another side of itself, one I've never properly seen before. The glimmer of the uncovered pool. Shape-shifting shadows. Crops that make a shushing noise in the slight breeze. The fresh smell of foliage. Skittering dry leaves in the parking lot, the first sign of impending fall. The beauty of it hurts me.

Noah stands next to me. "It's amazing, isn't it? Even without the floodlighting."

I nod. Now that I'm standing still, I'm even colder. What was I thinking, coming out here without a sweater? I rub my arms.

"You cold?" asks Noah. My skin itches with the thought of his skin touching mine, but he doesn't place his arm round me. He takes a small, slim iPad out of his pocket. The unlocker of secrets. Silver and perfect.

"Oh. Wow." Everything about this moment has an unreal quality.

"Hang on," says Noah. He peels off his hoody and hands it to me. It smells differently from clothes washed in the Creek laundry. It smells of his other life. Of a house, not a psychiatric facility, and of a washing powder that wasn't bought in industrial quantities. And of Noah himself.

"Are you sure?" I ask, but I have my head already inside it when I ask and he laughs.

Rather than wriggling into it, it sort of falls on to me because it's so big, and the hood flops halfway on my head.

I push back the hood properly and Noah hands me the iPad. "Thank you. Thank you a thousand times. No, a million..."

He smiles. "You're welcome."

As I look to see where to switch it on, he says, "Wait. Think about what you're going to search. We have to preserve the battery."

My mind races. Drew. HB. Callie Ridgeway. Dr Hunter Ballard.

"It'll be easier if we sit down," says Noah.

We sit on the towel that was sopping wet last time we were here. It's dry now, but greyer.

I tell him how I'm destined for Pattonville College, followed by a job in the Creek. Saying it out loud makes it sound even bleaker. "It's no longer about surviving two more years," I say. "It's about finding out what Hunter's doing to me, and to everyone else."

I stroke the iPad.

"I've been into the settings, and set up the wifi," says Noah.

Thank God for the patient who overheard Abigail tell

the password to the new receptionist. I just hope it hasn't changed since.

"Let's do this," I say. Except I don't know what to do. I'm still as clueless as I was in the computer store. I have to let Noah show me. He shuffles closer and leans in.

My stomach twirls like the glittering spirals in the vegetable garden to keep the birds away. He's pressing against my shoulder. His leg touches mine and I swear I can feel each individual leg hair against my skin. The iPad makes a soft chiming noise as it powers up. The outside world is breaking through into my Creek world. We both lurch forward to muffle the sound, and Noah flicks a switch at the side to mute it. We're so close our lips are less than a hand-width apart.

"Drew's last name?" asks Noah. He searches quickly, trying different social media, logging in as himself. An endless river of photos and messages, and snatches of video flows past. Noah points to a photo of a girl who looks a bit older than Greta, with the hairiest dog imaginable on her lap. "My sister. Our dog who thinks he's the most important member of the family."

I love the smile in Noah's voice but it makes me lonely.

"I can't find Drew straight off," says Noah. "Can you think of nicknames? Or places he might have gone?"

Drew will have to wait until another time. I do a search for HB, and wade through sites that show the initials are used for many products including pencils, ice-cream and cigarettes. I skim-read information about vitamin H and vitamin B. Minutes of battery-sucking time go by. I give up and move my focus to Callie Ridgeway, trying the first of the many ways I've thought her name might be spelled.

"I want to see if she knows anything about my real dad. She was mom's best friend," I explain to Noah.

Did you mean Callie Ridgeway-Morris? the search engine asks me.

I click on the name and there's a photo of her right in front of me. She looks about Mom's age. Petite with drawn-on eyebrows and blonde hair fanning out from a ponytail high on her head. More clicking. Through to a social media site.

I look at Noah, and I say, "Can I message her?"

"Sure. Let me set up a profile. You'll want an email address too." I watch his fingers move fast over the keyboard, creating an anonymous online version of myself.

Hi Callie,

You don't know me but I think you knew my mother when you were younger. Her name is Louelle Ballard but before she married she was Louelle Hill, and she had a brother called Frank. She loved horses. I think she knew some horses called Sunny, Barney and Rhonda.

I stop.

"Give her your date of birth," says Noah. "Tell her you're looking for your dad, and that you'd be grateful for any information about him."

So I do, and I ask her not to contact Mom under any circumstances. *It could be very difficult for me if you do,* I type. I change *difficult* to *dangerous.* Hunter is capable of making my life a living hell if he finds out about this.

My fingers tremble as I press SEND.

TWENTY-NINE

"You'll have to find somewhere safe to keep the iPad," says Noah. "Balance it on your toilet cistern?" He doesn't understand why I'm smiling. "What? I watch a lot of films. The sort where people hide things in toilets."

"I'm glad you came here," I say.

"Me too, though it's been surprisingly unrestful," says Noah.

"You're in better shape now, anyway. Eaten more healthily. Escaped your cousins."

You met me.

There's silence. I've killed the mood.

"Give me the iPad a moment," he says.

I hand it to him and squeeze my neck slightly to stop the pins and needles. I've learned it helps the prickling from becoming too bad. "What are you doing?"

"Starting your address book. I'm giving you my email

and my sister's email. If you memorize them you'll always be able to contact me at some point, even if something happens to the... Oh." He looks at his watch, then taps on the keyboard and frowns.

"What is it?" *Has Callie already replied? Is it Drew?*

It's almost as if he's forgotten I'm there.

"Noah? What's up?"

"What time does your watch say?"

"12.25. Why?"

"It's showing the right time zone on here but it says the time is 03.42."

"So the time isn't set up right on the iPad?" I ask.

Noah shakes his head. "I checked the time on a couple of websites. Your watch is wrong. Mine too."

"The *watches* are wrong? I'm surprised admin hasn't noticed."

"Yeah, it's strange," says Noah. "But it's way later than I thought." He gives the iPad back to me and stands. "Time to go."

I pull one arm out of the hoody sleeve but Noah says, "Hang on to it for now. Put the iPad in the pocket. Even if you get caught on camera, it's hidden."

I'm nervous again at the thought of the journey back to the apartment. We run as quickly as we can, crouching along the security building, crawling past the gate, back into the shadows of the trees towards Hibiscus. The stone is still in the fire door. We say goodbye by waving, not talking, and I slip inside, kicking the stone free and controlling the door so it closes with the tiniest of clicks.

I leap up the stairs, easing myself against the wall in the right places. I'm getting more adept, but the level of fear is still the same.

As I go past Ben, Luke and Joanie's apartment on the third floor, there's the sound of what might be a toilet flushing. Two more floors to go. My Converse make tiny tapping sounds on the marble stairs.

I stumble through our front door, closing it as quietly as I can with fumbling hands. Along the hallway to my room, and into the bathroom.

I have the cistern lid lifted when there's a knock on the door. Not my bedroom door. The actual unlocked bathroom door.

"Yes?" I call out. I can't risk putting the lid back in case it clanks, but it's hideously heavy.

"What's going on, Mae?"

Dad. Hunter. Did he hear the front door click, or the noise of my bedroom door closing?

"I can't sleep. Stomach cramps. Like my period's about to start." My period *is* about to start, and Hunter can check that out in my medical records.

"Well, keep the noise level down. Be mindful of others around you."

"Sorry." I wait until I hear him leave the room, then I carefully lower the lid to the bathroom floor, my muscles in spasm from holding it so long. I wait until I've stopped trembling, then I place the iPad on top of the plastic parts that stick up above the water and return the lid to the cistern.

When I come out of the bathroom, achingly tired but my brain racing, I see Noah's hoody on the floor. Hunter would have seen it. He'd have known it wasn't mine. Swapping clothes with patients is a no-no.

Why didn't he say anything? Is he watching me?

THIRTY

My watch alarm goes off at seven a.m. as usual. In the bathroom, I check the time on the iPad. It says 5.23 a.m. If the iPad's right, that means I've had very little sleep. I can't say anything to admin about the watches being wrong, of course, because then I'd have to say how I know, but I'm surprised they haven't figured it out themselves by now.

The home screen shows I have a message pending. I take a deep breath and click.

It's from Callie, sent an hour ago:

Oh my God!!! Louise's daughter got in touch!!! A bolt from the blue OR WHAT? Where do you live?

Yes I knew Louise until she ran off with the creepy guy at the clinic. Hugh he was called, or something like that. He made her cut off all ties with her family and friends, a real control freak. He was the one who renamed her Louelle. We tried to stay in touch but you can't keep on when you never hear anything back, can you?

Your mum never told you about your real dad? But she told you about the horses? That figures. I hope she's not in trouble and you are OK. Your email was very dramatic.

I moved away from the area when I got married so I don't know anything about her family these days. She was Louise Eleanor Hill – we called her Louise or Lou.

Call me, and I'll tell you about your dad. I'm not much of a writer as you can probably tell! lol!!

Underneath is a long row of numbers.

I search for Louise Eleanor Hill on the internet. There are loads, but no trace of Mom.

At breakfast, I look for Noah, but he's not there. Neither is Thet. They must have had earlier exercise times. It's no big deal, but my heart still squishes like a lump of soft clay.

As I sit down with my tray, I see Will leaving. I shouldn't do this – draw attention to myself – but I get up and follow Will out of the cafeteria. He hears me behind him and says, "Mae?"

I indicate that he should keep going down the corridor, past all the exercise studios, and then I usher him along until I'm pretty certain we're not on any cameras.

"Will. Sorry. Have you seen Noah this morning?"

He screws his face as he thinks. "Yeah, he had the first exercise session. He and Thet left the cafeteria as I came in – the supervisor told them not to be so slow next time. What's up?"

I breathe out. Noah's OK. "Thanks. I wanted to tell him something. Listen, I'm really sorry about Dr Jesmond and my dad not letting you go to Austin's funeral or memorial service. I wanted to go too. My dad told me it would be too far away." I hate calling him *my dad*, but it's better Will doesn't pick up on anything.

"I don't care about distance," says Will. "I'd go wherever it was."

"Could you discharge yourself?"

"That's the thing," says Will. His voice is low but angry. "I told Dr Jesmond I wanted to be discharged. You know what he did? He phoned my parents, right after that conversation. Told them I'd become fixated on Austin and attending the memorial service would set back my recovery."

"How do you know?"

"I kept telling Dr J that I needed to speak to my parents, and when I was finally allowed my call, they were like, *Your doctors say it's a no.* They wouldn't listen to me." He rubs his eyes. "I'm finding all this really hard."

"Do you mind me asking what medication you're on?" I ask.

"None. Your dad doesn't like people to be on other medication, does he?"

"Do they give you vitamins?"

"Yeah. Everyone gets them."

"Beige ones? How many?"

He thinks. "Er . . . three of those. Used to be two, and now it's three."

Three. "Do you know how many vitamins Austin was taking?"

"No idea, Mae. He once told me if someone shook him he'd rattle with those vitamins, so it must have been more than me. They gave him other things occasionally. To calm him down, they said."

All those pills, not rattling but dissolving into his bloodstream.

Will comes closer. "What do you know that you aren't telling me? Are you saying they aren't really vitamins?"

I'm scared what will happen if Will storms into Karl or Hunter's office to demand an explanation.

"Could Austin's death have been prevented?" he asks, almost in a whisper.

I look round. A member of the kitchen staff is carrying a large bowl of bananas from the other direction towards the cafeteria. "Please," I say. "Don't say anything. I'm trying to find out. I promise I'll tell you if I do. Just. . ." I know he thinks he's protected because his parents are loaded, but he's seen how easily Dr Jesmond manipulated them. "I don't want you to get hurt or ... punished for speaking out when we don't know anything for sure."

"I don't care," says Will.

"Not yet," I say, far too loudly. The woman with the bananas has stopped by the cafeteria entrance and is looking at us. I cut the volume. "Promise me? Will, you have to promise me. It's important."

Will slumps a bit. "OK."

Before lessons, I type back a quick message to Callie:

Hi again,
    I can't phone you. Please can you tell me my
dad's name and anything about him. You are the only
person who can help me.
    Yours,
    Mae

While Greta attempts to teach us simple algebra on the whiteboard, Ms Ray sorts out the stationery closet. Lessons have become a slow death. I hold my tongue as long as I can, waiting for Greta to notice that the answer to her sum is obviously wrong. She writes another one on the board and shouts at Luke when he can't remember what he has to do.

Ms Ray looks round from the closet. "Greta," she says. "It works best if you give more than one example."

"If you interfere again with my teaching, I'll report you," hisses Greta. She rubs her eye angrily, so that when she removes her hand it's much redder than the other one.

An uncomfortable silence descends, punctuated by Luke's sniffing.

"Luke?" says Greta.

"For goodness' sake, Greta," I say. "You got the first sum wrong, so how do you expect Luke to know what he's doing."

Greta leaves the whiteboard and walks up to my desk. "I don't like your attitude, Mae Ballard."

"I don't like your teaching, Greta Jesmond," I blurt.

Joanie giggles, Zach sucks in a lungful of breath, and I'm done for.

Greta swallows and straightens up. "Mae, take a book and sit outside for the rest of the morning. Tomorrow you'll be working in isolation."

As soon as I see Ms Ray's slight smile, I realize that for once, things might have unexpectedly gone my way.

As Greta has reported me to Hunter, I have to endure a talk about manners, gratitude and humility. "I imagine Greta needs more practice at teaching," says Hunter at dinner, as he delicately separates the fish flesh from the bones. "Your job is to support her, not undermine her. Until you can do that, I'm backing her recommendation that you do your work booklets in isolation. Tomorrow you will go straight to the office in the main building which you were in before."

I nod.

"Greta is an asset to Hummingbird Creek. Loyal and reliable. These are qualities I value. There seems to be an unpleasant air of discontent among some patients, and I will not have it spreading. As I am unfortunately having to remind some people, I have zero tolerance for those who are seeking to spoil our harmonious environment. Not even my daughter gets special treatment."

I clench my hands round my knife and fork. *I'm not your daughter.*

"I advise you to be careful, Mae."

Being in the office is a relief, but the memories of Drew crossing the lawn to leave the Creek bounce off the walls. It feels as if my life's been about survival ever since.

The desk is empty – no work booklet or writing equipment. I pull the chair up to the window and sit and watch the gardeners. I can't see into the schoolhouse but I spot Ms Ray when the main door opens and she walks down the steps with something in her hand. She looks up at my window and I wave. She doesn't act as if she's seen me, but carries on walking, past the golf buggies, to the side entrance of the main building. I expect she's been sent to deliver my work booklet.

I'm right – but Ms Ray delivers more than a work booklet and a pen. After handing it to me, with extra pages folded in to the centre, she leans against the closed door and says, "Mae, there's a school I know that's five hours from the Creek by car. Radley Bridge School. You could board there, and I think it would suit you. I can arrange for you to sit the entrance exam – you'd have to do it somewhere in Pattonville. There are scholarships available and you might well show enough potential to be awarded one. You wouldn't need your dad's money if you had a scholarship."

A school with proper teachers, five hours from here. It's nothing but a tantalizing dream. "There's no point. I'd never be allowed," I say. "It's arranged already. Hunter told me I have to go to Pattonville College, then come back and work here."

If she notices that I don't call Hunter "Dad", she doesn't give any indication. "You don't think he could be persuaded?"

"No. He always gets his own way." She's been here long enough to know that, surely?

"I thought you'd say that." She sighs. "Look, at age eighteen you're a legal adult and he can't force you to do anything. But we'd need your parents' permission for Radley Bridge. If you do well in their entrance exam, we'd stand a much better chance of persuading them."

Ms Ray has no clue, but I'm flattered she thinks I'm capable and worth bothering about.

"Radley Bridge do the exam a few times a year. The next one is in eight days." Ms Ray avoids my eye. "I won't be at the Creek for the exams after that one. I'm going to leave."

I nod. I'm surprised she stayed this long, if I'm honest.

"But I'm going to do my absolute best to get you to that entrance exam before I leave. That gives you seven days to prepare. I can help you."

"But. . ." It seems so hard to manage even that first step. "What's the point?"

Ms Ray looks stern. "The point, Mae, is that you have to try. You must never give up. You must seize chances. I want you to take the exam. We'll worry about the rest later."

I nod. "Thank you." At least the entrance exam will give me another glimpse into the outside world, and as peculiar as it would seem to the other staff kids, I like the idea of being tested academically.

"I have a ton of things for you to read and learn. I'm going to leave books in the library for you on the science shelf because nobody seems to touch that, and give you extra worksheets in your booklet."

"There are cameras in the library," I say.

She's taken aback. Our eyes meet. "You think it's that bad?"

"Yes." We need a better arrangement. "A swimming locker," I say. "We both swim, so it'll work. Use one of the top row ones and tell me the four-digit code. There are no cameras in the changing room, but we'll each have to wait until there's no one there. They only get deep-cleaned the last week of every month."

"OK, that's good." She starts to open the door; she can't be too long with me or Greta will have something to say. "One last thing. From now on it would be wise if neither of us spoke to the other unless we have to."

THIRTY-ONE

I sit on the toilet and read Callie's message.

Hi Mae!

Where do I begin? Your dad was good-looking and fun. Always up to no good and bunking off school!! Kids deserve to know who their parents are, so here goes.

Federico had a drug problem. Speed was what he was into. That's what we called amphetamine. Just had to look up how to spell that! Dragged your mum into the scene. Then – there's no easy way to say this – he went and died from an overdose.

I pause reading. *Federico* I say in my head, seizing on his name to counteract the knowledge that he's dead. A small deluded part of me was expecting my dad to be special, some sort of hero. Someone who might rescue me and Mom.

I don't think Fed knew your mum was pregnant. Truth is, he probably wouldn't have changed his ways and I'm sorry if I've upset you by saying that. Your mum was in a state but she didn't want an abortion. She went to a clinic, a rehab place, to get clean for your sake. That's where she met the doctor she ran off with. He was doing research into amphetamine but he took a shine to her and that was that. TBH I thought something really bad had happened to her!!! Glad she is still alive and kicking ☺ ☺ ☺

Don't want to bitch about her family because they were nice but they were messed up. Her mum was on loads of dodgy tablets and her dad and brother liked a drop of alcohol. We had some good times, me and your mum. All us teenagers used to hang out on some scrubland and your mum was mad about those horses who lived there. She was good with animals.

Long email to say your dad was called Federico Matthews. His mum was from South America somewhere. Never knew her name. His dad wasn't around. Rumour was he was doing time, but I don't know about that.

Gotta go now.

Callie x

I look down at my tanned skin, and pull my dark hair round to inspect the colour. I thought I'd got my darker colouring from Mom, but it must be from my South American grandmother too.

There are so many questions still to ask. About my grandmother Vonnie and my grandfather. Where mom grew up. What she was like before she met Hunter.

Federico Matthews. Half South-American. Good looking and fun. Drug addict. Oblivious that he had a baby daughter on the way. I think of the photo tucked inside the book on daffodils in Mom's office. *F with Barney, Sunny and Rhonda.*

F wasn't Frank, Mom's brother. He was Federico, my dad.

THIRTY-TWO

Boot camp with Mick. I block it out by going over the things circling in my head, things I've found out via my iPad.

Radley Bridge House. I saw photos of an ordinary building, but inside was a proper science lab and a massive library and rows and rows of computers. Lots of pupils, not a massive emphasis on sport, and a website without loads of slogans. Teachers allowed to help. No Creek watches. No Hunter, or Hugh, or whoever he is.

I have a new, exciting thought. If Hunter isn't my real father, does that mean that Mom might be the only person who needs to give permission for me to study at Radley Bridge?

Amphetamine. I read it's a stimulant, taken by people to keep themselves awake, energized and alert. It can cause death by placing too much strain on the heart.

I picture Federico in a field with horses, his heart stopped.

I keep checking the time on the iPad and comparing it to the time on my watch. I start writing down the time differences in the back of a notebook. It looks like a code. The battery indicator shows I've already used half the charge.

At my regular health check, Raoul is the nurse on duty. As usual I turn away from seeing the blood fill up the syringe.

"Does Greta still have blood taken?" I ask.

"Of course," says Raoul.

"She could say no, couldn't she? She's an adult now."

"But why would she do that?" He looks appalled.

"I'm not saying she would, but if she refused, what would you do?"

"I'd tell her daddy that he needed to have a talk with her. Best health facility for miles, you have here. You are all lucky, lucky, lucky." He smiles his super-white bright smile and takes my watch off to plug it into the laptop.

"Raoul, is it true that some of the patients are acting up?"

He loses his smile. "Who did you hear that from?"

"My dad."

He sighs. "Some patients are too restless. They want trouble. They need to be more busy."

"Do the watches ever tell the wrong time?" I ask.

"Why do you ask that?" Raoul pulls the needle from my arm and brings the full syringe up to his face, as if the colour or viscosity of my blood can tell him what's in my head.

"I don't know," I say. "I thought mine had gone wrong the other day but I must have been mistaken."

"What made you think that?"

I swallow. "It seemed too early to get up."

"Watches don't go wrong here," says Raoul. "This is Hummingbird Creek. We have excellent technology." He shakes his head as I strap my watch back on.

I'm shown into Karl Jesmond's room. "Hello, my dear," he says. "I hear you're giving my daughter a hard time."

"She's giving me a hard time," I say and he laughs as if I'm Joanie who's said something unintentionally funny.

"Okaaaay," he says. "Time for the questions. Ready?"

"Yes," I say, and I answer them smoothly.

He jots a few scribbly words down on his piece of paper. "You're starting to push the boundaries, huh? Disturbing the learning environment? Why's that?"

"I..."

He's stopped listening. He's looking at his computer screen now. "What's this?" he asks sharply. My stomach twists. Has something shown up on my data? "You think your Creek watch has gone wrong?"

Raoul must have sent that through.

"Oh. I . . . I was wondering if they ever did." Surely other people have questioned it at various times?

Karl looks at me and thins his lips. He no longer looks like an overfed, kindly uncle. "A word of advice: there will always be people who challenge the smooth-running of Hummingbird Creek. Who think that things aren't working properly, or who focus on the negative and not on the many positives of a facility like ours. They think things are always better somewhere else."

I wonder what precise point he's making. He rests his elbows on the desk and leans towards me. "It would be better for you not to be like that. We have to keep a very close eye on those people. Do you understand?"

THIRTY-THREE

The next few days consist of scribbling a few answers in my work booklet each morning for Greta's benefit, and then I study hard. When I'm doing exercise, I'm going over what I've learned in my head, testing myself.

At dinner, I force myself to swallow the beige pills. I hate them, and I hate that I need them.

I swim a lot. Furious laps up and down the indoor pool, followed by periods of getting dressed really slowly because I'm waiting for the changing room to clear so I can access locker 87. I meet Thet in the pool, and I tell her that there's a chance, slim but still a chance, that I might leave the Creek too. I make sure we keep our watches underwater. I wouldn't be surprised if they had microphones in them and they recorded our conversations.

"I've heard Will and a couple of others demanding to know why Austin wasn't allowed to take it easy after he had that weird outburst on the basketball court," she says. "He's started asking why the Creek is so hung up on vitamins when Austin should have been given better treatments." She twists her little orange earring as she thinks. "I'm worried for you, Mae."

"I'm going to find out what HB is," I say. "And I'm going to leave here. It might take me years, but I'll do it."

"I'll help you," says Thet. "I'll be on the outside helping you." She bites her lip. "I shouldn't say this, but however bad this place might turn out to be ... it feels like home right now. I've become better here. I can be myself. I'm scared to leave."

"You can be yourself somewhere else too," I say.

"But I still have so many stupid fears."

"They're not stupid," I say. "Irrational, maybe, but not stupid. If things go wrong, there'll be other people who can help. People who aren't as secretive and controlling as the Creek staff."

"I know." The water is up to our chests. Thet takes her foot and pulls it into the stretch that we do in aqua-aerobic classes. "I used to be able to hold this for ages with weights round my ankle." She lets her leg splash down into the water. "Maybe it's because I'm doing less exercise."

"Maybe it's because you're not on the same dose of vitamins," I say.

"I'm down to an eighth of a pill now," says Thet. "I feel fine. But still tired."

I know now that the tiredness isn't just caused by

exercise. I lift my legs and try to float. "You'll be OK on the outside, Thet, and when we meet, I won't be Mae Ballard. I'll be Mae Hill. Mom's name before she married."

"Mae Hill," repeats Thet.

It sounds good.

We have a secret schedule, Noah and me. We meet from three to three-thirty every afternoon. Sometimes it really is thirty minutes. Other times when I go back to the apartment and check the iPad, I see it's longer. We meet on the rooftop and he helps me study. I place clothing or the towel over our watches to muffle the sound of our talking – Noah says I'm being paranoid, which shows how crazy it's become.

The time my alarm wakes me up in the morning varies wildly, but the earliest is five a.m. For the patients who exercise earlier, it must be much earlier. The morning exercise session usually lasts far longer than the hour it's supposed to. Creek time and real time often merge at midday after a long lesson session, which is when visitors or contractors turn up to work. The shutters go up and down at varying times, and when our watches show 22.00, the time I'm supposed to go to bed, it's usually later than that. Creek time works to a twenty-four hour cycle, and we sleep for very little of it.

When I have my weekly internet session, the time on the computer is the same as my watch, and I have no access to websites where I can check it. My emails from pen suppliers come through, and I notice for the first time that they have a date on them but not a time.

My eyes blur, my muscles ache and my neck prickles. I have a nosebleed during brain training. I spend a lot of time afterwards wondering if it's a new side effect or just a nosebleed.

There are only three days to go before the entrance exam, and I'm back on the roof with Noah.

"I don't even know if I'm going to be able to take it," I say. "I haven't heard anything."

"Ms Ray will manage it somehow," he says.

I wish I had his optimism. To not even have the chance to take the exam will be agony. I close my textbook with my pen inside it. For a few moments I don't want to think about the exam. I want to hear more about life on the outside, particularly Noah's life. He tells me that the previous summer he worked in an old people's home to earn money.

"Why did you do that?"

"My parents own a chain of them as one of their businesses. They wanted me to earn money. Not be a spoilt rich kid. Some of the old people were great. Others were miserable sods."

"I've never met anyone my age who's earned their own money."

"That's because you live in a Creek bubble."

"A bubble makes it sound like a fragile place," I say. "Like a soap bubble or a glass bauble that you put on a

Christmas tree. It's more like a prison or a cage. If I stay here too many years, I won't even know how to behave in the outside world. I've never been to a party where there weren't orderlies monitoring behaviour. I've never danced in a couple."

"I'm rubbish at parties," says Noah. "I skulk in the corners."

"Don't you dance?"

"Only if I've had some alcohol." He smiles. "Don't look so disapproving. Here. I'll show you how a slow dance goes." He leaps to his feet and holds out his hands. For me to hold? I'm not sure. I stand but I keep my arms by my side.

"Mae?" He steps closer and takes my hands and I hope he can't feel that mine are trembling. He squeezes them. "If this was a party, I might put my hands on your waist like this."

Solid warmth on my waist.

"And you might put your arms on my shoulders."

Slowly I do it.

"Or we could do this." He moves his hands so that one is on my shoulder and the other is holding mine. "This feels more your classic ballroom, I reckon."

I don't want to say anything stupid so I keep quiet.

"If we were at a party right now, we'd be the cool guy and the hot girl." He adjusts his hand grip to something looser. "To be honest, it would be geeky guy, hot cool girl. In real life you'd be way out of my league."

I frown.

"You're … you know, really … more attractive than me."

He's complimenting me and I should thank him, but I'm embarrassed. I pull away. He's not sure what's happened and neither am I.

"You thinking of Drew?" he asks.

I shake my head. Not in the way he means. It's more that I've never felt special or desirable until now. Drew never made me feel this way.

With Hunter, I try to be like I've always been. I listen to what he says and nod and smile as required. On Wednesday night I'm jittery. The exam is on Friday and there's been no word from Ms Ray. She delivers booklets to the office before I get there, and I never see her in the swimming pool changing room. The notes she writes are things like

Make sure you understand this.

Good effort but look where I've added information.

This is a classic mistake.

Keep going. I see an improvement.

Hunter talks to Mom and me about the possibility of a temporary ice-skating rink at the Creek in December. "We'd have it on the lawn near the security building, on the right as you drive in," he says. "Imagine what a fantastic photo that would make with the main building as a backdrop." He takes a bite of vegetable flan, and I look away so I don't have to watch his jaw go up and down any more.

It would be hard to go up on the roof with an ice-skating rink next to the security building.

"Lucky you, Mae," says Mom. "You'll learn to skate."

I shiver at the thought of still being here in December. No Ms Ray, Drew, Thet. Or Noah. Maybe not even Will if he can find a way to be discharged.

"What's up with you?" asks Dad.

"I don't like to think of it being cold," I say.

"By the way, I've heard that you've been spending a lot of time with Noah Tinderman. I think it's best you avoid him in the future – he's not a stable influence."

The hoody. He saw the hoody in my room.

"It's not a good example to Zach, Ben, Luke and Joanie. Be polite to patients, but don't get involved. You don't understand their needs, and you never know what might set back their recovery. You're also to cut down contact with Thet. I shouldn't have let you two spend so much time together. She's leaving. I don't want any overreactions when that happens. Understood?"

Mom looks across the table at me. There's worry in her eyes.

"Understood," I reply quietly.

"Eat up your food," says Hunter. "The rules have been too lax lately."

I force the food into my mouth, bit by little bit. I chew and swallow elastic bands and cardboard.

*

The next morning, I don't wave to Thet. I refuse to meet Noah's eye as I walk out of the cafeteria. I have to lie low for a bit. In the office I go through the chemical equations Ms Ray's set me. I study the geography case histories and write a mock essay comparing two poems. I cram my brain with facts and theories, ideas that are bigger than the Creek, and I block out everything else.

As I walk into the schoolroom to deliver my booklet, I'm shoved in the side by Joanie. "Did you hear? Did you hear?"

"You nearly knocked me over. What?"

Greta's standing on a chair replacing one of Ms Ray's posters with a large sheet of paper titled *Rules of the Schoolroom*. Zach, Ben and Luke walk past us on their way to lunch.

"It's not that big a deal, Joanie," says Zach. There's a sour note to his voice. "I'll be surprised if Mae's allowed to go."

"She's on full privileges, aren't you, Mae?" says Ms Ray.

"Just. What's going on?"

"Ms Jesmond read an announcement," says Joanie.

Ms Jesmond? Is that what we have to call Greta now?

Joanie squawks, "You and me! We're going to a trampoline training day tomorrow!"

"It's for home-school educated girls in the Pattonville area," calls Greta. "You and Joanie can work on your routine for the next open day."

"My first trip outside." Joanie beams.

"Nice," I say. This is a way of leaving the Creek for the exam. Ms Ray has either found a real event that ties in with the exam or she's dreamed up a fake one and managed to get it through admin.

"I'll see if Mick's free to take you," says Greta, as she jabs the last thumbtack into the sheet of rules. "Be in the parking lot at nine o'clock."

"No," howls Joanie. "Not Mick. I want Ms Ray."

Joanie, I concede, hasn't turned out too badly so far. Greta tenses one side of her mouth to show she thinks Joanie's being difficult, but it probably suits her to have Ms Ray out of the schoolroom for a day.

At lunchtime, I make an effort being civil with Greta because I don't want anything to jeopardize me leaving the Creek with Ms Ray tomorrow. I listen to her ideas about feeble projects to tie in with booklet topics. I ask questions about her apartment and she describes the bedroom that will be mine when I move to Pattonville. She's found some wallpaper hand-printed with hummingbirds.

I'm aware of Thet and Noah looking at me. I could get a message to them through Will, but I don't want Greta to see me talking to him. Since his outburst at the barbecue about Hunter and Karl not letting him go to Austin's funeral or memorial service, she thinks he's a bad influence.

I wait until later, after my afternoon exercise, but I

can't find Will anywhere. When I'm certain I'm not on a security camera and I'm not being watched, I ask a patient if he's seen him, and he tells me Will spends his free time in Larkspur smashing table-tennis balls against a wall. "I gotta go," he says, "before someone sees us. We're not allowed to talk to staff kids now. Otherwise we get fined."

THIRTY-FOUR

Joanie skips ahead of me in her Lycra shorts and vest top. She tells me this is the best day of her life.

Ms Ray is standing by one of the silver Creek cars. "Morning," she says. "Climb in the back, you two." She's wearing a white long-sleeved shirt and navy trousers. Serious clothes. I'm in loose yoga pants, and a T-shirt with a cartoon on the back of someone bouncing high in the air. The pants have a pocket, and I've brought my Dunhill-Namiki pen because I'm hoping the golden dragon will bring me luck.

I wonder what time the exam starts. I'm so nervous my throat has narrowed and I can only manage shallow breaths. Joanie slaps my hand away when I lean across to buckle up her seatbelt. "I can do it myself," she says, fumbling around for ages until she manages to click it in far enough.

Before I left the apartment I checked the time on the iPad. It was showing half an hour earlier than my Creek watch. Normally the difference is far greater. That must be why the Creek doesn't like to arrange trips; if one person's watch has to be altered, everyone's has to be.

I think of when patients first arrive. How the induction process takes so long, how they often have their first meal in their room. How they're given a watch but it takes a few hours to "go live". That must be to allow for them not to notice the time difference. I wonder how much Greta knows, and remember that she's not allowed to turn up spontaneously from college, but has to schedule her visits with admin. Perhaps her watch takes time to go live too.

Ms Ray leaves the car in front of the gates while she goes into the security building to pick up her cell phone and sign us out. When we drive through the gates, the car moves agonizingly slowly. I don't feel free until I turn and see the gates have banged shut behind us.

After being awed into silence by the huge fields, Joanie starts an excited commentary. Pointing out trees, cars, buildings. She laughs when she sees a dog in someone's front yard. She drinks in the sights without feeling cheated that she's not been allowed to see them before. I feel sorry for her because she's got that realization to come.

"We're going to a library first of all, Joanie," says Ms Ray. She catches my eye in the mirror.

"Where there'll be trampolines," says Joanie, kicking

her legs into the back of Ms Ray's seat. I hold her legs still and give her a what-do-you-think-you're-doing look.

"Not there," says Ms Ray. "We'll do some drawing while Mae is busy in another room. We'll draw trampolines. Then afterwards we'll go do your routines on some real ones." While she lowers Joanie's expectations for the day, I touch the smooth metal door handle. Mick once told me that Creek cars had child-locks so no one could fall out by mistake. Or escape.

There are things about Hummingbird Creek I've grown up with and never properly questioned until very recently. The shutters that come down at night and prevent us from seeing outside. Mornings spent away from natural light in the basement. The endless testing before and after exercise. Being cut off from the outside world so everyone has to rely on Creek watches to tell the time. Watches that don't tell the truth.

I'm not a patient, but I have blood tests every two weeks. Endless questions about how I feel. Health stats taken at every opportunity. Why else would Hunter want me to go to Pattonville College, where he can keep an eye on me, if he's not collecting data from me? Not data to keep me healthy, but to monitor the effect of the drug. Statistics that Peter, someone from the military, is so interested in. A drug that makes people stronger and fitter, with more stamina. One which has side effects and is dangerous in large amounts. Noah will hopefully smuggle out a vitamin for his sister to analyse. Then what? How, if I ever get any concrete evidence, do I confront Hunter without him covering it up or something bad happening to me?

"How did you manage to sort this?" I say quietly when Ms Ray's parked the car and we're waiting for Joanie to unbuckle herself.

"I sent a letter to a friend and asked her to contact the Creek about a trampoline day. I wasn't sure if it would work out in time."

"Weren't you worried about your letter being read?" I ask.

Ms Ray's forehead creases. "I worded it carefully."

I think of Will's black-market operation and about the elaborate code Drew told me he uses in his letters unless he can send messages with patients who leave.

"I'm told your mom often writes letters to an English address but security shreds them," says Ms Ray. She cringes as I reel from that news. "I shouldn't have said that, Mae. I'm so sorry. You should be focusing on the exam." She holds her hand out to Joanie who is about to jump from the car. "Come on, you."

The exam room is a community hall attached to a library on the edge of Pattonville. The building is shabby and poorly lit. Before I go in, Ms Ray hands me a biro, pencil, ruler and eraser. I show her my golden dragon pen. "I could use this?"

"If you like," she says. She squeezes my shoulder. "Best of luck."

Joanie squeezes my hand. "I hope it doesn't hurt," she says. She must think I'm having some sort of medical exam.

About fifteen of us file in to the room and sit at single desks, in rows. A strict-looking woman with greyish cropped hair hands out papers.

"You may turn your papers over," says the woman. She writes the end time on the board at the front. The room comes alive with movement and I'm all panic. The first questions are math and the numbers jiggle. I try to calm myself.

Write your name at the top of the paper. Take a breath.

I tunnel my hands round the corner of my eyes for a moment, blocking off everyone. I slow-motion my brain so that I work through each step and move steadily through the questions. Panic flares again when I catch sight of the page the person diagonally opposite me is on.

Ignore them.

The English questions are more enjoyable. My hand moves across the paper writing words that seem to flow from my brain down my arm.

"Mae Ballard?" The grey-haired woman is leaning over my desk. "Please can you step outside for a moment."

Have I done something wrong?

My chair makes a noise as I push it back with my legs and everyone turns and glares. Ms Ray is in the doorway. Her face is grey, the sleeves of her shirt rolled up above the elbow. Joanie, beside her, stares at the rows of desks.

"Mae, I'm sorry," says Ms Ray and the woman gives her a death stare until the door is shut behind me. "I had a garbled call on my cell phone. From someone on Creek reception. Something's happened."

Stomach-lurch.

"An iPad was found in your bathroom."

Nausea.

"Noah said it was his. Your father's placed him in solitary, and now he's trying to locate Thet. She's missing."

Solitary. Missing. The words scare me.

"It sounds as if the situation is out of control. The place is on lockdown. He's found out that you're here through a search on the iPad and Mick's been sent to fetch you. It's not safe for you to go back to the Creek. We need to get you out of here before Mick arrives. I've called the police."

Each beat of my heart is one of fear. I wonder if the only reason Hunter let me leave the Creek today was so that he could have my room and bathroom pulled apart to see if I was hiding anything. "I have to go back. Noah and Thet can't take the blame for me. It's very dangerous for them." I know how bad this could get. Hunter's already covered up Austin's death. Noah and Thet mean nothing to him, and he's an expert at manipulating parents. I'm the one he really wants. He has years of data on me. I'm too precious for him to lose. If he lets the other two leave the Creek, he can have me.

"Mae, I have a cousin who grew up in a cult," says Ms Ray. She sees my confused expression. "Cults are groups that follow strange teachings and tend to do anything their leader tells them to. Hummingbird Creek is a bit like that. We need to hurry. I have a friend who lives in Pattonville. We'll be safe there."

"I can't." I feel oddly calm. If I waited this out at Ms Ray's friend's house I would never forgive myself.

Joanie puts her hand in mine. "I want my mom. I want to go home."

We forgot she was there, listening to us. "OK, we'll go home," I say. "We'll work on our routine another day."

Ms Ray rolls down the sleeves of her white shirt and slides her hand into her bag for the car key. "As long as the police are there before us," she says under her breath.

THIRTY-FIVE

As Ms Ray drives out of the library parking lot, she says, "Shall we talk about this?"

I shake my head. I don't want Joanie to overhear, and if I tell Ms Ray about HB and the time differences, about Hunter not being my dad and Austin's death being covered up, she won't drive me back.

I force myself to think about the exam, to concentrate on my favourite questions, but my mind slides back each time to Noah in solitary and Thet missing. I wonder if Will knows what's going on, and if Mom will do anything to save me when she realizes that I've been hiding an iPad.

"I guess there's no turning back now, even if we wanted to," says Ms Ray in a low voice, glancing in her mirror.

Looking through the rear window, I see we're being tailed by an identical silver car to the one we're in. It's Mick. Joanie sinks down in her seat. Fear pecks at me, but we have Ms Ray and the police are on their way.

We pass the sign that says:

Hummingbird Creek
Private Psychiatric Facility
for Adolescents
1 mile

I was at least ten before I understood what psychiatric and adolescents meant, not that I cared. My life was about exploring the Creek with Drew.

There's a Creek security guard on the road, in front of the gates. No police.

I'm not sure that when I go through those gates I'll ever be allowed out again.

The guard indicates that Ms Ray should lower her window. He peers into the car. "All three of you? Good. Go straight to the security building, you can park in front."

We drive through the gates, followed by Mick. Joanie unbuckles her belt and scoots over to me. It's not unusual for the grounds to be empty during lesson time or when all activities are taking place away from this front part of the Creek, but there's usually a gardener or a member of the support staff around. Today there's no one and every sound is magnified. The thud of the car doors behind us. Our feet on the concrete of the parking lot. The call of birds hidden in the trees. Ms Ray and I take hold of Joanie's hands. Mick walks a few paces behind us.

"Let's get this ironed out," says Ms Ray in a voice that's too loud.

Fear is throbbing through my veins now. It's hard to think straight but as long as Noah and Thet don't suffer for being my friends, that's all that matters.

Two different guards watch us approach. One says, "Mick will escort Joanie to her apartment."

Joanie cowers from Mick. "I don't want to go with him! Don't let him take me!" Her screams terrify me.

"I'll take her home," I say.

"No need." Mick pulls Joanie away from us. She's immediately silent with shock. She walks towards Hibiscus with Mick's hand on the back of her head.

The guards escort Ms Ray and me into the security building. The monitors have been upgraded since I was here. They're super-thin and cover an entire wall. A female guard is watching them. She looks at us as we're led past her, through a door to a corridor where the lights are on because there are no windows. I count four closed doors.

"You," says one of the guards to Ms Ray. "Come with me."

"Where to? What's going on?" She laughs in a nervous way. It's frightening how small and vulnerable she looks, like a new patient. I regret the silent journey back here. I should have thanked her for trying to help me.

The guard points to a door at the end of the corridor. "In there. And I'm going to be the one asking the questions. Not you."

The other guard knocks on a different door, and I'm led in. Earl is sitting behind a polished wood desk. I remember the rumour about him strangling someone. He stares at me for several moments, watching my legs shake violently, then he says, "So here you are. Mae Ballard. What trouble you've caused." His gold cufflinks glint at me.

I'm barely breathing.

"Tell me about this iPad of yours," he says.

I shake my head. I have to know that Noah, Thet and Ms Ray will be OK before I say anything they want to hear. "Where's Hunter? I'll tell him." My voice is a croak.

He stands up and circles behind me. "Where did it come from?"

I say nothing.

"Who knew about it?"

Silence.

There's a knock on the door. It's the guard who showed me into the room. "Dr Ballard is in admin, sir. He's been informed that Mae is here and he's asked that we send her up."

Earl nods. "Any sign of the other girl?"

"No, sir. Not yet."

There's a moment's pause, then Earl says, "The heat-seeking equipment is on its way. Let me know if the police turn up. I told them everything was under control but you never know. Take Mae to her father."

Outside the air is shimmery. I walk up the path to the main building with the guard by my side. A movement to my right catches my eye. I glimpse Will, tucking himself round the side of the building. As I climb the steps to reception, I glance back slightly and he's there, watching.

Help me, I plead silently.

There's no one in reception. The hard tiles beneath my canvas shoes are cold.

Jenna must have known about the time differences. Everyone who worked on reception taking phone calls must have because they were dealing with the outside world. How much was their silence worth? Did they think they were doing the right thing – helping Hunter with his research? Who else knew? Who guessed something wasn't quite right and turned a blind eye?

The guard pushes me into the elevator and the confined space freaks me out. A mini solitary room.

The doors open to more silence, and then I see Abigail leaning against a window. Her face is teary-red.

"Do you realize what you've done?" she spits at me. "Hunter's been under a lot of stress recently and you've tipped him over the edge."

We keep walking. The guard swipes me through the glass door. Admin is empty. Normally there should be a dozen people working at the desks. I spot Hunter crouched over a computer screen in the far corner, the area where the most senior admin staff sit.

The guard coughs loudly. "Dr Ballard," he says. "I have Mae for you, sir."

Hunter turns. His eyes are hard and wild. I take a step back and hear the click of the glass entry door, which tells me I'm on my own now with him.

"You little *bitch*," he says, standing up and coming towards me. He points at the chair nearest me.

I sit. Upright and trembling.

"Mae, don't insult me by denying things I know to be true. Noah confessed to bringing in the tablet under the noses of security."

He didn't betray Will.

Hunter continues, "You used Creek wifi, so I have a complete record of your searches."

There's a lightness in my body, as if I've become insubstantial. Less of who I was.

"I have a number of questions for you, but let's start with this one," he says. His voice is ice. "I see you searched HB. Who told you about it?"

My head is on fire. Should I pretend to know more about HB than I do, or should I say nothing at all until he guarantees not to punish Noah and Thet?

"I read my medical records on your laptop," I say finally. There's satisfaction in seeing the incredulity on his face. He can't believe it was his own security breach that allowed me access. "So I also know you're not my father."

The sensation of throwing words like sharpened arrows is exhilarating.

Hunter blinks. He recovers quickly. "I gave you a life that has been infinitely better than it would have been otherwise. I've given you so much and have had such little gratitude in return."

My heart is bruised from thumping so hard. "You can keep me for your data purposes but let Noah and Thet go home. They've done nothing."

"I have to disagree with you there," says Hunter. He sighs. "I think they know more than they should."

"All they know is that people are starting to ask questions about the vitamins."

I've hit a nerve. I keep going.

"They want to know why Austin died. It was the HB, wasn't it?"

Hunter frowns. "By helping with my research he finally did something useful with his life." He steps towards me and I shrink from him. His voice is calm and controlled, but I can see the anger pulsing in a vein in his neck. "You've become a liability, Mae."

"Ms Ray spoke to the police before we came here. They're on their way." I gabble, clutching at anything that might prevent what he's about to do to me.

"Oh, Mae, you are so naïve. The police are used to us having a spot of trouble with our more difficult patients. We have an excellent relationship with them, and they're always very understanding." He laughs. A false, high, mocking laugh. "It was so foolish of Steffi Ray to call the police. She'll never get a decent job again after an abduction charge."

"No!" I stand up but he uses just one finger to push me back down on to the chair.

"Noah's parents have been informed that his paranoia has worsened and he's come up with all sorts of conspiracy theories about the Creek. Very disappointing. It's best if he stays for a much longer period, and we can negotiate new payment terms if that's a problem. We do have access to funds through Everleigh's charity. They're aware he's in solitary confinement for his own good."

"You—" I say. *You can't do that*. But I realize he's prepared to do whatever it takes.

"And Thet. Well, her loyalty to you is a problem. Her grandmother will understand if I tell her that Thet's had a major relapse and won't be able to start her new school. She can stay here until I find a suitable place for her too. That leaves me with you. Of course nobody is indispensable."

I can't swallow. Can't talk. My head's almost lopsided with heaviness. I'm no match for Hunter. There's nothing I can do.

Hunter picks up a phone receiver and presses a button. "Earl? Come on up. I want her moved to the medical suite. Now."

THIRTY-SIX

I half-stumble, and am half-dragged by Earl to the elevator. The ground floor is still empty.

No police. Nobody apart from a security guard who stands near the front desk of the medical suite speaking into his radio. As we pass I hear him snap, "The location where you found her watch is irrelevant. Check the grounds, inch by inch. She can't have vanished into thin air."

In that instant, I think I know where Thet is: on the roof of the security building, even though she'd been afraid of climbing the ladder. I picture her. Scrunched up. Maybe tapping her arm.

Stay there, Thet.

Raoul is at the desk. He nods at me, and says, "I'm disappointed in you, little lady. I'll take your health stats before solitary but first I must talk to your father."

I sit in the waiting area with the security guard watching over me while Raoul speaks in hushed tones with Hunter and Earl. I hear Noah's name. Snatches of psychiatric terms.

Hunter is tapping a syringe against his hand as he speaks, like someone else might do with a pen. How easily he gets what he wants. His charm ensures most parents, patients and staff are taken in by him. His willingness to be ruthless, and his access to money to pay people off, have been invaluable.

Breathing hurts. There's too much pressure in my chest. Noah is behind the padded door in solitary, only a few paces away. His life is in danger, and he was only ever helping me. To calm myself, I feel in my pocket for my pen. I rub my thumb against the raised golden dragon on the barrel.

I could make a run for it, but I'd be caught by the security guard in seconds. Sedated immediately. I don't know what's in that syringe Hunter has, but it's bound to be heavy-duty. Or lethal.

"Right," says Hunter. He's winding up the conversation. "Mae is all yours, Raoul. Into solitary after health stats. Earl, let's have a word with Karl. We'll get our story straight with him in case the police decide to make an appearance." He tells the security guard to patrol the corridors, then strides into Karl's office and Earl follows.

I let Raoul take my blood in the treatment room,

hardly flinching when he jabs me hard. I hold the pad of cotton wool against my arm afterwards and stare at the ridge of bruising he's caused. I say nothing while he takes my watch and downloads the health statistics. When he hands it back, it's him who breaks the silence and says, "I thought you were a person with peace and gratitude in your heart. Why did you cause so much trouble for your father?"

I look at the photo of the young boy by the silver laptop. Raoul's little brother.

Act young. Act the little lady.

"I don't know what you're talking about. I asked Noah for the iPad because I wanted proper access to the internet. So I could keep in touch with him."

Raoul rolls his eyes. He might be buying it.

"It's kind of embarrassing," I say. "My dad doesn't think I'm old enough to have a boyfriend." I bite my lip theatrically. "Noah's given me his email and everything."

"Dr Ballard is correct. You are too young," says Raoul. "Right. Let's go."

"Please, Raoul. I'd like to say goodbye to Noah – can I? Just for a minute?"

"You cannot wrap me round your finger, little lady." His face is grim as he takes me by the arm.

I'm coming undone at the thought of solitary, but the pain of never seeing Noah again and him never knowing how sorry I am overrides everything. "Please, Raoul. One minute with Noah. That's all. Do it for me."

He grips my arm more tightly. "I have only contempt for you," he hisses as he unbolts the door of the second solitary room.

With my free hand, I feel for my pen and unscrew the cap. I have nothing to lose. With all the force that I use to slam a tennis ball during a serve, I plunge the fine steel nib into Raoul's thigh. As he bellows in pain and clutches his leg, I let go of the pen, push him into the solitary room and bolt the door. There is immediate silence; the room has exemplary sound-proofing. Shaking with the shock of my own violence, I run across to the other solitary room, and I bash my hand as the bolt flies open but it barely registers.

Noah is curled up with his head on his knees, his back to the door. "Piss off," he says without turning round. "I've got nothing else to say."

"Noah?" I say.

He turns and stands all at once. "Mae!"

We collide halfway across the room in a hug. His arms, my arms, holding on and breathing in, heads touching. Knowing, although I can't see his face, that he's choking back tears too.

"I'm sorry," I say softly.

Noah pulls away to hold my face so that I'm looking into his eyes. Seeing the him that's really him. "Don't be sorry," he says.

My lungs are saturated with sadness. We hold each other tight again and it feels as if I'm drowning, gasping for breath. Somewhere embedded into the ceiling or wall will be a camera and we'll be on a monitor in the security building. "We have to go," I manage to say.

We only make it a few paces into the waiting area before we hear the security guard yell for assistance, and see him run towards the gap between the front desk and the wall to block our escape.

The door to Karl's office flies open.

"What's going on?" Hunter's voice is high-pitched in disbelief. In his hand is the long syringe. Karl and Earl are behind him. "Where's Raoul?"

There's the sound of an argument outside. Shouting.

I seize the moment to push Noah against the wall and stand, shield-like, in front of him.

"Let Noah go home," I say in a tight voice. I'll need to be unconscious before he's dragged from me. I imagine that long needle piercing my skin with a concentrated, painful searing sting. The spinning of the walls, the fuzzing of my resolve and strength. I picture myself biting Hunter. Kicking him in the groin. Scratching his face until my fingers have no more power.

I hear Will screaming about justice. All at once, a crowd of patients surges through the automatic doors, some of them kids who hate crowds or loud noise. A few are crying, but most, like Piper, are chanting about wanting the truth.

"What happened to lockdown?" asks Hunter, turning to Earl. "Where's Raoul?" he repeats.

Will comes to stand next to us. He holds a golf club in front of him, as a barrier. He must have broken into the sports equipment room. Other patients stream in. Mick and Abigail are at the back, telling everyone to go back to Larkspur immediately.

"We want answers!" shouts Will.

Earl moves towards him, but Hunter places a politely restraining arm against him. "Let me deal with this," he murmurs. There's a hush when Hunter puts his hands up in the air. The syringe is like an extra finger on one hand. "Listen up! Everyone needs to calm down. There have been ridiculous rumours going round, and there is only one thing you need to know. Mae, Noah and Thet have caused a massive breach of security which has compromised us all. You have to trust me and Dr Jesmond to sort it out."

"He's been testing a drug on us," I shout into his self-satisfied pause.

Angry noise erupts, then dies down again when Will speaks. "Was that the drug you gave Austin?" he asks.

"We offer highly professional bespoke treatment here," says Hunter smoothly. "I can't discuss individual cases." He thinks he's got this.

"It's called HB," I shout. "We're all on different doses."

"She's delusional, I'm afraid," says Hunter. Although I can't see it from here, I bet the vein on the side of his neck is pulsating like crazy. "We've been doing important research on sleep. Unfortunately, it's not quite ready yet to be talked about openly. It's certainly nothing to be worried about."

"So we're your lab rats, are we?" asks Piper angrily.

"Seems you've been working out all sorts of things," says Noah in a loud, clear voice. "Like how much food someone needs to eat for your drug to work properly. Anorexics are ideal for that, aren't they? You've been testing our limits. And Austin—"

"What did you do to Austin?" shouts Will.

"Let Mick and Abigail through please," says Hunter. "They'll help everyone get back to Larkspur."

The crowd doesn't move. Earl mutters into his radio, then says, "Why isn't my radio working? Anyone know why my radio isn't working?"

"They gave Austin too much HB," I say.

Hunter's face is taut with rage. "Austin was a very troubled young man and he didn't cope well with the regime we gave him. Will, you're being overemotional. You're seeking some sort of misplaced revenge for a boy you think you loved. You're acting out a grotesque leadership fantasy, believing you're helping others when really you are setting back your own recovery."

"Maybe you don't understand," says Will, "how tightly some of us bond here. The other patients here are my family."

His words trigger something in me. I let go of Noah's hand and I unstrap my watch. As if I'm demonstrating an arm movement in an exercise class, I raise my hand high. Unfurling my fingers, I drop it. It hits the hard floor and bounces off at a strange angle. Noah's eyes flash conspiratorially and he unstraps his own watch. As he lifts his arm, as deliberately as I did, other patients copy. Watches clunk on to the floor like a shower of huge hailstones.

"That's enough!" shouts Hunter. He moves fast, pushing aside terrified patients, but I'm fast too, and strong, thanks to HB. As he attempts to force the needle into my upper arm, I grab his wrist and turn his arm. He's already pushing the plunger with his thumb. I jerk his hand forward, pressing down on top of his thumb. And with a bit of help from me, he injects the contents of the syringe into his own neck.

There's a blood-freezing scream. Choking.

"That dose is too much for him," Karl shouts.

Hunter is on the floor, his face red and his eyes bulging. He twitches for a couple of seconds before his body goes limp. I think I might vomit.

Some patients flee, others move forward to see what's happened. Karl repeats over and over that he can't find Hunter's pulse. Earl screams down his radio. Abigail's on her knees. Mick is shouting at the remaining patients to leave the area, and Will begins trashing whatever equipment he can with the golf club.

"Quick," says Noah. We run fast, with the stamina that's been built up from hours and hours of physical training, towards the woods near the boot-camp area.

There are no fully formed thoughts in my head, only words. *Hide. Secluded. Escape. Hunter. Killed. Perimeter fence. Security guards busy. Across fields. Run. Run. Run. Freedom.*

We run without talking and then Noah stops. I see what he's seen a split second before me: two police marksmen on the ground. Guns pointing at us.

Overload of adrenaline. Hands on our heads. Loosening of emotion. Sobs. Sinking to the grass. I throw up.

The police are on their radios, using a frequency which works. There are more of them, moving stealthily towards the main building. One of them asks our names. Asks what we've witnessed. Our words trip over themselves.

We're led along the perimeter fence past the cycle track, the basketball court, the grounds staff office, the schoolhouse and the back of Hibiscus. We see the blue flashing lights of police vehicles. More police. Security staff in handcuffs. A straggle of patients and staff talking and crying about what they've seen.

I need to find Thet. Thet and Mom. Thet and Mom and Ms Ray.

"We have a friend," I tell a policewoman. "A patient. I think she's hiding on the security building roof. Can I go up there? She trusts me."

There's a discussion on the radio. The policewoman asks Noah to give a statement to a colleague while she accompanies me to the roof.

I run to the ladder, and call, "It's me, Thet. Did you hear the police? You don't need to hide any more."

There's no reply. I scale the ladder, tapping with my nails as I go, and step on to the roof. She's at the far end. Crouched against the wall, she's made herself tiny, but the bright pink of her dress is impossible to miss.

"Thet – it's over."

She stands up unsteadily, and brushes away the dust from her legs in jerky movements.

The police officer says, "Are you OK?"

Thet nods and walks six steps, then into me, slamming against my heart. I close my arms round her small body. Will's words come back to me. *Maybe you don't understand how tightly some of us bond here.*

I have to wait before I can cross the grass again to Hibiscus to find Mom. I sit among a bewildered group of patients and support staff on the scrubby verge outside the gates, huddled between Noah and Thet. We see a body brought out on a stretcher by paramedics, covered in a red blanket. It's loaded into an ambulance.

"Hunter," murmurs Noah, and he squeezes me closer.

Abigail follows, accompanied by a flak-jacketed policeman. She's distraught. I think of Hunter's meetings and conferences outside the Creek, the time I hid in Abigail's car and I overheard her say, *Well, if it isn't my favourite doctor,* and how Hunter would always take her side. How he never took much notice of Mom.

Staff are led to police cars. Greta is there among them, white-faced and uncomprehending. I almost feel sorry for her. She's arguing with the police; she still can't believe anything bad of the Creek.

I want to know that someone is looking after Will. When I ask, I'm told the paramedics are with him. Computers, other equipment and files are carried out of the security and main buildings, wrapped in clear plastic.

"Mae!" Ms Ray is standing by the gates. Her face is shiny and tear-stained. The sleeves of her shirt have been rolled up and down so many times today they look stripy from the creases. "Thank God you're OK." She hugs me and I'm overwhelmed by how much physical contact this day has contained. How much comfort there is in arms being wrapped around me.

A little while later, I walk with the policewoman from before, across the lawn and into the front door of Hibiscus which has been wedged open so that there's no need for the security code. When I sprint up the five flights of stairs, she can't keep up.

"Mom!" I call as I burst through the door.

She's lying on her bed in our ruined apartment. It's about the one piece of furniture that hasn't been smashed up.

"He's gone," she says weakly.

I nod. I don't know what the police have told her, but I don't tell her how he died. Not yet. I'm still processing it.

"He went crazy," she whispers as she sits up, crunching herself against the headboard. "He thought I knew about your iPad."

I sit on the bed. One side of her face is bruised and cut, and she's clutching her shoulder.

"He kept asking me if I knew you were at the library in Pattonville. After he left, I persuaded reception to give me an outside line to the library. It was the new receptionist. The man. I told him Hunter had asked me to make the call and he put me through."

"It was you who called to warn me?"

She nods, and her voice cracks as she speaks. "I was scared it would be really bad for you this time."

"Did you know about the vitamins?" I ask.

Her eyes brim with tears. "I wanted a better life for you than I had. I thought Hunter would give it to you. We needed him; he needed us."

"Why did you trust him for so long?" I ask. It's not really a question, and she has no answer. I saw it happen – how she wasn't allowed to make decisions, was confused by other drugs, and how he controlled every aspect of her life.

"I found Federico's photo," I say. "I know he's my dad."

She closes her eyes. "I'm sorry, Mae. Neither of your fathers were any good."

I allow myself to hope that without Hunter, in a different place and with her meds sorted out, she might be less of a shadow and more of a person. I hope that Radley Bridge School will give me another chance to sit the scholarship exam. I hope all at once for many things but

I'll manage whatever happens. I have Thet and Noah and Ms Ray, as well as Mom, to help me.

The policewoman is watching us from the door.

"Let's go," I tell Mom. "We need to give a statement to the police."

She nods. She sits and swings her legs round. The floor is covered with smashed-up things and broken glass, fragments of our previous life. I reach for the sandals that she must have kicked off earlier.

Tears roll down her cheeks as she fumbles at her wrist.

"Let me help," I say, and I remove her watch.

EPILOGUE –
ONE YEAR LATER

My first flight. Terrible food. Awesome movie selection. Since leaving the Creek, I've become claustrophobic. Any place I can't leave easily makes me nervous. I glance at the screen in front of me. Less than two hours until we reach our destination. That's something else. I like to check the time a lot, but I never wear a watch.

I tuck my arm under Mom's. She's asleep. She doesn't need total blackout, like me. My brain is still too used to shutters.

But letting my mind wander to dark places has become a bit easier. Hunter died. It wasn't my fault; it was self-defence. I still get nightmares about it, and I think I always will. But it's getting better.

A lot has come to light over the past year. HB was developed to be a vastly superior kind of amphetamine. Hunter hoped it would allow people to stay awake for long periods while functioning at eighty per cent capacity as their body underwent processes that normally occurred when they were asleep, such as tissue repair, toxic waste disposal and hormone regulation. Early tests showed it gave users strength and stamina, but also serious side effects, some of them long-term. Anybody who's ever taken HB will need to be screened for heart problems for the rest of their lives.

It turned out that Hunter named the drug after his initials. HB represented nothing more than the size of his ego. And Mom and I were not much more than two specimens for him to experiment on. He didn't think anyone would come looking for us.

His investor, Peter, is a now-disgraced army general who saw the potential of HB for the military. His trial, along with those of Karl, Earl, Abigail, Mick and Raoul, hasn't got to court yet, but there have been hearings and financial rulings.

Austin's parents sued and went to the papers, as did those of other patients. Will met Austin's parents and messaged me to say that they've asked him to be involved in a foundation in Austin's name. He gets to help decide which teenage mental health projects the money is spent on.

An air steward walks past, and checks I have my seatbelt on underneath my blanket. "Not long now," he says. He can tell I'm nervous being on a plane. But I also can't wait to get there.

I discovered Mom's dad died years ago, before we left England. But we're going back, and in a few days' time we'll visit Uncle Frank and then Callie. I'm intrigued to meet them, but it's Noah I want to see most. We've messaged loads. He's happier at school. Happier generally. Still into human rights, but he's able to switch off more. He knows I found Drew online, but Drew didn't want contact. He said he had to put the Creek and everyone associated with it behind him. I'm still recovering from that, if I'm honest.

Noah knows how much I like Radley Bridge House, and I tell him pretty much everything about my new life, but there are things I'm looking forward to saying in person, like how much I miss him. I have friends at Radley Bridge, but I'm different to the other pupils. It doesn't matter. That difference makes me strong. It makes me determined to achieve things.

We live near my school, Mom and I, in a tiny rental property. We don't like it too tidy, and although we eat healthily, we always have a few emergency packets of potato chips in the kitchen cabinets. Mom works for a gardening enterprise that supports people with special needs and volunteers for an animal rescue charity.

Noah, Thet and I sometimes have three-way Skype conversations. Noah teases Thet about talking too much, but I'm happy about that because it means she's OK. She finished her novel and she's started another one, which is just as brutal. We don't talk much about the Creek because we don't want our lives to be defined by what happened there, but also I think because it's only been a year. When Thet and I met at Christmas, we cried for a solid evening and then we did that friends thing I always dreamed of: we lay on her big bed in her grandmother's house and laughed about things that wouldn't have been funny to anyone else.

Ms Ray says I have to concentrate on getting into a good college. When she's not sending me articles to read or researching the requirements for different colleges she's retraining to be a lawyer. She helped Ben, Luke and Joanie's parents find new employment. The kids are at a proper school now, and Joanie kept sending me weird drawings until she settled in properly. Nobody knows where Everleigh, Greta and Zach are, but Greta didn't return to Pattonville college and the Hummingbird Sports Hall is called something different these days.

The plane lands on the Tarmac with a worrying bump, and we emerge into the cold of the airport terminal. There are endless corridors. Long lines. Questions about the purpose of our trip here.

"Pleasure," I say. "Visiting friends and relatives."

The immigration official asks why it's me who speaks and not Mom. I tell him it's because Mom takes a bit of time to reply. She has a condition, but she's getting better every month. He wishes us a good trip, and we follow everyone else to baggage reclaim. There are bright lights, lots of people, many different languages being spoken, noise. But we manage.

We pull our wheeled suitcases towards the sliding door. It opens and Noah's there.

ACKNOWLEDGEMENTS

A heartfelt thank you to Becky Bagnell at Lindsay Literary Agency.

Major thanks to Lucy Rogers and Linas Alsenas – this book is so much better because of your suggestions and editing skills (credit to Linas for the vintage pen finale). Lena McCauley, thanks for being there at the early stages. Sean Williams, another storming cover from you. Lucy Richardson, you've been an excellent publicist. Thank you to the rest of the supportive Scholastic team, particularly Olivia Horrox, Fi Evans and Pete Matthews.

Much gratitude to Caz Buckingham for my new author photos. I know it was a tricky assignment.

Kristina Collins, I'm indebted to you for your close read.

I've met many inspirational bloggers, vloggers, librarians and booksellers in the last year. Special mention to Vivienne Dacosta, Michelle Toy, Faye Rogers and

Christopher Moore, Kate Priestley at Kingston Libraries, Jamie-Lee Turner at Waterstones Birmingham, Margaret Wallace-Jones at the Alligator's Mouth, Richmond, and Pat Freestone-Bayes at Regency Bookshop, Surbiton.

To everyone involved with the Society of Children's Book Writers and Illustrators, Book Bound and Kingston Writing School, I'm grateful for all I've learned and the friendships. Sara Grant, thanks for the encouragement. David Rogers, thanks for the opportunities.

My lovely critique buddies, NM Browne, Zena McFadzean, Sarah Day, Az Dassu, Camilla Chester and Annie Harris, thank you for your behind-the-scenes support.

My fellow #LostandFound debut authors, Olivia Levez, Kathryn Evans, Patrice Lawrence and Eugene Lambert – you are fabulous and kind.

Huge thanks to Cath Howe for helping me so much with plot and life crises.

Thank you to many other great friends for cheering me on.

To my family – I appreciate you immensely.

Phoebe, Maia and Sophie – I love you.